# HAGATHA KETCHEL UNHINGED

*The Slaughter Minnesota Horror Series Book 2*

Chris Bliersbach

**Smashwords**

The characters and events portrayed in this book are fictitious. Any similarity to real persons, living or dead, is coincidental and not intended by the author.



ISBN: 9781005320096

Cover design by: Tatiana Fernandez, Vila Design

*"Beloved, believe not every spirit, but try the spirits whether they are of God: because many false prophets are gone out into the world." 1 John 4:1*

*"For nothing is secret, that will not be revealed, nor anything hidden that will not be known and come to light." Luke 8:17*

*"To everything, there is a season and a time to every purpose under the heaven. A time to be born and a time to die. A time to plant and a time to pluck up that which is planted. A time to kill and a time to heal. A time to break down, and a time to build up." Ecclesiastes 3:1-3*

*"Prepare slaughter for his children because of the iniquity of their fathers. Lest they rise up and possess the land, and fill the face of the world with cities." Isaiah 14:21*

# PROLOGUE

Hagatha's descent from a blissful life of privilege to the depths and darkness of despair felt precipitous. In fact, it happened over two years, from 1892 to 1894. Nonetheless, the erosion of her marriage to Enoch Slaughter was so devastating that she lost her mind. And despite 24 years of treatment in an insane asylum, most would agree, Hagatha never recovered. Actually, most would probably say it made things much, much worse.

Hagatha Ida Ketchel was born in 1872 to Otto and Ursala Ketchel, who emigrated from Germany to Grand Rapids, Minnesota, in 1871 to open Ketchel's Bakery. Hagatha was a beautiful child with blond hair and piercing ice-blue eyes. And while blond, blue-eyed people were plentiful in the area given the predominance of Scandanavians, Hagatha's beauty was exceptional. So much so that when she was 16-years old working in her parent's bakery, a young man named Enoch Slaughter took a shine to her. Not that that was uncommon. Fending off the attentions of lumberjacks who frequented the bakery was a daily occurrence. But Enoch was different.

Enoch was little more than a boastful dreamer when Hagatha first met him. He was known for talking big but couldn't back up his lofty ambition with actual accomplishments. Nevertheless, he was bound and determined to strike it rich with what he called "the new gold." He had heard about iron ore in the area and was convinced that he'd become wealthy if he could find it. It would take almost two years and falling off a horse before he literally stumbled onto the motherload. He liked to refer to himself as a mining tycoon, but he didn't know the first thing about mining. In truth, he made his wealth selling his iron-ore-laden property at a premium to a family of brothers in Duluth. They, in turn, would be credited with starting the iron ore mining boom in Northern Minnesota. With his riches, he bought 320 acres of land just east of Grand Rapids with eyes on two things – creating a town in his name and courting Hagatha Ketchel.

He was successful in both endeavors. First, he developed what was once a lumberman's sleeping camp into a small town. Naming it Slaughter, Minnesota, and declaring himself Mayor. Second, he leased portions of his land to the lumber and mining industries, exponentially increasing his wealth. But no matter how much wealth he amassed, all of it would be for naught if he didn't have descendants to carry on his legacy. Enter Hagatha Ketchel.

Enoch reacquainted himself with Hagatha, who was now 18 and still working at the bakery. Over time, he endeared himself to both Hagatha and her parents. Eventually, with Hagatha's parent's blessing, he proposed to her on the steps of his mansion on 5-acres overlooking town. She accepted, and they were married.

Their marriage was a happy one. Made only more so when Hagatha became pregnant. Many customs were followed in that day and age, supposedly helpful in dictating whether one gave birth to a boy or a girl. And Enoch and Hagatha had their hearts and minds set on having a boy. They even had a name picked out, well in advance – Enoch Junior. Hagatha's water broke, and she started having contractions weeks before she was due to deliver. Enoch rushed her to the hospital in Grand Rapids, where she gave birth to a tiny baby girl struggling to survive. She wasn't expected to live. Regardless, Hagatha chose a strong German name, Hilda, which meant battle armor. Hilda beat the odds, but by the time she was strong enough to leave the hospital, Hagatha's marriage was in shambles.

The moment Enoch found out Hagatha had a baby girl, the marriage took a decided turn for the worse. Enoch was incensed and blamed Hagatha for not being committed enough to have a baby boy. He ignored her and the baby for weeks. Hagatha protested, begged, and pleaded to be given another chance. He finally relented. They tried to have another child for several months, but when Hagatha didn't become pregnant, she went to see a doctor. The news was devastating. She was declared barren.

Enoch's response was swift and brutal. He threw Hagatha and the baby out of the house and had the marriage annulled. If that was not enough, he used his connections and money to ensure that their marriage and the child's birth records were not just expunged but destroyed. Enoch never spoke of Hagatha or the baby again. His intent? To erase what he considered an embarrassing chapter in his ascent to a life of greatness and adulation.

With nothing but the clothes on her back and Hilda in her arms, Hagatha started walking to Grand Rapids. Her initial thought, and the last rational one, was to seek solace and shelter with her parents. But along the way, something snapped in her head. Not only was she distraught, but now her thoughts became disordered. Suddenly she knew that the only way to save Hilda and herself was to deposit the baby in the Mississippi River. You might think this crazy, and it was. But Hagatha now felt like Moses' mother, Jochebed, who placed her baby in the reeds along the banks of the Nile river to save him.

Instead of walking to her parent's house, she walked to the banks of the Mississippi. There, she threw Hilda, swaddled in a blanket, into the water. This is where the stories of Moses and Hilda radically diverge. Moses was fortunate to have a mother who took great pains to place him in a floating vessel – guaranteeing his safety. Hagatha took no such precautions. Despite this, Hilda once again cheated death.

Evelyn and Charles Shepherd happened to be on the river bank relatively close downriver. Witnessing Hagatha's horrific act, Charles jumped in the water, nabbing Hilda before the river became her watery grave. It was fortunate that the muddy Mississippi is only slightly murky in those parts, not far from the crystal clear headwaters. They got a wailing Hilda out of her cold, wet clothes and wrapped her in their picnic blanket. They would adopt Hilda and raise her in a loving home. Unfortunately, they didn't know the baby's name or her birthday. Estimating she was about 1 year old, they designated the day they rescued her as her 1st birthday. They named her Pandora after Evelyn's mother – Dori, for short. In time, they would learn her given name. But for now, she was Dori, and they couldn't have been happier.

Hagatha's future was not nearly as fortuitous or bright. Not only did Evelyn and Charles rescue Hilda, but they reported Hagatha's actions to the police. And this is where Hagatha's story of pain, persecution, and payback begins.

# CHAPTER 1

The police found Hagatha pacing and babbling unintelligibly on the Pokegama Lake Dam, a concrete and timber crib dam constructed 10 years earlier. By now, Hagatha's break with reality was in full swing. So when she saw the cadre of police officers approaching, she thought they were Israelites seeking protection from Pharoah. In response, she invoked a line from the Book of Exodus.

"I will take you as My people, and I will be your God. Then you shall know that I am the Lord your God who brings you out from under the burdens of the Egyptians."

But apparently, the police officers didn't feel they needed saving and escorted her off the dam. Fortunately, Hagatha didn't protest. All the way back to the police department, Hagatha recited snippets of what sounded like biblical quotes. They probably didn't need a doctor to tell them she was crazier than a loon. But they followed protocol and had a doctor examine her at the hospital.

The hospital in Grand Rapids in 1895 was little more than a house staffed by volunteers from the church, a nurse, a midwife, and one doctor. Their primary patients were pregnant women with complications and lumberjacks injured in the line of duty. They didn't have the capacity or competency to do major surgery, provide overnight care, or treat patients deemed to be insane.

The police also had Evelyn and Charles Shepherd confirm that she was the young woman who tossed the baby into the river. No matter how the police tried, however, they were unable to learn the woman's identity. Every time they asked her name, she responded, "I am that I am. I am has sent me unto you," once again referencing the Bible.

Ironically, it was much easier to commit Hagatha to the closest insane asylum 185 miles away than to incarcerate her in prison. There were only two prisons in Minnesota, one of them in Stillwater and the other in St. Cloud. However, neither were equipped to accept women. Committing Hagatha to the Fairdale Falls State Hospital was easy. Getting her there was another matter. The trip required a torturous two-day journey involving a day-long horse-driven carriage ride from Grand Rapids to Duluth, then 8-hours on a train, topped off by another horse-driven carriage ride. This was a challenging trek even for the most well-adjusted individuals, and Hagatha was nowhere near well-adjusted. In fact, she was decompensating rapidly, making the trip to the asylum that much more difficult.

Her perception of the police suddenly changed on the carriage ride to Duluth. No longer was she the savior of the embattled children of Israel. Now she was the persecuted victim who saw them as the enemy. She lashed out, kicking, clawing, biting, and spitting at her captors. Simple handcuffs were insufficient. They eventually used rope to tie her arms and legs and put a canvas bag over her head. Totally restrained now, it also eliminated the chance of being bit or spat upon. It also eventually stopped the stream of profanity as Hagatha struggled to get enough oxygen.

Their crude restraints combined with the continuous jostling of the carriage ride resulted in the rope rubbing the skin on her arms and legs raw by the time they reached Duluth. Oxygen depletion also did nothing to improve her already tenuous grip on reality. They took a side trip to the hospital in Duluth to treat her abrasions. They also commissioned one of the doctors armed with chloroform to accompany them on the remainder of the journey should Hagatha require sedation. They would not need the doctor's services, however, as Hagatha became completely catatonic. She wouldn't or couldn't move or talk. Her eyes were open but were in a perpetual vacant stare that didn't seem to focus on anything. She was so debilitated that they needed to carry her onto and off of the train. She wouldn't eat, didn't sleep, and apparently didn't require a bathroom for the remainder of the trip.

In 1895, the Fairdale Falls State Hospital was just a hint of the impressive Romanesque castle-like structure it would become over the tenure of Hagatha's stay. When Hagatha arrived, it consisted of one large, long, lonely, white 4-story building on a slight elevation in the middle of bucolic farmland next to a small, unnamed lake. That lake would ultimately be named Devil's Lake, which might give you some idea of what people thought about its nearby residents at the State Hospital.

Fairdale Falls wasn't an incorporated town. It was a made-up name to give the State Hospital an identity without associating it with any official municipality. It was built five years earlier, purposely equidistant between Pelican Rapids and Fergus Falls. State officials would have told you the location was selected because the peaceful and quiet environment soothed the patient's disordered minds. It was more likely the case that no one wanted a bunch of crazy people residing in their backyards. Regardless, it was Hagatha's new home for the foreseeable future. Not that she seemed to be aware of it when she got there.

# CHAPTER 2

Caring for lunatics, as they were referred to in the 1890s, was thought to be quite advanced. But, of course, almost anything beyond the abject abuse and neglect suffered before the advent of asylums would appear moral and innovative.

On the evolutionary scale of mental health treatment, the toolbox was still relatively empty. And what tools they did have were rather crude and of questionable benefit. Fresh air, abundant sunlight, and exercise were some of the more innocuous interventions. Forced labor, restraints, seclusion, and ice baths were some of the more extreme measures. You could say the only positive thing was at least they weren't drilling holes in skulls or bloodletting to exorcise demons anymore. And they had yet to discover and use insulin comas or lobotomies. In this regard, Hagatha and the 200 other lunatics who occupied the Fairdale Falls State Hospital were somewhat fortunate.

Hagatha's catatonic state persisted for the first few days of her stay. Unable to identify who she was, they called her Iam, the only response she gave to police before her catatonia. She was the most manageable patient on the ward. Ward staff could transport her in a wicker rolling chair, the precursor to self-propelled wheelchairs, and she'd sit quietly until they thought to retrieve her. Unfortunately, it also made her the most vulnerable patient on the ward. Staff had to be constantly alert that other patients didn't take advantage or take their aggression out on her. She may have been mute, unmoving, and crazy as a bedbug, but she was still an attractive 23-year old woman who drew attention – most of it malicious.

Of course, this didn't necessarily prevent some male ward staff from taking liberties - mainly during the night shift. While most of the males who took advantage of Hagatha were satisfied just to see her naked or cop a feel here and there, one named Tobias took full advantage of her, you might say. In fact, Tobias made Hagatha his living sex doll. He could pose her as he wished. There wasn't an orifice of Iam's he didn't use or abuse he boasted to his colleagues.

He mistakenly thought she didn't know what was happening or who was doing these things to her. This went on for several nights until her catatonia suddenly resolved. On the occasion of Hagatha's recovery, Tobias happened to have his manhood in her mouth. Suffice to say, he left her room with a dismembered member ending not only his employment at the hospital but any hope to ever produce offspring. In this respect, Hagatha did society a big favor.

On the other hand, the incident set Hagatha off like a Roman candle. She quickly went from the most manageable patient to the least. Now, she couldn't remain still. She talked, muttered, or yelled incessantly, often to imaginary people, who she claimed, were out to get her. Often reverting to her familial and second language – German. It was the language her parents predominantly spoke in the home, which she had learned by osmosis growing up. She had violent outbursts. The first being, right after she orally castrated Tobias. When he stumbled out of her room screaming as blood spurted from his groin, she followed. She ran to the activity room. After spitting Tobias's penis onto one of the tables, she promptly threw a chair through a window. Three staff members ran out from the Nurse's station, thinking she was trying to escape. Instead, they could hear their colleague, Tobias, screaming from down the hall. Other patients started to emerge from their rooms to see what the commotion was. One of the male orderlies went to attend to Tobias. The other two staff, a male and a female, stayed to contend with Hagatha, who had picked up a shard of glass and wielded it like a knife. The duo braced for an altercation. Instead, Hagatha sat down at the table and used the glass to cut Tobias' penis into slices. Then offered pieces to the staff. They hadn't a clue about what she had done or what she was doing and slowly crept closer to see.

“Das ist gute Blutwurst, ja?” she said in German, popping a slice of what she believed to be delicious blood sausage in her mouth, chewing and swallowing.

When the staff realized what she was dissecting and eating, they both vomited. At the same time, the male orderly returned from down the hallway, frantic about Tobias's injury. He ran into the common area, hollering.

"Quick, Tobias needs a doctor. She bit off his," he started to say, then stopped when he saw what Hagatha was doing. That and seeing his colleagues spew the contents of their stomachs on the tile floor caused a predictable response. Thereby tossing his cookies into the vomit fest.

While the staff gagged and yakked out bilious chunks of partially digested food. Hagatha continued to eat until nothing remained of Tobias' manhood.

"Ich bin satt," she said, with a resounding burp, patting her belly.

Then she put down the glass shard and quietly got up from the table. She walked calmly past Tobias, still writhing in pain on the floor. Entering her room, she got into bed and fell asleep.

Hagatha's sleep would be abbreviated, and her dreams would not be sweet. She was wracked by persecutory nightmares. Visions of her ex-husband, Enoch, castigating her for having the audacity to deliver a baby girl, belittling her for being barren, and physically throwing her out of the house. If he wasn't chastising her, it was Hilda's inconsolable shrieks that she heard. Or inexplicably, her baby's frantic mewling of Mutti, Mutti, as she started sinking into the murky Mississippi River. All contributed to Hagatha wanting one thing – to kill herself and make the visions and messages stop.

No sooner had the staff dispatched Tobias to the infirmary, cleaned up the mess in the common area, and got the other patients back into their rooms when Hagatha emerged in a frenzy. Throwing herself repeatedly at the walls and scratching at her arms and face, opening up bloody abrasions. She made a dash for one of the windows in the common area, but staff grabbed her before she was able to crash through it. She was like a wild feral cat, biting and scratching at the orderlies holding her. The blood on her arms making them slick and difficult to restrain.

The lone Nurse in the facility overnight, fresh from treating and transporting Tobias to the infirmary, administered chloroform, rendering Hagatha unconscious. This enabled them to clean and dress Hagatha's wounds, fit her with a strait-jacket, and place her in a locked and padded seclusion room. She had caused enough damage and calamity for one night, and the Nurse wasn't going to allow her any more opportunities.

One thing was for sure, though, after that evening. The male orderlies were much more respectful of Hagatha from that point forward.

# CHAPTER 3

That Ursula and Otto Ketchel hadn't heard from their daughter in nearly a week was not unusual. Telephones were still uncommon in the U.S., so there was no quick or easy way to stay in touch. But Hagatha's failure to come to church with their granddaughter on Sunday raised a red flag.

They were so concerned that after church, they took their bicycles, which Enoch had bought for them while he was courting their daughter, and rode all the way to Slaughter. Upon arriving at the Slaughter mansion, they were greeted by a less than welcoming Enoch.

"What are you doing here?" he asked, his bleary eyes and whiskey breath telegraphing his condition.

"Is that any way to greet your father and mother-in-law?" Otto protested. "We're here to see our daughter and granddaughter. They didn't come to church this morning as usual."

"Well, she ain't here," he said. "Now go away."

"We'll do nothing of the sort," Otto replied, putting a hand on the door to prevent Enoch from shutting it. "What do you mean, she's not here? Where is she?"

"How the hell do I know. She left me a few days ago and never came back."

"She left you? Why? What did you do to her?" Otto said,

eyeing him with suspicion.

"I ain't done nothing to her. She just left, baby and all," he answered, as a young female voice called out from behind him.

"Enoch, dear. Who is that at the door?"

Otto and Ursala, not recognizing the voice, looked at Enoch with disapproval. But before they could question him further, he responded to her question.

"No one. No one's at the door," he said, slamming it in Otto and Ursala's face.

Now Otto and Ursala were not only more worried but also incensed at how their son-in-law had treated them. Their concern for their daughter and granddaughter was paramount. So instead of giving Enoch a piece of their mind, they got back on their bicycles. They stopped a few people in Slaughter to ask if they had seen their daughter, to no avail. When they finally got back to Grand Rapids, they were at a loss.

"Do you think we should check the hospital? Maybe she's sick," Otto theorized.

"Oh, I can't believe that. If she was sick, don't you think she would have asked us to take care of Hilda?"

"Maybe she didn't want to worry us and has a friend in Slaughter who's looking after Hilda. She knows we're always busy at the bakery," Otto replied.

"I guess it won't hurt to ask," Ursala relented.

When they got to the hospital, they learned the bittersweet news.

"We're looking for our daughter and granddaughter. Have you treated a woman named Hagatha Ketchel in the last week?" Ursala asked.

“Hmmm, that name is not familiar to me. What does she look like?"

“She's young, 23, and has long blond hair and the bluest of

eyes you'll ever see."

"Why yes, we did see someone matching that description a few days ago," the Nurse replied, unsure of how to tell them about her condition.

"Oh, thank God. Was she sick? Is she better?"

"Ah, she wasn't physically sick. She was acting strange."

"Acting strange? How so?"

"She couldn't give us her name. I think she thought she was Moses or something. She kept reciting scriptures, saying she was going to lead the children of Israel out of Egypt."

"I think you must be talking about someone else. That couldn't be my daughter," Ursala exclaimed.

"Well, there is a lot of blonds with blue eyes in town. But she had piercing blue eyes just as you described."

"Do you know where she is now?"

"No. Well, yes, I guess I do. The police were going to transport her to Fairdale Falls State Hospital."

"The police? Why the police? And where is Fairdale Falls State Hospital?" Ursala asked frantically.

"You'll have to ask the police about why they brought her here. As for Fairdale Falls State Hospital, it's an insane asylum just south of Pelican Rapids."

"An insane asylum? Our daughter's not insane! And where is Pelican Rapids?" Otto joined in.

"It's about 200 miles southwest of here. It's supposed to be quite nice, I hear," she added, hoping to tamp down Ursala and Otto's rising anger and frustration.

"200 miles? That will take days to get there. I don't care how nice it is. That's just too far. And what about her baby? How is she going to see her baby?" Ursala cried.

"Come, Ushi. Let's go speak to the police and get this straightened out," Otto said, wrapping his arm around his tearful wife.

If Ursala and Otto Ketchel thought they were annoyed leaving the hospital, they didn't know of the further insults they would experience speaking with the police.

# CHAPTER 4

Hagatha woke up, realizing she had soiled herself. She was in a dim, stuffy, unfamiliar room that was not much larger than a closet. The walls and the door were padded with straw-stuffed canvas. There was no detectable ventilation, and the only light came from the outside hallway through a small gap at the bottom of the door.

She was in a straitjacket making her shoulders, elbows, and wrists ache from her arms being tightly crisscrossed around her body for what must have been hours. The jacket had a canvas strap that went between her legs, cutting uncomfortably into her groin. She was able to move her legs and attempted to stand. Doing so without the aid of her arms was a challenge. In the process, she repeatedly rolled in her own feces and urine. She eventually succeeded in standing. However, there was nothing to see once she was standing. She could hear voices. After convincing herself they weren't just in her head and were generated by real people, she started hollering for release. When this failed to produce results, she started kicking the door. Eventually, she heard keys jingling on the other side of the door.

Hagatha was blinded by the light when the door opened. She had to close her eyes, not having the use of her hands to shield them.

"Woo, what a stinking mess you've made," exclaimed the

female orderly, plugging her nose. "We need to get you cleaned up. Are you going to behave yourself?"

Hagatha nodded, now squinting to see who was offering her freedom.

"My name is Margaret, but everyone calls me Maggie. They tell me your name is Iam. That's an unusual name. I've never heard of it before. Is it an old family name? I was named after my great-grandmother."

Maggie was clearly unlike all the other staff members Hagatha had encountered. Not only was she talkative, but she seemed to have a genuine interest in her. When Maggie got Hagatha to the washroom, she unbuckled the soiled straitjacket. Once released, Hagatha felt a tingling sensation as circulation returned to her arms. Next, Maggie started the shower and assisted Hagatha out of her fouled clothing.

"We need to make you presentable. The doctor will be in today and will want to see you. You must have been pretty upset last night. I always find that a good hot shower makes everything better. Don't you?" she asked, conversationally as she guided Hagatha under the warm spray. "That's not too hot, is it?"

Hagatha didn't say a word, but Maggie didn't seem to require a response and just continued her diatribe.

"I'll get you some soap and a washcloth so you can clean up. And don't forget to wash your hair. You have such pretty hair. I wish I had long, blond hair. But no, I have my mother's mousey brown hair."

Even if Hagatha wished to speak, she would have found it difficult, given Maggie's verbosity. But oddly, it seemed to calm the demons that were in her head. Or perhaps Maggie's incessant talking only temporarily drowned out the imaginary persecutory voices. Either way, Hagatha was granted a brief reprieve from the torturous thoughts that had been accosting her, for which she was grateful.

Once Hagatha was cleaned up, Maggie found some clean clothes for her to wear. Hagatha had come to Fairdale Falls with just the clothes on her back. Fortunately, the hospital had an inventory of donated clothing. The day's fashion was mainly long gowns with puffy sleeves, under which knee-length knickers or a full-body undergarment, called a combination, were worn. While not a perfect fit, they were clean and serviceable.

"Now, don't you feel better, Iam?" Maggie asked.

"Yes, thank you," Hagatha replied. This being the first socially appropriate and normal response she had uttered in weeks since coming to the hospital.

"Didn't I tell you a shower works wonders? Now I have to get you to Dr. Rosenstern's office. Follow me, Iam."

Hagatha cooperated.

"Why do you call me Iam?" she asked as they were talking down the hall.

"That's what the police said your name was when they dropped you off here. Why? Isn't that your name?"

"No. My name is Hagatha. Hagatha Ketchel," she replied in a moment of lucidity. Causing a flood of emotion as she suddenly recalled losing her married name of Slaughter and having to revert back to her maiden name.

"Hagatha? That's an unusual name too," Maggie exclaimed, not recognizing that Hagatha was starting to decompensate behind her.

Maggie got to the exit door when she realized that Hagatha was no longer beside her. She looked back down the hall and saw that Hagatha had crumbled to the floor, silently crying. By the time Maggie got back to Hagatha, her silent tears had turned into mournful wails.

"Oh, no, what happened? Why are you crying?" Maggie asked when she got to Hagatha's side.

Hagatha could not put her distress into words. All she could think about was how her life had fallen apart. Added now to her despair was the realization that she had a baby named Hilda, but she couldn't recall where she was or what happened to her. She had gone from being numb and paralyzed from her grief to having it breakthrough her consciousness, overwhelming her with painful thoughts and feelings.

Had Sigmund Freud been Hagatha's doctor, he would have diagnosed hysteria and melancholia and prescribed psychoanalysis and cocaine. But Freud's ground-breaking techniques for plumbing the depths of people's subconscious minds and his novel treatments weren't yet practiced in America. Instead, insanity was felt to be primarily a function of environmental and physical factors. Of which Dr. Rosenstern was a fanatical proponent. Nothing a little fresh air, vigorous exercise, backbreaking work, and the judicious use of ice baths, seclusion, and restraint couldn't fix.

And so it was, Dr. Harold Rosenstern met with Hagatha, and in 5 minutes, he had formulated a precise treatment plan. Never mind that Hagatha cried the entire time and didn't hear a word the psychiatrist said. Or that her treatment plan was interchangeable with the 200 other patients within the walls of Fairdale Falls State Hospital.

Dr. Rosenstern's recipe for curing lunacy included an hour of calisthenics first thing in the morning. Followed by 8 hours of work in the fields, gardens, stables, kitchen, or housekeeping. And concluding with another hour of calisthenics before lights out. This schedule was followed every day except Sundays or one of the six Holy Days of Obligation dictated by the Catholic Church. On these days, the patients would be obligated to hear mass in the Chapel.

The patients would be granted luxurious15 minute breaks to eat their breakfast, lunch, and supper. Unless, of course, it was a day of fasting or abstinence, like all Fridays, all days during Lent, certain Holy Days, or one of a handful of Vigil Feast days. In which case, only one evening meal was served. Moreover, eating meat was prohibited on fasting or abstinence days. And meat and fish could never be served and eaten at the same meal.

For any patient unwilling to follow this treatment, attend mass, or observe the dietary plan, liberal use of ice baths, seclusion, or restraint was employed.

"An occupied body and a God-fearing mind have no room for the devil's madness," was Dr. Rosenstern's motto.

Woe betides the patient who failed to subscribe to his transformative treatment. For Dr. Rosenstern, who fancied himself as God's gift to the lunatics of the world, was only too happy to mete out the punishment and the pain for their grievous mortal sins. Selling his approach as the only way to exorcise the demons that their weak and immoral constitutions had wrought.

At the time, many considered Dr. Rosenstern's methods ground-breaking, on a par with discoveries made by other notable psychiatrists of the era. But, eventually, his approach would be seen for what it was – a dismal failure. Nothing more than an attempt at absolution through abuse. But by then, the damage to Hagatha and others would be done. And then, for Hagatha, there would be no turning back.

# CHAPTER 5

"How dare you put my daughter in an insane asylum!" Otto shouted as he and Ursala barged into the police station. "I demand that you return her immediately."

It was a good thing that the police officer on duty was familiar with Otto and Ursala, as their bakery had recently become a favorite stop for the officers. Ironically, had they frequented the bakery while Hagatha was still working there, they would have known who she was and taken a decidedly different tack.

"Mr. and Mrs. Ketchel, I didn't even know you had a daughter. The woman we put in the asylum couldn't tell us her name. And I assure you, she definitely needed to go there."

"Well, you know now. And just exactly what makes you qualified to determine she needed to be in an asylum?"

The police officer was between a rock and a hard place. He had two irate parents, and what he was about to tell them would only make matters worse.

"Let's go talk about this in my office," he suggested, hoping to delay the inevitable.

"No. Here is just fine. Talk!" Otto spat.

The officer was out of options.

"Fine. But I'm afraid what I have to say is going to be,"

"Just get on with it already!" Otto fumed.

"A young couple came in here last week holding a baby girl. They claimed that a woman had thrown the baby into the river, and the young man had rescued her."

Otto and Ursala's anger was temporarily tempered by concern.

"Who is the couple, and where is our granddaughter?" Ursala asked.

"Charles and Evelyn Shepherd, and I suspect the baby is with them in Duluth."

"Duluth? How do you know they didn't steal the baby from my daughter?"

"They gave us their address and told us that if we identified the rightful family, they'd return her."

"And how do you know that the address they gave you is really where they live?"

"Ah," he stammered. "I don't. They looked like honest people. And the young man's clothes were all wet. So I don't think they lied to me," he said, in defense of his decision.

"Well, you better hope so," Otto said in a threatening tone.

"And what about our daughter? What was she doing that made you think she needed to be in an asylum?"

"We found your daughter on the Pokegama Lake Dam. She was mumbling, reciting scriptures, and not making any sense. We feared she might be trying to kill herself. We had the doctor examine her, and it was upon his recommendation that we took her to Fairdale Falls State Hospital."

Enoch Slaughter's story about their daughter just up and leaving with the baby was now starting to make sense. Although they found it hard to believe, what other explanation could there have been? Perhaps she had gone mad, left unceremoniously, tried to dispose of her baby, and then attempt to kill herself. Only to be saved by the police. She would have had to be more than a little touched not to seek help from them. Ursala and Otto's reaction softened.

"Please understand. I'm grateful you rescued our little girl off the dam. But maybe she was just temporarily confused, or maybe she was just distraught over what she did to her baby. Perhaps if she knew that Hilda survived, she wouldn't be so sad. And we could get her baby back," Ursala suggested.

"Maybe so, but that would be something you'd have to take up with Fairdale Falls State Hospital now. I'd be remiss if I didn't tell you that on the way there, she became quite agitated. She scratched and bit one of the officers and spit on us. We had to bind her arms and legs and cover her head. I tell you this just so you know that we had cause to take the action we did."

"Oh, heavens, that's awful. I'm sure she must be feeling terrible about that now. Our apologies in her stead," Ursala exclaimed.

"Yes, that is dreadful," Otto added. "Please tell your officers that coffee and strudel are on the house. We raised our little girl to be respectful, and what you endured is so out of character for our sweet, gentle Hagatha."

Some would say that Otto's generous offer of free strudel and coffee was the event that spurred the tradition of shopowners offering police officers free coffee and donuts. Which would become endemic 100 years hence. But records of such matters in the 1890s either didn't exist or were lost to the sands of time. Thus, no one really knows. But it was a welcome gesture that the Grand Rapids police officers took full advantage of.

Ursala and Otto requested and received the address of Charles and Evelyn Shepherd. Intent to write them a letter requesting that they return Hilda. But before they did that, they had to liberate their daughter from Fairdale Falls State Hospital.

# CHAPTER 6

It was perhaps fortunate that Hagatha's lucid moments were just that – moments. Otherwise, the overwhelming anger, shame, and guilt she had would boil over like an unattended boiling pot of water - scalding anything and everything around her. During these moments of clarity, her actions were highly unpredictable and frequently destructive. She was just as likely to strike out at others as to try to harm herself. On occasion, her emotions became so intense that she would become paralyzed and mute.

While Fairdale Falls State Hospital had a small, locked forensic unit for male offenders, kept separate from the general population, all the other wards were coed. Likewise, daily exercise sessions and therapeutic work, as it was called, included both men and women. As you might suspect, this introduced a whole nother variable into patient management. How could you not have shenanigans when you had men and women living, working, and playing in proximity to each other. Especially men and women ravaged by the scourge of the Devil's madness, as Dr. Rosenstern put it. But the coed units and activities were part of the treatment philosophy. Segregating the sexes would introduce an unnatural environment. An environment that patients wouldn't find in everyday society if they were discharged and expected to behave as civil human beings. Thus, segregating the patients would do them a disservice.

The exercise regimen that Dr. Rosenstern prescribed for all patients wasn't all that novel for male patients. The benefits of men exercising was a well-established practice, even in the 19th century. However, women exercising was innovative, and some thought it dangerous. Moreover, it went against the precepts of the day, which dictated that women should refrain from exercise after puberty. The reasoning was that women were thought to have fragile emotional constitutions and feeble arm strength, making them unfit for such endeavors.

When the weather was conducive, exercise sessions would be held out on the front lawn or down by the lake if swimming was involved. From a patient management perspective, calisthenics on the lawn was easier to supervise than swimming. Trying to observe and control 20 to 30 patients splashing around in the water from the shoreline was trying at best. Consequently, nothing prevented a patient from trying to swim across the lake. Not that staff feared this presented a flight risk. Except for where the hospital complex stood, the lake was surrounded by vast fields of flat farmland. Making escape nearly impossible. Some tried, but high-tailing it on foot was no match for staff on horseback.

No, the primary concern with swimming across the lake was that they may not make it and drown. Of course, this possibility only became a concern when it happened one day when Hagatha and her ward mates jumped into the lake to cool down after exercising. Everything was going swimmingly until Hagatha felt intrusive hands fondling her nether region underwater. She shrieked, but amid the laughter of the other patients and the splashing, it didn't register as a concern. The culprit surfaced next to Hagatha with a devious look of satisfaction.

"You're all wet down there," leered Gerald, a middle-aged patient who looked older than his age.

Gerald was a 45-year old farmer from southern Minnesota

who had been transferred to Fairdale Falls from the over-crowded asylum in St. Peter. Graying hair and missing front teeth, and lateral incisors made him look at least 20 years older. He had lost his teeth when one of his sheep kicked him in the mouth. Accidents happen to farmers, but this was no accident. The ewe didn't take kindly to being violated by Gerald. After felling him with a well-placed kick in the groin, she followed up with another to his mouth. Gerald's wife, Martha, also happened into the barn and saw his disgusting act. She landed a few well-placed kicks of her own before reporting his bestiality to the police and having him carted off to the asylum in St. Peter.

"Go drown yourself, Gerald," Hagatha replied angrily.

After which, something seemed to take hold of Gerald. He started swimming out towards the middle of the lake. Staff called for him to return, but he didn't stop. One staff member ran to the stables to get a horse in case he tried to elope. The other staff continued to yell to him from the shoreline. Several of the patients joined her in calling for Gerald, forming a chorus. Finally, when he got to the absolute middle of the lake, Gerald stopped swimming. He turned and looked back at the gaggle of people calling to him. He had a terrified and desperate look on his face. As if he had swum out there involuntarily. And then he slowly started to sink, screaming for help, until he disappeared under the surface of the water.

They would recover Gerald's body a couple hours later. The coroner, who in those days was not a physician, ruled the death a drowning. Surmising that he probably got a cramp, rendering him unable to swim.

Hagatha surmised otherwise. She wasn't remorseful of the outcome, given the liberties Gerald had taken. However, she was definitely shocked when he seemingly couldn't help but cooperate with her angry response. She didn't mean it literally. She had said it as a kind of cuss, but its effect was a deadly curse. She couldn't even really fathom it at the time. It would be her first inkling that there was something dark, mysterious, and powerful inside her.

# CHAPTER 7

The young lady's voice that Otto and Ursala Ketchel heard the day they visited a drunken inhospitable Enoch Slaughter belonged to Lila McInerney. Lila was 17 years old, 13 years Enoch's junior. He had met her shortly after jettisoning Hagatha and baby Hilda from his life. No one would have mistaken their initial meeting as ever having a chance to become a burgeoning romance - quite the opposite.

Lila may have been young, but she was no shrinking violet. She grew up as the only girl in a family with six older brothers who loved her but mercilessly teased and taunted her. So she had no choice but to learn how to stand up for herself. Whereas Enoch had been able to intimidate Hagatha and always get his way, Lila was not so easily dominated. She had a stubborn streak and a fiery temper that rivaled his. When she got her Irish up, she could give it right back to him and then some. In fact, that is what infuriated and attracted Enoch to her when they first met.

Lila's family ran McInerney's Mercantile, Slaughter's General Store. On the occasion of their first meeting, Lila happened to be the only shopkeeper. Her father and one of her older brothers were busy running errands. She was assisting a customer with their order when Enoch sauntered in as if he owned the place. He picked an apple out of a barrel, rubbed it on his sleeve, and bit into it with a resounding crunch. This would not have been an issue had Lila's father been there. He was accustomed to Enoch not observing the store's rules. But since Enoch was the Mayor, Lila's father never confronted him – even when he left without paying for what he had consumed.

Lila, however, didn't know Enoch, and even if she had, she was a staunch rule-follower and fierce rule-enforcer. She looked up from what she was doing and laid into him.

"Excuse me, sir. Kindly respect the store rules. No eating until you've paid for your items. That will be 2 cents. Now pony up," she demanded, holding out her hand indicating that she intended to collect what was owed.

Enoch chuckled and took another bite out of the apple. With his mouth still half-full, he replied.

"Don't you know who I am, young lady?" he asked as pieces of apple flew from his mouth and onto the floor.

"No, I don't, and I don't care beans if you think you're the biggest toad in the puddle," she replied angrily. "Now pay up, and then you can wipe up the mess you just made on my floor."

The customer Lila was helping was aghast. He knew who Enoch was and feared for Lila's well-being in trying to hold him accountable. He cringed, knowing he was in the middle of an encounter that was likely to turn ugly.

"You obstinate, ignorant little wench," Enoch blustered. "I'm the Mayor of this town, and I can shut this store down as quickly as I gave your father permission to open it. As for stooping to clean your disgusting floor, that's work befitting a woman. Although there doesn't seem to be a proper one around here."

"You rude, poor excuse for a man. I will not tolerate your insults any further. Leave this minute or so help me, God, you'll have to be carried out."

"And how is a little spit of a girl like you going to do that?" he laughed heartily.

Lila reached into the folds of her dress and produced a .45 caliber Derringer.

"I don't know, would this do the trick?" she asked, flashing the gun along with a wry smile.

"Now, now, you take it easy, young lady," Enoch pleaded, taking a step back and raising his arms in surrender. "My apologies. I will settle with you for the cost of the apple. Now put that down."

"And clean the floor?" she asked, keeping the gun trained on him.

"Yes, ma'am. Now please put that away before someone gets hurt."

"I'll put it away when I see two pennies on my counter and your filthy spittle removed from my floor."

Enoch looked lost. He was not accustomed to cleaning, let alone what the store used to maintain their wood plank floors. Which were spotless, contrary to his previous derogatory comments, except for the bits of apple and spit.

"There's a mop in a bucket in the corner," she said, pointing in the direction he should head. "And make sure to wring it out good before you use it. Too much water will warp the flooring."

Enoch walked to the appointed corner of the store. Upon seeing the mop sitting in the bucket of water, he turned and looked at Lila with a questioning look.

"Ah, how do I?" he said, trying to formulate a question.

"Do you mean to tell me that you don't even know how to wring out a mop?

"Ah, er, well, I never," he started to stammer.

Lila put the gun back in the pocket of her dress and marched over to where Enoch and the mop bucket stood.

"Move!" she commanded, making Enoch jump aside.

With practiced movements, she expertly wrung the mop

out with her hands. Careful not to spill a drop on the floor. Then held the mop out for Enoch.

"Here! Now, go mop up your mess."

Enoch took the mop, holding it at arms-length like he was afraid it might bite him. Then, when he got to the area that needed cleaning, he started to dab the area, repeatedly dropping the mop head on the spot in an up and down motion.

When he looked back to Lila, she just stood there shaking her head in disapproval.

"What?" Enoch asked.

"You can't even mop a floor, and you're the Mayor? God help us!" she said, exasperated.

"Here, let me show you," she said, marching over and liberating the mop from Enoch, who was now thoroughly humiliated. As the man, who Lila had been helping, continued to look on in amusement.

Enoch was also somehow wholly taken by the petite but ferocious and self-assured young woman. And by the time he had paid for the apple and left the store with his tail between his legs, he had convinced himself that he would marry that little fireball – come hell or high water. The clock was ticking on his desire to ensure his family legacy. After their inauspicious start, you would have thought Enoch would take an easier path than pursue Lila McInerney.

In doing so, however, he guaranteed himself a tumultuous and passionate relationship. They would fight and love hard, always either on the edge of ecstasy or the brink of disaster. Fair winds and following seas had no place in their relationship.

# CHAPTER 8

Ursala Ketchel desperately wanted to communicate with Charles and Evelyn Shepherd for the return of baby Hilda. However, Ursala and Otto had a dilemma – how to keep the bakery running while someone took what would be at least a 4-5 day trip to Fairdale Falls State Hospital and back.

"I wish we could go together. We could stop at the Shepherd's on our way and surprise Hagatha when we all get to the hospital. Imagine how happy she'd be to see that she didn't drown her baby!" Ursala gushed.

"Yes, Ushi, that would be ideal, but we cannot afford to have the bakery closed for nearly a week," Otto replied.

"Maybe I should go and pick up Hilda and go to the hospital on my own," Ursala suggested.

"Ushi, my love, I'm not going to let you go by yourself. It's a long trip, and who knows what kind of people are out there. Plus the baby. I don't think it's a good idea to travel with her all that way. And what if our daughter is truly sick? What then? We can't take care of a baby and the bakery on our own."

The disappointment on Ursala's face evolved to resignation.

"I guess you should go while I run the bakery. And if you get Hagatha out of the hospital, perhaps you could stop at the

Shepherds' home on your way back."

"Now that makes more sense," Otto said, putting his arm around his wife. "I know how much you miss them, Bubala. I'll make arrangements, and be sure to give me the Shepherds' address. I plan to bring our daughter and granddaughter back before the week is out."

Otto's confident response buoyed Ursala's flagging spirits. Although confidence was the last thing that Otto was feeling. He didn't know what he was walking into. An insane asylum? He couldn't even believe his beautiful daughter was in such a place, let alone alleged to have tried to drown her baby. So there must have been some mistake, some misunderstanding. Or maybe it was something that his son-in-law, Enoch, knew more about or had caused.

Otto needed to get to the bottom of this, and now that he knew where his daughter was, he would try to approach Enoch once more. His reasoning was sound. He and Ursala were not wealthy and could barely afford the cost of the trip. On the other hand, Enoch had far greater resources and influence. So who better than Hagatha's husband to help get her and the baby back?

Otto convinced himself that perhaps he and Ursala had caught Enoch at a bad time on their last visit. Maybe he was drunk and distraught because his wife had left him. And as for the woman's voice in the background? Perhaps she was a family member or friend just there to provide him support. Otto had only known Enoch to be a doting and loving husband. And if that was the case, he would want to help Otto get her released from the hospital and recover Hilda. If, on the other hand, Enoch turned him away again, then maybe his daughter's break with reality was caused by something that transpired between her and Enoch. All he knew was that he needed more information before he trekked 200 miles in an attempt to bring his daughter back home. And there was only one way to do it – to meet mano a mano.

# CHAPTER 9

As its name proclaimed, Fairdale Falls State Hospital was a government-funded institution. As such, you would expect there to be a separation between Church and State, as was Thomas Jefferson's intent in crafting the First Amendment of the United States Constitution. However, this was clearly not the case. Dr. Rosenstern's treatment philosophy, which was based on the assumption that lunatics were possessed by the Devil, required the healing salve of strict religious principles and dictates.

In addition to Catholic church services and dietary practices, each patient room was equipped with a copy of the King James Bible. This was the one and the only form of reading material supplied. Patients were assigned Bible readings each day. Staff enforced compliance by randomly quizzing patients at the end of the day. Progressive discipline was applied if the patient failed to answer the question correctly. The first time resulted in a stern warning. The second and third offenses were a day of abstinence from food. After that, every subsequent offense was either an ice bath, seclusion, or restraint at the staff's discretion.

Ward staff also had discretion on the difficulty of the questions. While some might ask something simple like, "What were the names of the two people in the Garden of Eden?" Others might ask a patient to recite from memory a specific verse within the required reading. If you think that the difficulty of the question was random, you'd be sorely mistaken. It was often related to how sadistic the staff member felt that particular day or their frustration level with the specific patient.

In the case of Hagatha, both male and female staff reveled in giving her the most challenging questions. However, for different reasons and for other ends. Female staff envied her beauty and how male staff and patients alike would constantly ogle her. They asked difficult questions intending to put her in seclusion if she failed to answer correctly. Out of sight, out of mind was their mantra. The male staff just wanted the opportunity to lay hands on her and plunge her into an ice bath. Where more than just Hagatha's nipples would become erect. Of course, the men knew better than to let their excitement get anywhere near Hagatha's mouth.

The repeated instances of seclusion and ice baths continued for months. Eventually, Hagatha became so well-versed with the Bible that staff would have to ask her multiple questions before getting something wrong and ending up in seclusion or the ice bath. The long-term abuse and feeling between a rock and a hard place had predictable results. Hagatha's frustration and resentment evolved into blinding anger and hatred. No longer would she be a victim of their cruelty. Instead, she would find a way to get back at them. All she needed to do was learn how to tap the powers she had used to compel Gerald to drown himself.

In the meantime, Hagatha just took names and continued to endure the abuse. As she was repeatedly thrown into the seclusion room, or men pleasuring themselves to her nakedness in the ice bath, she would growl, "To me belongeth vengeance and recompense. Their foot shall slide in due time, for the day of their calamity is at hand, and the things that shall come upon them make haste."

But that retribution verse from Deuteronomy would not be the only scripture she would recite. She would inevitably commit to memory and utter all the biblical references to revenge. And even make some up that sounded biblical but were manufactured by her tortured mind. The staff found great amusement in this. Laughing in the face of her threats. That is until the day Hagatha delivered on her promised payback.

# CHAPTER 10

Otto went to visit his son-in-law, filled with hope. Buoyed by the assumption that once Enoch knew what had happened to Hagatha, he would come to her aid. As Otto crested the hill upon which the Slaughter Mansion stood, Enoch was high-tailing it out the door. He looked happy to see Otto this time and ran to greet him.

"Otto," he panted, out of breath. "So good to see you."

Before Otto could respond, he heard the sound of a woman yelling and dishware shattering coming from the house.

"Is everything all right back there?" Otto asked, peering over Enoch's shoulder.

"Oh, that's nothing. It's just my clumsy housekeeper. She's constantly breaking things. Let's take a walk," he said as Otto got off his bicycle.

Enoch led Otto away from the commotion in the house and back down the hill towards town.

"What brings you out here? I haven't seen you in ages."

Otto looked at him quizzically.

"What do you mean? Ursala and I just visited you last week. And I must say, you weren't very pleasant. You seemed to have a brick in your hat. And it was only mid-morning."

Enoch returned a look of surprise.

"Huh, I don't recall that. Are you sure?"

"Yes, you told us that Hagatha had left you. You were in quite a huff."

"Ah, it's coming back to me now," Enoch acknowledged. "My apologies. I did get a little liquored up. I couldn't believe she left me. And then to learn that Hilda wasn't even mine. That was the last straw," he added.

"What? Are you saying my Hagatha had amorous congress with another man?"

"Yes, I was entirely hornswoggled. All the time leading me to believe the child was mine."

"I can't believe that. Maybe that explains why she did what she did," Otto thought out loud.

"Why she did what?" Enoch asked.

"That's the reason I came here to see you. When we couldn't find Hagatha, we went to the police. They told us that she tried to drown Hilda in the Mississippi River. Fortunately, a young couple was able to rescue her. Hagatha was later found on the Pokegama Lake Dam, talking nonsense. The police think she was trying to kill herself. A doctor examined her and sent her to an insane asylum. I was hoping that you would help get Hagatha and Hilda back. But now, knowing what you just told me, I don't suppose you're inclined to do so."

"You'd be right about that, Otto. And just to let you know, I have annulled our marriage. I'm sure you understand. I couldn't abide by her false-heartedness. Even if I was inclined to help, I no longer have any legal standing as I am not her husband. Nor am I or was I ever the baby's father."

"I understand your reasoning, Enoch. But I do not understand my daughter's behavior. We raised her to be a proper, God-fearing lady."

"Nor do I, Otto. I'm sorry I can't help you. Now I better get back to the house and make sure my housekeeper doesn't destroy everything."

"You might want to consider getting a new housekeeper," Otto suggested.

"I might just do that. Thank you, Otto. Have a safe ride home."

Otto pedaled off back in the direction of home. The hope he had arrived with was shattered by the inconceivable information Enoch had shared. Now, he questioned whether traveling to the asylum was even worth it. Perhaps his daughter truly was insane. In which case, the Fairdale Falls State Hospital was the right place for her. As for Hilda, maybe being raised by a young couple who obviously cared for her was the best thing. However, he was not looking forward to having to break the news to Ursala.

Meanwhile, Enoch turned and smiled as he walked back up the driveway towards the mansion. Congratulating himself on making up the story about Hagatha's adultery and Hilda's illegitimacy. He was happy to close the chapter of his life with Hagatha and dispense with his former inlaws. As he approached the mansion, he also hoped that Lila had cooled down from their earlier argument and that they still had some unbroken dishware on which to dine.

# CHAPTER 11

Work was an integral part of the patient's treatment plans at Fairdale Falls. Like everything else, Dr. Rosenstern dictated that all patients would cycle through all the various jobs regardless of aptitude. His reasoning was that inflexibility of mind, body, and spirit contributed to insanity. Thus, rotating patients in and out of different work roles forced one to adapt and build new competencies. Just as exercise made the body limber, and the worship of God freed their spirit from the paralyzing clutches of the Devil.

Hagatha's first work assignment was working in the stables. Horses were the lifeblood of transportation and farm work in the late 19$^{th}$ century. Fairdale Falls State Hospital had a team of twenty horses to supply for all of their needs. Unfortunately, working in the stables was difficult and uncomfortable regardless of the time of year. And the combination of mentally unstable individuals and skittish horses was not always a marriage made in heaven.

For this reason, employed and trained grooms primarily managed the horses. This entailed feeding them and preparing them for their duties in the early morning. Horses not assigned to carriage or farm duties had to be exercised or brought out to pasture during the day. At the end of the day, the grooms rubbed the horses down to remove dirt and sweat and gave them their evening feeding. In between times, they had to manage the patients to ensure that the critical tasks of mucking out the stalls, forking hay down from the hayloft, watering the horses, and bedding the stalls were correctly done.

The irony of having patients presumably possessed by the Devil given pitchforks to accomplish their tasks was apparently lost on the hospital's management. To Dr. Rosenstern, the benefit of the work far outweighed "the occasional misadventure," as he termed it. Tell that to the patients, grooms, and horses that would suffer being impaled over the years. However, only a few would die from their injuries, usually from the infection that ensued from the manure-tinged tines.

What made the work that much more unpleasant was the summer heat and humidity. Not to mention the ripe aroma of urine and manure, the itch-inducing hay, the sinus-clogging dust, and the ever-present infestation of flies. The job and the environment would be challenging enough for anyone. But for Hagatha, that was not all. In addition, she had to contend with near-constant harassment by one male patient.

Richard was from a different ward and was also assigned to stable duty. He had been committed to Fairdale Falls after setting himself on fire. To look at him was like looking at two different people. That's because the burns from the fire were confined to the left side of his torso and head. So half of him was a hairless collection of scar tissue contorting the left side of his body and face. His left eye had no brow or lashes and was partially covered by a hood of scar tissue. His lips on the left were huge and swollen. He could not close that side of his mouth, causing him to drool and giving him a perpetual sneer. The right side of his face looked absolutely normal. Giving you the sense that at one time, he may have actually been quite handsome. It was a disturbing image that made people gravitate towards standing on his right side to avoid looking at the hideous half-mask he wore on the left.

But as Hagatha would learn, Richard's problem wasn't that he tried to kill himself. No, his problem was much more complex.

Meeting Richard for the first time was difficult for anyone. Hagatha had all she could do not to stare or let the horror she felt inside transmit to her face. Once she got over the shock, then curiosity took its place, and she had to fend off the desire to ask him what happened to cause his dichotomous appearance. Everything about Richard just made you want to avoid him. And this was even before Hagatha got to experience firsthand his fetish.

The first day they worked together was relatively uneventful. Hagatha was stationed to the right of Richard as they mucked stalls. Thereby when she happened to look his way, she saw the normal side of his face. The only mishap was Richard running into Hagatha's hip with his manure-filled wheelbarrow on the way to the manure pile.

"Oh, I'm sorry. I didn't see you there," Richard exclaimed, setting down his wheelbarrow. "It's my left eye. The scar tissue blocks my peripheral vision."

"You're forgiven," Hagatha said, her face a mask of pain as she rubbed her backside where he had run into it.

She didn't think anything of it. She appreciated the apology, and his reason for the accident was believable. It wasn't easy navigating a loaded wheelbarrow, and she could only imagine the additional challenge of doing so with partial vision.

"I hope I didn't hurt you too badly," he added as a stream of drool escaped from the left side of his mouth.

"I'll be fine," Hagatha responded, quickly looking away to hide the disgust she felt as he slobbered like a St. Bernard. "I'll try to be more cautious where I stand next time."

"Thank you for understanding," he replied and continued his journey towards the manure pile.

The incident would soon be forgotten, replaced by the revulsion for the job itself and the unbearable heat and humidity. A long dress with long sleeves may have been the order of the day, but it wasn't optimal for barn work. Hagatha was disheveled and exhausted when she got back to the ward.

"Welcome back, Hagatha. How was your first day of work?" Maggie, the talkative orderly who had rescued her from seclusion, asked.

Before Hagatha could respond, Chester, one of the male orderlies, interrupted.

"Scripture test," he announced.

"But I haven't had time to read the Bible yet," Hagatha protested.

"That is not my problem. Recite Philippians chapter 4 verses 6 and 7."

Despite not having done the day's reading, Hagatha was familiar with the biblical reference.

"Be careful for nothing, in everything by prayer and supplication with thanksgiving, let your requests be made known unto God. And the peace of God, which passeth all understanding, shall keep your hearts and minds through Christ Jesus," Hagatha replied, as Chester read along in the Bible.

Maggie smiled, thinking Hagatha had passed the test.

"Oh, I'm sorry. You missed a word. It's "Be careful for nothing, BUT in everything by prayer." You missed the but. I'm afraid your butt's going in the ice bath," he laughed at his play-on-words and grabbed Hagatha's arm gruffly.

Two other male orderlies joined Chester in parading Hagatha off as Maggie was left to protest.

"Chester, that's not fair. She misses one word, and you give her an ice bath? I'm going to speak to Dr. Rosenstern."

"You do that, Maggie, and you'll be the next one we take

to the ice bath," Chester called, to the amusement of the other two orderlies.

Maggie knew that Chester's threat wasn't idle words and decided against tattling to Dr. Rosenstern.

Meanwhile, Chester and his boys got Hagatha to the ice bath and stripped her down.

"Whoa, look at that bruise," Chester exclaimed upon seeing an angry purple contusion on Hagatha's right butt cheek. "What happened at the stables? Did the stallion try to mount you?"

They put her in the ice bath and strapped her wrists to the tub to prevent her from escaping. To their chagrin, she didn't put up a fight. Nor would Hagatha dignify any of their taunts with a response. Part of her was happy to be plunged into the ice bath after suffering the sweltering heat of the stable. Even if it meant the indignity of being naked and having Chester and his gang masturbate while ogling her.

She knew that retribution would be her reward, eventually.

# CHAPTER 12

Enoch walked into the kitchen to find Lila sobbing amid a blanket of shattered snow-white china covering the floor around her.

"I love you," Enoch said, taking her in his arms and kissing her cheek.

"I hate you," she snuffled in response, pounding on his chest half-heartedly with her fist.

"Let's get married."

"You're crazy. We'll never last."

"You're beautiful. I'll die without you."

"I might just kill you if we get married."

"So be it. Just give me some baby boys, and then you can kill me."

It was a unique way to propose marriage. But entirely in keeping with Enoch and Lila's relationship, which had never been conventional. Nevertheless, she accepted his proposal. Several weeks later, they hosted an extravagant wedding on the grounds of the Slaughter Estate.

Both families and nearly half the town were invited. Enoch's parents, Elias and Ruth Slaughter, traveled up from the Twin Cities. It had been their loan that enabled Enoch to literally fall into his wealth. Elias Slaughter always had high expectations for his oldest son, Enoch. And up until he failed to produce a son in his marriage to Hagatha, Enoch had lived up to his father's lofty hopes. He far surpassed his younger brothers, both in wealth and station in life as Mayor of the town he created. Yet Enoch felt his supremacy over his brothers was rapidly diminishing.

Enoch's two younger brothers, Jeremiah and Abraham, and their wives and children were also in attendance. Enoch may have had financial riches, but his two younger brothers were way ahead of him in the sweepstakes that really mattered. That being having boys who would be able to carry on the family name and legacy. Jeremiah had a 7-year old son named Jacob, and his wife was pregnant. Abraham had a 3-year old son named Noah. And while his wife wasn't pregnant, it was well-known they planned to have more children.

It galled Enoch to see his parents fawning over their two grandsons. To say that Enoch resented his brothers would be putting it mildly. If not for Lila's insistence, he wouldn't even have invited them to the wedding. And as only Enoch and Lila could, their differences on the matter caused a barnburner of a fight. Which was like most of their arguments. Lila would hold her ground. Enoch would get frustrated and storm out to the dram shop for a few drinks. Then crawl back and surrender to Lila's wishes. He'd grovel for forgiveness. Lila would pardon him, and they would reconcile in what would eventually be their marital bed. It was not the most efficient or diplomatic way to settle differences, but it seemed to work for them.

The big wedding was another argument Enoch lost with Lila. Having been through getting married before, Enoch wanted a small, quick, private ceremony. Lila, a 17-year old with her head in the clouds marrying the town's wealthiest resident, wanted a big, audacious party. And as was becoming readily apparent, what Lila wanted, Lila got. Consequently, Enoch suffered through the pomp and circumstance of the lengthy wedding ceremony. A couple of drinks helped loosen him up during the reception. And as the party wound down, he carried Lila over the threshold, and they consummated their marriage.

Nine months later, Enoch and Lila welcomed Enoch, Jr. into the world. While Lila was elated and basked in the glow of motherhood, Enoch still felt as though he was playing second-fiddle. Jeremiah's wife bore him a second son, Jedidiah, three months earlier. Elias Slaughter's expectations for his eldest son never extended to competing with his brothers in the race to produce male offspring. Instead, Enoch put that pressure on himself. And we would not rest until he dominated his brothers in every aspect of life.

# CHAPTER 13

Hagatha found that the drudgery of working in the stables was minimized when she could lose herself in thought. Specifically pondering how to recapture and harness the power she exercised over Gerald to compel him to drown himself. Except now, she wanted to turn that power against others who continued to torment her – like Chester. Being able to dispose of people without so much as touching them would be a valuable skill.

Unfortunately, every time she would be deep in reflection and think she was on the brink of a breakthrough, a groom or Richard would say or do something to distract her. And then she'd have to start the thought process all over again. It was maddening, and the last thing her tortured soul needed was more madness.

Hagatha thought Richard's running into her with the wheelbarrow was an accident. However, every day Richard seemed to find a way to cause her pain. One day he ran into her, almost knocking her over. Another day he stepped on her foot. Yesterday she had been following him up the ladder to the hay-loft, and he slipped, kicking her in the head in his effort to find a rung and not fall. She had come to the stables worried about being injured by the horses, only to get daily bumps, bruises, and abrasions from Richard. Even when she gave him wide-berth, he seemed to find a way to injure her. While mucking a stall the other day, he found an empty water bucket. He tossed it out at the exact moment Hagatha passed by, and the heavy metal container hit her in the mouth, splitting her lip and loosening a couple of her teeth.

Each time these things happened, Richard was quick to apologize. However, the look on his face and a marked increase in his drooling made Hagatha wonder if he was sincere. It almost looked as if he enjoyed it. However, Richard's face was hard to read because half of it was permanently frozen in a grinning sneer.

Eventually, a day came when Hagatha no longer questioned whether all these incidents were accidental. Several times a day, she and Richard would need to climb into the hayloft to fork the forage through trapdoors into cribs below. On this occasion, Hagatha was careful not to follow Richard too closely up the ladder. However, when she got up to the loft, she was hit on the head, temporarily rendering her unconscious. She came to, only to find her wrists bound by ropes tied to the hayloft beams. She was naked. Behind her stood Richard, holding a leather whip typically used by the carriage drivers. She knew what was coming and started screaming before he even swung the whip.

There were either no grooms in the stables, or if they were, they ignored her cries as Richard cracked the whip repeatedly on her back, buttocks, and legs. Each time he swung the whip and heard her scream in agony, he grew more excited. He'd occasionally stop to run his hand painfully over Hagatha's lacerations, smearing her blood on his face. At times he would even lick the blood on her back and off her buttocks. Moaning in ecstasy as he did so.

The whipping went on for what seemed like hours, and Hagatha, now hoarse from shrieking, eventually passed out from the pain. This time when she came to, she was in the infirmary lying flat on her belly. Her wounds had been dressed with sterilized gauze dressings, a relatively new invention for that day and age. She was excused from the usual daily schedule of activities and spent the next week lying prone on her bed.

Ironically, Hagatha's pain brought progress. All she could do was lie still and cogitate on how to kindle her powers of retribution and destruction. Now, of course, Richard rose to the top of her hit list. Her first job was to ponder a suitable mechanism of death. As Richard seemed to get off on inflicting pain. She wondered how much he'd enjoy it if the shoe were on the other foot. What death would be slow and painful?

Suddenly, she got an idea. Slowly and with great pain, she reached for her Bible. She recalled a verse in Genesis about birds eating flesh which sounded like an excruciating way to die. Finally finding it in Chapter 40, she recited, "Yet within three days shall Pharaoh lift up thy head from off thee, and shall hang thee on a tree. And the birds shall eat thy flesh from off thee."

"Hmm," she said to herself. "Beheading and hanging are much too quick. Perhaps I will only use that last part."

Hagatha started repeating, "And the birds shall eat thy flesh from off thee," while concentrating on Richard and all the pain he had caused her. She didn't stop, even when she had to bear the pain of getting up to relieve herself in the bucket ward staff had placed in her room for convenience. Day and night, she did nothing but recite the phrase while focused on her tormentor. She refused meals and didn't even allow herself to sleep. Finally, after three days, totally exhausted, she fell into a deep sleep. Only to be awakened 12 hours later by a vivid nightmare of Richard being attacked by a murder of crows.

Her wounds and welts had healed, and she was cleared to resume her regular schedule. She didn't know what to expect when she got to the stables after being away for a week. She could only hope that the mantra she had recited had worked its magic. She didn't know how she would ever face Richard again without trying to impale him with her pitchfork.

Maggie escorted Hagatha down the path towards the stables. As usual, Maggie talked up a storm. Hagatha was too anxious to listen or respond to Maggie. Her angst was only temporarily assuaged when they passed the beautiful lush green pasture with the splendor of several horses feeding and frolicking in the distance. The pastoral scene and Maggie's incessant monologue were suddenly interrupted by a large crow swooping in and lighting on the three-rail wooden pasture fence.

The crow seemed to be eyeing them as they approached. Maggie was uncharacteristically quiet and nervous. Needless to say, Hagatha's anxiety grew, recalling the mantra she had recited for days on end and the horrific nightmare that had awakened her. She nearly jumped out of her skin when the bird let out a series of caws, only to have six more crows swoop in, seemingly out of nowhere, and take up places on the top rail.

"Just keep walking and don't make any sudden moves," Maggie whispered uneasily. "And don't run."

Maggie's advice was unnecessary. Hagatha was too petrified to speak, let alone run. When they finally entered the stable, Hagatha's anxiety shifted from the mysterious gathering of crows to her fear of seeing Richard. When he wasn't there, she felt like she could finally breathe again. And Maggie once again found her voice.

"Phew, that was scary. I hope they're not there when I walk back to the ward."

Maggie could not restrain the impulse of communicating what she was feeling or what was on her mind. Even when doing so would be unsettling to the patients, whose emotional stability was already fragile.

"Why did you tell me not to run?" Hagatha asked as Maggie

was about to leave.

Maggie paused. Looking as if she was having an internal debate about how to respond to her.

"Well, I probably shouldn't tell you this," she said conspiratorially. "But, another patient was attacked by crows a couple of days ago. They attacked him when he tried to run away."

"Really? Who was the patient, and what happened to him?" Hagatha asked, unable to believe that her efforts may have been successful.

"I didn't know the patient. He was from another ward. And I probably shouldn't tell you what happened to him," Maggie said, although Hagatha could tell by Maggie's face that all it would take is a little prompting.

"Come on, Maggie. You can't just tell me half the story."

"Well, as long as you promise not to tell anyone that I told you."

"I won't tell a soul," Hagatha replied.

"He died. They pecked him to pieces. By the time someone could shoo them away, they had poked out his eyes, and his entire body had little bloody craters from where their beaks had bitten chunks out of him. I got sick to my stomach."

"You saw him?"

"Yes, but I wish now that I hadn't. I can't get the image out of my head. He didn't even look human. It was gross. I better get back to the ward. Wish me luck," she said, turning and heading back in the direction they had come.

"You'll be fine, Maggie. You'll be fine," Hagatha called.

"Hope you're right," Maggie said without turning but giving a wave of acknowledgment.

"Oh, I'm right, Maggie," Hagatha said under her breath and smiled. "You're one of the good ones. But Chester, your day of reckoning will come soon."

Hagatha grabbed a pitchfork and sunk it into the manure-filled bedding, willing her mind to begin to focus on the next spell she'd cast.

# CHAPTER 14

When Otto returned home from his visit with Enoch, Ursala knew immediately something was wrong. Otto hadn't told her where he was going. He just told her he was going on a bike ride. Consequently, she couldn't imagine what may have caused the hangdog expression on her husband's face.

"What's the matter, Otto? You look so sad."

"I'm afraid I've learned something disturbing about our little girl."

"On a bike ride? What could you possibly discover on a bike ride?" she asked.

"I went to see Enoch. I'm sorry. I should have told you."

"Why did you go to see him? Especially after his rude reception on our last visit."

"I wanted to tell him what we knew about Hilda and Hagatha's disappearance. I thought it might make him come around and help us get them back," Otto replied, pausing and shaking his head.

"And? What was his reaction?" Ursala prompted when Otto didn't continue.

"He told me that Hagatha committed adultery and that Hilda isn't even his baby."

"What? That's not possible!" Ursala exclaimed, denial being a typical parent's first reaction to news about their child they can't or don't want to accept.

"He swears by it. And he's already annulled their marriage."

"No!" she screamed as tears came to her eyes. "Otto, this can't be true. We didn't raise our little girl that way. How could she have gone so far astray?"

"I don't know, Ushi. Maybe the doctor was right. Perhaps she went insane."

"What are we going to do?" Ursala asked, wringing her hands as her denial gave way to reality. "Did Enoch say who the man was?"

"No. And I didn't ask. I don't know that I want to know. Besides, if it's true, then Hilda is illegitimate, and he has no claim on her." Otto replied, biting his tongue, not wanting to say what he knew would break his wife's heart.

Children born out of wedlock and their unwed parents in that day and age were shunned by society. The children were called bastards and thought to be more susceptible to being deviant or feeble-minded. Adopting illegitimate children was also frowned upon.

But Otto didn't have to say the words. His wife knew the ramifications of what he was telling her.

"Perhaps it's best that Hilda stay with the Shepherd's then," she said in resignation.

"Yes, I agree," Otto sighed, happy he didn't have to convince his wife otherwise.

"Are you still going to visit Hagatha?" Ursala asked.

"I don't know. Maybe it's best Hagatha's where she's at, as the doctor recommended. We could write a letter and ask them how she's doing," Otto suggested.

"I think that's a good idea, Otto. I will do that," Ursala replied.

Meanwhile, in Duluth, Minnesota, Charles and Evelyn Shepherd were startled out of their fitful sleep that evening. Baby Dori let out a howl and screamed and cried inconsolably through the night. It was the first time she hadn't slept peacefully through the night. Unfortunately, it wouldn't be the last.

# CHAPTER 15

Ice baths were becoming a routine evening event for Chester and his band of literal jerk-offs. Most evenings, Chester would have to ask Hagatha multiple scripture questions before he could trip her up and cart her off.

She didn't protest his deceitful treatment for his obvious ulterior motives. It just lent more fuel to the bonfire of vengeance that burned inside her. The other reason she went willingly was to adapt her abilities to focus and craft spells despite the most extreme and discomforting circumstances. The lack of putting up a struggle also made the process less exhilarating for Chester and his gang. She hoped they would tire of her and find some other female patient to fuel their fantasies. Regardless, she'd eventually create a spell that would put a certain end to it.

After Chester and his cronies satisfied their appetites for self-flagellation, they released her restraints and pulled her out of the frigid water. Then, as they had done on previous occasions, they wrapped her in the towels into which they had ejaculated. Her body, numb from the cold, couldn't feel the warm stickiness of their emissions. However, she could definitely smell its faint ammonia-like scent.

Masturbation in the late $19^{th}$ century was considered immoral. To do it was not only a sin against God but was thought to cause any number of physical maladies. Once Hagatha was dressed and returned to her room, she did as she had done before – she sought out guidance from her Bible. Seeking a scriptural reference that she could repeatedly recite that would prompt an appropriate reckoning for Chester and the others.

"Onan spilled his seed on the ground, displeasing God who slew him," she whispered, paraphrasing a verse from a chapter in Genesis.

"But how did God slay him?" she wondered out loud. "No. Death is too easy. He must suffer. Suffer in such a way that he remembers. And instead of pleasure, the memory causes him pain."

She smiled a demented smile and couldn't help but laugh demonically. So began a process whereby Hagatha would cobble together biblical phrases to meet her objectives. Convinced that God had chosen her to bring fire and brimstone down upon the sinners of the world. Never mind that she took great liberties with the context and original meaning or intention of the scriptures she was contorting. She wasn't doing the will of God. She was doing the vengeful will of Hagatha. Couching the punishment in words from the Bible giving the illusion she was acting on God's authority.

In Chester's case, Hagatha decided that he should suffer a long and painful life. Death was too good for Chester. Among the long list of things masturbation was thought to cause were blindness and sores on the skin. It took her several weeks to find what she was looking for in the Bible. In the late 19$^{th}$ century, there wasn't any easy way to find specific topics in the King James Bible – no topic-based indexes, no computers with Internet search engines. Even with Hagatha's familiarity with the Bible, it took her a week just to find the verses she required. Finding snippets from Leviticus and another from the Gospel of Matthew. Then she joined them to fit her desire to have Chester's manhood fall off from leprosy and go blind. But that was not enough. She also wanted Chester's compatriots to go blind. And thus was born, Hagatha's new mantra.

"The scab spreadeth in the skin of the man whose seed goeth from him. Behold, the blind will lead the blind, and he will be unclean with leprosy."

This, however, was the easy part. The hard part was concentrating on Chester and his friends and reciting this mantra over and over. When she had been laid up for a week after the brutal whipping Richard had given her, it was easier. She laid in bed, and with nothing to distract her, she accomplished her mission in several days. Now she would have to concentrate and recite this phrase while participating in the daily schedule of activities and work.

Had Hagatha continued to work in the stables, this might have been possible. Mucking out stalls and hauling fresh water in for the horses was fairly mindless work with few distractions. However, it was harvest time, and she had been reassigned to the farm. While following the horse-drawn reaper through the fields was not overly taxing on the brain. Constantly tying the sheaves of wheat and stacking them in stooks was physically demanding. Sapping her ability to attend to the internal process necessary to bring Chester to justice.

If Hagatha was not working in the field, she was assigned to work at the steam-powered threshing machine. Neither feeding the wheat into the thresher, bagging the clean grain, or baling the straw was overly complex, but it was dangerous. And the steam engine and thresher created quite a racket, making it hard for Hagatha to think. But, after two weeks, nothing had happened to Chester or his buddies, and the near-nightly ice baths continued.

Hagatha had only one choice. She needed to do something to get herself locked away in the seclusion room. And based on Hagatha's experience and observation, the quickest way to get yourself into seclusion was to attack a staff member. It almost always guaranteed a 24- to 48-hour stay in the tiny little dim closet.

Other than Chester and his self-pleasuring companions, Hagatha didn't want to harm the other ward staff. She considered asking Maggie to lock her away. But Maggie was a straight-arrow. One of those rule-followers who couldn't be swayed to bend the rules. Maggie was also one of the few ward personnel who actually seemed to have compassion for the patients. Hagatha knew that Maggie would never agree to lock her up based just on her request. There had to be a reason. So on a day when Maggie was working, and Chester wasn't, Hagatha launched her attack.

The best time to cause a seclusion-worthy disruption was during breakfast. Any time all the patients were congregated together, staff were quick to address misbehavior. Fearing that not doing so may spur others to misbehave, causing an uncontrollable insurrection.

Betsy was an elderly patient who carried on a near-constant conversation with herself consisting primarily of unfavorable assessments about all those around her. She was an equal opportunity disparager, sparing no one as she muttered profanities. Most just ignored her as she cycled through her insults. But on this occasion, when Betsy called Hagatha a "ratbag hedge-creeper," 1890s-speak for a dirty prostitute, Hagatha took offense and threw her breakfast plate at Betsy. Narrowly missing Betsy but causing a resounding crash as the plate shattered on the floor. Then Hagatha got up and retrieved a shard of the broken plate. Wielding it like a knife as staff closed ranks on her.

When they got too close, she made threatening thrusting motions with it. She purposely gripped the shard tightly so that it cut into her hand, causing blood to spill and splatter as she wielded it. They evaded her jabs and eventually outflanked her. When she thought she had done enough to warrant seclusion, she let them restrain her and remove the bloody shard from her hand.

After a stop in the infirmary to bandage her hand, they placed her in seclusion. As a precautionary measure, they also put her in a straitjacket. Worried she might unwind the bandage and try to choke herself with it.

Finally, Hagatha had what she wanted. Time to seal Chester's fate.

# CHAPTER 16

Ursala crafted a heartfelt letter to the Fairdale Falls State Hospital inquiring about her daughters' condition and the expected duration of her treatment. Correspondence by mail, however, was hardly a quick or easy way to communicate. The postal system at the time was very rudimentary and consequently slow and unreliable. Her letter could be expected to take two weeks to arrive at its intended destination if it arrived at all.

Otto and Ursala Ketchel didn't have time to mourn their daughter's fate or the fact that Hilda was not their true granddaughter. Business at Ketchel's Bakery was picking up with the growth of Grand Rapids. Without help, they both worked six 16-hour days a week. They procrastinated on hiring someone to help them. Holding out hope that Hagatha would soon recover from her condition and perhaps agree to come back and work in the bakery. Now that she was no longer married or burdened by what they thought was a bastard child.

Enoch's town of Slaughter was also the beneficiary of the population growth in the area. His sleepy little town was quickly expanding into a bustling community with new businesses. As a result, the one-room schoolhouse was replaced with two new school buildings – Slaughter Elementary and Slaughter High School. Both schools were significantly larger than what people considered necessary. But Enoch, true to his bold nature, predicted the town of Slaughter would quickly grow into them. He was right, and if anything, even a bit too conservative.

Enoch Jr. was just starting to walk and talk. Enoch and Lila's marriage ran hot and cold, as it would throughout their marriage. They were two hot-blooded and headstrong individuals who seemed to revel in their roller-coaster union. So it wasn't a shock to Enoch when Lila gave him the third-degree when he walked into the kitchen one evening.

"Now you've gone and done it again," she said in an accusatory tone.

"What? What did I do?" he asked defensively. Trying to think what he might have done to deserve her ire.

"You don't know? Please tell me you're not that simple-minded."

"I haven't done anything, woman!" he blustered.

"You most certainly have, man!" she bristled in return.

"Are you going to tell me? Because if you think I'm going to guess, you have another think coming."

"Oh, is that so?"

"You're damn right it is!"

Lila, seeing she had Enoch worked up to a full lather, started laughing.

"What the hell is wrong with you, woman?" Enoch asked, shocked by the sudden change in her demeanor.

"I guess it's the baby in my belly, you oaf!"

"Baby? You're pregnant?"

She looked at him and laughed.

"See? Didn't I tell you that you did something?"

"Yes, you did. But you didn't need to make me think I did something wrong."

"Now, what fun would that be?"

He laughed.

"Come here, woman," he said, pulling her into an embrace and kissing her.

"I love you.  Even if you drive me mad."

"I know," she said, smiling.

# CHAPTER 17

Two days after being secluded, an orderly attempted to remove Hagatha's straitjacket and release her from the seclusion room. For his efforts, she kneed him in the groin, guaranteeing her continued restraint and seclusion for another couple of days.

Hagatha didn't want to risk the chance of leaving the peace and quiet of the seclusion room prematurely. She only wanted to exit when she was reasonably sure Chester and his boys wouldn't be able to abuse her further.

Seclusion didn't mean she was neglected. She was offered food three times a day and the opportunity to use the restroom. However, she refused both. Accepting only small sips of water. Unwilling to interrupt her silent reverie, reciting her mantra over and over.

"The scab spreadeth in the skin of the man whose seed goeth from him. Behold, the blind will lead the blind, and he will be unclean with leprosy."

Most of the time, she focused on Chester as she spoke her spell. But she committed some time to the others who had pleasured themselves in her nakedness. It was a grand experiment. Trying to bring justice to several people in one fell swoop.

Nor did Hagatha sleep. Instead, the exercise of repeating

the exact same phrase put her into something akin to a hypnotic trance. At times, she wasn't even sure whether she was speaking the words or if they were just echoing in her head. Her eyes may have been open, but all she saw was the image of Chester and the others as they furiously stroked their erections. Gazing upon her naked and numb body like a pack of ravenous wolves.

Occasionally, her mind would stray to Enoch and how he had unceremoniously abandoned her. All because she hadn't given him a son. As if the only thing that mattered was his family legacy. While this added to the rage burning inside her, she knew she needed to refocus. Forcing herself to return to Chester and his band of merry masturbaters.

She felt used and abused. And in her mind, she was at a crossroads. She could accept she was worthless and only suitable for being her captors' seminal receptacle. Or she could reject that notion altogether and fight back. Show them, and all who dared cross her, that they would have hell to pay by not showing her the proper deference. Refuse the role of their chattel – their sex slave. Put the fear of God in them or banish them altogether from this world.

Dr. Rosenstern's theories of insanity aside, Hagatha's struggle between self-hatred and self-aggrandizement was the crux of the matter. Both could not exist together. One had to win out. And the arc of Hagatha's life depended upon which self-perception would win the battle.

If she gave in to the persecution and could not defend herself, a lifetime of self-loathing would be her destiny. On the other hand, all glory would be hers if she rose above the oppression and punished those who did her harm. Self-hatred would likely abbreviate her life. While self-aggrandizement would likely preserve it.

So it was no small matter when Hagatha finally emerged after 4 days in the dark seclusion room into the glare and the commotion of the ward with its menagerie of lunatics. But Hagatha was least concerned about the patients. It was the ward staff present who would determine her fate. If Chester appeared, she would be devastated and attempt to kill herself rather than suffer the continual degradation. If he didn't appear, she would find hope for a long and fruitful life.

When she didn't see him, she didn't immediately claim success. Perhaps it was his day off. Instead, Hagatha found her one and only ally – Maggie.

"It is good to see you, Hagatha," Maggie exclaimed with a genuine sense of relief. "I was worried about you. How are you doing?"

"I'm fine," Hagatha replied disingenuously. "Do you know where Chester is?"

Maggie didn't respond immediately. Which for Maggie, who usually suffered verbal diarrhea, meant something. Her face communicated conflict. As if wrestling with whether to divulge a secret. Finally, she spoke.

"He's not here, but I can't tell you why. At least not out here where others can hear," she whispered.

Maggie looked around, scanning for any other ward staff in the vicinity. Seeing none, she continued.

"I'll visit you in your room just before lights out. All right?"

Hagatha nodded, buoyed by Maggie's secrecy but still not entirely satisfied.

Although it was supper time and Hagatha had not eaten in four days, she just sipped on a cup of tea. Her stomach was in knots, even though neither Chester nor his self-flagellating compatriots were nowhere to be seen. Evening calisthenics were performed on the ward due to the inclement weather. It was October, and winter was providing a preview of things to come. Hagatha's hand lacerations were still healing, and her shoulders, elbows, and wrists ached from prolonged restraint in a straitjacket. Fortunately, given the close quarters, exercises were confined to stretching and running in place.

Calisthenics gave way to Bible reading. However, Hagatha could not concentrate on her reading, anxiously awaiting Maggie's visit. Nevertheless, she easily answered the scripture-based question. She began to think that Maggie had forgotten when there came a soft knock on her door. Hagatha knew it was Maggie because only Maggie observed the respectful practice of knocking before entering a patients' room.

"Come in," Hagatha called.

Maggie entered and quickly closed the door behind her. Hagatha was taken aback. This was strictly against protocol which called for staff to always leave the door open when visiting a patient room. For Maggie to break a rule was tantamount to hell freezing over.

"I hope you didn't mind that I couldn't tell you about Chester earlier. We're not supposed to tell the patients," she whispered.

Hagatha was conflicted. She didn't want Maggie to get in trouble, but she also didn't want to go one more minute without knowing the cause of Chester's absence.

"I won't tell a soul. I promise," Hagatha replied.

"I know I can trust you, Hagatha. That's why I'm bending the rules. Besides, I know what Chester and his friends did to you, and it was not right."

"Thank you. So tell me," Hagatha asked anxiously.

"Well, the word is that Chester and three others went to a doggery in Pelican Rapids after work two days ago. Apparently, they had themselves quite the spree. They got liquored up and ended up seeking sexual congress with an adventuress," Maggie exclaimed with a look of disgust on her face.

"From there, the details get a little fuzzy. All we know is that something happened to cause the woman to seek medical attention. While Chester and the others remain quarantined in the hotel room."

"Quarantined? Why?" Hagatha asked.

"That's the fuzzy part. We're not sure. We had a visit from a doctor yesterday who asked us some odd questions."

"Like what?"

"Like whether any patients or staff had any complaints of visual problems, unexplained rashes, unusual hair growth, or sloughing off of body parts. Can you imagine? Thank God we haven't. How awful! We think that maybe Chester and the others have some rare contagious disease. It would serve them right, taking up with that hussy."

"Did he say whether they would be able to come back to work?"

"No. All we know is that he sent them to a specialty hospital. When I learn more, you will be the first person I tell."

"Thanks, Maggie," Hagatha replied despite the disappointment of not receiving more definitive news.

Maggie smiled in response. "I better get back to work before I get in trouble. Now get some rest."

As Maggie exited, rest was the last thing on Hagatha's mind. She didn't want to take any chances that Chester and his gang would come back. She began to chant silently.

"The scab spreadeth in the skin of the man whose seed goeth from him. Behold, the blind will lead the blind, and he will be unclean with leprosy."

# CHAPTER 18

Charles and Evelyn Shepherd were becoming increasingly concerned about Dori. Her episodes of awakening in the middle of the night screaming were occurring much more frequently. In addition, she was now old enough to put words together in response to her parents' questions.

"Did you have a scary dream?" her mother asked, stroking her hair.

Dori, eyes wet with tears, nodded. The acknowledgment causing her to bury her head in her mother's bosom.

"What did you see?" she asked after Dori seemed to relax in her arms.

"A scaywe man," Dori said, sniffling. "He was bweeding."

"He was bleeding? Where was he bleeding?"

"Here," Dori replied, patting her groin.

"That must have been really scary," her mother said, no longer interested in pursuing further details. "Sometimes we have scary dreams, but they're not real."

Dori looked up at her mother with doe eyes and nodded. Wanting to believe her but uncertain because the imagery was so vivid and life-like.

"I don't wike scaywe dweams," she replied, once again burying her head in her mother's chest.

"I don't like scary dreams either, Dori," her mother cooed, once again stroking her daughter's hair.

Dori eventually fell back asleep, and Evelyn padded back to bed. But she couldn't sleep, haunted by the disturbing nature of Dori's dream. Finally, after tossing and turning, she woke Charles up.

"What?" he grumbled, still half asleep.

"Wake up, Charles. We have to talk about Dori. Something is not right," she replied. Shaking his shoulder.

"Can't we talk about it in the morning?" he said, rolling over and trying to ignore her.

"No, Charles, we can't! Now turn back over and talk to me," she demanded.

Charles grudgingly obeyed. Rolling over and sitting up in bed.

"All right, what is wrong with Dori?"

"Dori had a scary nightmare."

"Doesn't every child have nightmares?"

"Yes, but she seems to be having them more frequently. And this one was truly gruesome."

"She was able to tell you?"

"Yes, in a way. She said she saw a scary man who was bleeding from his, she paused. "From his," Evelyn stammered, not sure how to say it. "From down there," she finally said, pointing to Charles' groin.

"What? Why would she have such a nightmare?" Charles exclaimed in shock.

"Exactly what I thought. See, I told you we needed to talk."

"Well, maybe it was just a one-time thing. I mean, we don't know what traumas she might have had before we saved her. It was bad enough her mother tried to drown her."

"True. Maybe we should try to find out who her mother and father were. Not to give her back or anything. Just to get a sense of who raised her," Evelyn suggested.

"And how do you propose we do that?"

"There must be records of her birth. And if not, maybe she was baptized. We could learn about her real birthday and what her original name was. Make a little vacation out of it before the snow falls."

"Hmm, that sounds like a good idea. Now, can I go back to sleep?" he asked, yawning.

"Yes, you can go back to sleep. Thanks for talking to me. Maybe now I can get some sleep too."

Charles smiled and gave her a kiss, and they snuggled together and fell fast asleep. Blissfully unaware of the dastardly psychic connection that had fueled their daughter's night terror.

# CHAPTER 19

Hagatha lived on pins and needles for several weeks before Maggie gave her the whole story of what happened to Chester and his colleagues. Being what it was, human nature guaranteed that word of sensational occurrences eventually spread, despite not having modern conveniences like telephones, still 20 years from becoming commonplace. The area didn't even have a local newspaper until the Pelican Rapids Press produced its inaugural issue 2 years later. No, the story spread through word-of-mouth. And it was surprisingly effective.

As Chester and his buddies were wont to do, they left the doggery and took the prostitute to a hotel room. While Chester was in the act of intercourse, he lost his vision, his manhood broke off inside her, and a rash covered his entire body. Watching and pleasuring themselves, his friends were horrified when a geyser of blood sprang from Chester's penisless groin. If that was not disturbing enough, they feared Chester's lesions may be contagious. As Chester stumbled around blind and bleeding, they checked themselves for skin lesions. Instead of rashes, they noticed the palms of their hands which had been stroking their erections, were rapidly growing hair. They also started experiencing visual disturbances. One had severely blurred vision. Another had to keep his eyes closed to stop the spinning that was causing him severe vertigo. While the third could only see things in black and white.

It was pandemonium, and the woman, covered in blood and carrying an extra body part inside her, ran from the hotel screaming. Seeing the woman and hearing the commotion, the hotel manager suspected that the men must have tried to kill her. So he sent his wife to get the police. Gun in hand, he guarded the door to prevent the men from leaving. However, the men were in no condition to do so and didn't even attempt to exit.

Meanwhile, the prostitute sought out the aid of the town doctor. He was appropriately shocked by her physical dilemma and her description of what had happened to her male suitors. After extracting the stray penis that had taken up residence in her, the doctor's curiosity and medical obligation compelled him to investigate the woman's claims about the men's symptoms.

The police were only too happy to defer to the doctor when he arrived. While Chester's bleeding had abated, he lay unconscious on the blood-soaked bed. His naked body, covered by a sea of angry red weeping pustules. The other men were sitting in chairs bemoaning their visual maladies and the condition of their hands, each now having one that looked more like a hairy paw. The doctor was flummoxed and knew what he was looking at far exceeded his medical training and experience. Subsequently making arrangements to transfer them to a specialty hospital in southern Minnesota.

Before doing so, however, the doctor, suspecting some rare and potentially contagious disease, learned that the men all worked at Fairdale Falls State Hospital. This prompted his visit to the hospital the next day to investigate a potential cause. When his investigation turned up empty, he suspected the prostitute may be the carrier. However, other than the mental distress of temporarily having Chester's dislodged penis in her vagina, neither she nor the subsequent clients of her services demonstrated any ill effects.

Human nature also demands that when there's a vacuum of information, the rumor mill must fill it with suitable explanations. Consequently, over time and fueled by contributions by the adventuress herself, the reason for the men's misfortune became attributed to the scourge of masturbation. Before long, it was common knowledge and accepted that masturbation caused blindness, hairy palms, and skin eruptions. This explanation not only aligned nicely with how masturbation was viewed in that day and age, but it was a boon to the adventuress's business. Better to pay her for one's so-called stress relief than to pay with disabling physical conditions.

Fairdale Falls State Hospital staff never heard from Chester and the three other men again. Which, of course, caused more speculation and rumors about their fate amongst staff and patients alike. All except Hagatha, who knew the truth and wasn't about to divulge it.

To Hagatha, God had chosen to bless her with a gift. The power to rid the world of sinners and those who sought to cross her. But the lines between good and evil get blurred sometimes. Hagatha had a gift, but perhaps the gift-giver wasn't God at all. As her trusty Bible read, "Beloved, believe not every spirit, but try the spirits whether they are of God: because many false prophets are gone out into the world." The Devil has a way of making the descent into Hell feel like the ascendency to the right hand of God.

# CHAPTER 20

Charles, Evelyn, and Dori arrived in Grand Rapids on Dori's 2nd birthday - the first anniversary of her rescue from the swirling waters of the Mississippi River. The day-long carriage ride from Duluth left them with little energy to celebrate. They checked into the hotel and made arrangements for dinner at the hotel's restaurant after they washed up from their long, dusty journey.

Dori's eyes were at half-mast when the restaurant delivered a small cake with two candles to their dinner table. While the cake and candles were a well-entrenched birthday tradition in the late 19$^{th}$ century, the birthday song was not. Back then, the tune for the birthday song existed as "Good Morning to All," which was a welcoming song to students before class began. Nevertheless, the cake and candles woke Dori up.

"Now you have to make a wish," Evelyn prompted her.

"A wit?" Dori asked, as her language development skills weren't evolved enough to correctly pronounce words with more complex sounds.

"Yes, a wish," her mother repeated. "Something that you want," she clarified.

Evelyn and Charles expected that Dori's wish would be something very rudimentary. And having failed to tell her not to say her wish out loud, they were shocked when she responded.

"No scaywe dweams," she announced.

It took Evelyn and Charles a second to recover from her response. It had been several weeks since her nightmare of the man with the bleeding groin. But, obviously, it was still tormenting her.

"No more scary dreams. That's a great wish," Evelyn exclaimed, trying to put on a happy face. "Now blow out the candles so that your wish comes true," she instructed.

Dori looked at her mother, confused.

"Blow. Like this," she said, demonstrating by directing a soft puff of air through her pursed lips, making the candlelight dance but not go out.

Dori tried to copy her mother but couldn't quite master how to position her lips or produce a stream of breath. The candlelight barely danced. Evelyn encouraged her to try again. But this time, Charles surreptitiously assisted her, causing the candles to go out. Evelyn and Charles erupted in cheers, and Dori smiled, thinking she had accomplished the task.

"Now your wish will come true," Evelyn exclaimed.

It was the right thing to say at the moment, but eventually, she would forever regret that she did.

Dori eagerly devoured her cake, and when they got back to their hotel room, Evelyn and Charles gave Dori her first doll. Dori loved it and promptly named her Dolly. They would become inseparable. Evelyn and Charles declared their first birthday celebration with their daughter a success. Tempered by what was looming in the back of both their minds. That their little girl still suffered torturous memories from her nightmare.

Dawn broke the next day, and the Shepherd family, including Dolly, prepared to set off to conquer the day. Their agenda included visiting the library, the hospital, and the church, in the hopes of learning more about their daughter. Of course, Dori was not privy to any of this. They told her they were just exploring. But what seemed like a good idea a few weeks earlier when they made plans for this trip didn't seem so anymore to Evelyn.

"I don't know why we're doing this," she whispered to Charles as they were getting ready in the bathroom as Dori occupied herself playing with Dolly. "I think it might be better if we don't know. I mean, what are we going to do? Change her name? Change her birthday? She's been through enough already."

"We won't have to do anything. It will just be to help us know more about our little girl," Charles replied.

"I suppose. But we already know her mother was crazy. What if we learn the father is crazy too. Or he's an ax murderer or something? Like that Lizzie, whatever her name was in Massachusetts? It will forever taint our perception."

"Lizzie Borden?" Charles asked incredulously.

"Yes, her."

"I think it's more likely that we will learn that her father is a fine upstanding, successful, and brilliant man? In which case, our perception will be tainted favorably."

"Well, I hope you're right."

Fortunately, all of their destinations were within walking distance of the hotel. Their first stop was the library, where they hoped to comb through the local newspaper archives for birth announcements. The plan was for Charles to do the research while Evelyn took Dori to the children's section to read her stories.

"Oh, look, a bakery," Evelyn announced on their way to the library. "Let's stop and get something."

As they hadn't had breakfast, Charles was quick to agree.

Ursala Ketchel was not prepared to see her granddaughter

in the arms of the young couple when they came through the door. She had all she could do not to squeal with delight and divulge her identity. Fortuitously, Otto was in the back baking.

"May I help you?" Ursala asked, trying but failing to take her eyes off of Hilda, who had grown considerably since she last saw her.

"Oh, my, everything looks so good," Evelyn exclaimed. "I think I'm going to need some time to decide."

"No hurry. What a cute baby girl! What's her name?" Ursala asked, trying to act as she naturally would with any couple with a child.

"Why, thank you. This is Pandora. But we call her Dori," Evelyn replied. "Dori, can you say hello to the nice woman?"

Dori immediately responded. "Hawo," she said and held Dolly out towards Ursala.

Ursala's heart nearly broke. She wanted to hold Hilda. Knowing she couldn't, she did the next best thing. She reached out and accepted Dori's offer, giving Dolly a big hug.

"Oh, Dolly is a beautiful girl. Just like you," Ursala cooed.

Dori smiled.

"Say thank you, Dori," her mother prompted.

"Tan you."

"You're very welcome. But I think Dolly wants to go back to you," Ursala remarked, holding Dolly out.

When Dori took Dolly back, Ursala purposely let one of her fingers touch her granddaughter's hand. It was all she would allow herself, fearful that if she was allowed to hold her, she would never want to give her back. To hear Hilda talk, even with her articulation challenges, added to Ursala's heartbreak.

"My, I'm amazed she let you hold Dolly. We haven't been able to pry it away since we gave it to her."

Ursala smiled. "In that case, I am honored. Would you

mind if I gave Dori a cookie?

"Oh, I'm sure she'd be delighted. Yes, you may give her one."

Ursala stepped away from the counter and went to a nearby display case. There she grabbed a few spritzgebäck cookies, almond spritz cookies topped with pink sugar. Ursala had to fight back the tears. She had given Hilda these cookies in the past and knew she loved them. She put a few in a small bag and returned with one in her hand.

"Would you like a spritzgebäck cookie, Dori?" Ursala asked, reaching across the counter.

Dori quickly took the offered confection and put it in her mouth. While Ursala handed Evelyn the small bag.

"I put a few more in a bag for later. I hope you don't mind."

"Mind? Not at all. She obviously loves it," Evelyn replied as Dori made quick work of the cookie.

While Evelyn and Dori were occupied, Charles had made a tour of the display cases. Then, returning as Dori was eyeing the bag of cookies in her mother's hand.

"I don't know how anyone can make a decision in here," he exclaimed. "It all looks so good."

"Thank you," Ursala replied. "I'll be happy to help you make a decision. Or I can put together an assortment for you."

Evelyn looked at Charles. "I say we go with the assortment. Is that all right, dear?"

"That's fine with me."

As Ursala marched off to fulfill their request, she called to them. Asking questions to which she already knew the answer.

"Are you new in town or just visiting?"

"Just visiting," Evelyn replied.

"Have you been to Grand Rapids before?"

"Yes, about a year ago."

Despite knowing the answer, hearing her say it was like a stab to Ursala's gut. The tears threatened to overflow their banks this time, and she decided not to ask any more questions. Instead, she pulled herself together as she closed the box of goodies and tied it with string.

"Here you go," she said, handing Evelyn the box. "I hope you enjoy what I selected and your visit."

"I'm sure we will. Thank you. What do we owe you?" Charles asked, reaching for his wallet.

"Oh, it's my treat. You don't owe me anything," Ursala replied.

"My, that's mighty generous of you," Evelyn exclaimed.

"It's my pleasure. And it was my pleasure to meet you and your dolly," she said, turning her attention to Dori. Once again, feeling the waterworks looming just below the rim of her eyelids.

Evelyn and Charles thanked her profusely and said their goodbyes. Ursala held it together until they were exiting, and Dori turned back.

"Bye-bye," raising her little hand that wasn't holding Dolly.

Ursala crumbled as the door closed, sobbing as all the emotion she had been holding back breached their banks. Hearing his wife's wailing, Otto rushed out from the back to find Ursala on the floor. He first thought she had fallen and hurt herself. But Ursala's injury wasn't from a fall. Instead, it was much deeper and more painful than any physical damage ever could be.

# CHAPTER 21

Dr. Harold Rosenstern strolled into his office to find an envelope from Ursala Ketchel on his desk. While letters were the primary means of communication in those days, it was rare to receive letters from patients' family members. Instead, most of the correspondence he received was from the two other insane asylums in the State requesting permission to transfer patients to Fairdale Falls. In addition, the construction of another patient wing and a central administrative building were nearly complete, doubling the hospital's capacity.

He read Ursala's heartfelt letter, which she had written a month earlier. Most people would have read the letter and been touched by its content. But Dr. Rosenstern read it with a cold, clinical eye. His bias was that most lunatics were a product of lackadaisical parenting and wayward upbringings. Thus, his reaction to the letter was more skeptical. To Dr. Rosenstern, all of Ursala's expressions of concern rang hollow. Thinking she was probably trying to hide the guilt she felt for the lack of care she provided her child until it was too late. While he wanted to set the letter aside unanswered, he decided to craft a response to her questions about their daughter's condition, treatment, and anticipated length of stay.

"Dear Mrs. Ketchel,

Thank you for your letter regarding your daughter, Hagatha. I can assure you that she is being treated well and with the utmost care. While I understand your desire to learn of her condition, medical ethics prevent me from divulging the details. However, I can assure you that our treatment at Fairdale Falls is second to none, and your daughter is in good hands.

As for her anticipated stay here, that is a much more difficult question to answer. In my experience, the insults to a person's emotional stability are usually from prolonged and repeated exposure to destabilizing forces in their lives. Thus, the time required to reverse their maladaptive thoughts and behavior frequently requires lengthy treatment.

Although I understand your desire to visit your daughter, I would strongly advise against it. Your daughter needs to focus all of her attention on the healing components of treatment. While I'm sure you love her very much, your visit could unwittingly set her treatment back."

Dr. Rosenstern re-read his letter and determined it to be adequate. He signed the letter and gave it to his assistant to mail. Then made his usual rounds to the wards, consulting with the Head Nurse of each for updates on the patients.

Dr. Rosenstern didn't meet with patients regularly, relying on the Head Nurse of each ward to determine if and when they thought a patient needed a therapeutic visit with him. However, Ursala Ketchel's letter had piqued his curiosity. So when he got to Hagatha's ward, he asked the Head Nurse about her.

"She's doing much better of late," she replied. "No instances of restraint, seclusion, or ice baths."

"And what do you attribute that to?" Dr. Rosenstern asked. "My treatment regimen?"

"Yes, doctor," the Head Nurse replied. "I think the exercise, farm work, and Bible readings are working. She has especially taken to the Bible readings."

"Very good. I just received a letter from her parents. Do

you think you could have her come to my office? Perhaps after supper?"

"Yes, I'd be happy to arrange that, doctor."

As a Head Nurse at Fairdale Falls State Hospital, you learned to emphasize the good news and hide the bad news from Dr. Rosenstern. If you didn't, you didn't stay employed very long. Thus, while the staff on Hagatha's ward knew her previous ice baths were due to Chester's abuse, that information was never conveyed to Dr. Rosenstern. Instead, the stock answer to Dr. Rosenstern when a patient required restraint, seclusion, or an ice bath was to say they were "failing to fully participate in the required treatment." This would be accepted by Dr. Rosenstern without question. To say anything else was to risk intense inquiry, which often resulted in Dr. Rosenstern finding fault with the person doing the reporting. In other words, Dr. Rosenstern had no problem shooting the messenger.

The first and only time Hagatha had met with Dr. Rosenstern was shortly after her arrival when she was a blubbering mess. Distraught over how her life had fallen apart and unsure of what had happened to her baby. So it came as quite a surprise when the Head Nurse told her she would be meeting with him after supper. She immediately wondered what it was she had done to prompt the meeting. She was more than a little nervous. So much so that she didn't even touch her supper.

Having Maggie escort her to Dr. Rosenstern's office was the only thing that kept Hagatha's anxiety from paralyzing her.

"Why do you think he wants to meet with me? Did I do something wrong?" she asked as they walked down the hall towards his office.

"If you did something wrong, I'd know about it. And I don't. So stop worrying. He meets with patients occasionally," Maggie replied, sensing Hagatha's uneasiness.

Dr. Rosenstern's assistant had gone home for the evening,

so Maggie knocked on his door when they arrived.

"Come in," they heard through the door.

"Ah, thank you for bringing Miss Ketchel, Maggie," he said, getting up from behind his desk.

"You're welcome, doctor. Would you like me to wait outside so I can escort her back?"

"Oh no, that won't be necessary, Maggie. I will get Miss Ketchel back to the ward."

Hagatha's anxiety shot through the roof. Her experiences being alone behind closed doors with men hadn't been exactly therapeutic. As Maggie exited, Hagatha began to tremble.

"Sit, sit," Dr. Rosenstern said, motioning towards a chair on the opposite side of his desk. That he seemed content to stay on his side of the desk was the only reason Hagatha was able to obey his command.

"My job as Chief Psychiatrist is to make sure our patients are well cared for. And while I have complete faith in the staff we employ, I try to meet with our patients occasionally to see how they're doing."

He paused, and Hagatha didn't know if he expected her to respond to what he had said. She was surprised at his vote of confidence in his staff. How could he not know about how some of them had exploited her? She chose to keep her mouth shut for the time being.

"How are you doing? Are you finding our treatment helpful?" he asked.

Her jitters gave way to growing anger. How could he think her treatment had been beneficial after what Tobias, Chester, and the others had done to her? She needed to set him straight. Unlike the staff, Hagatha had no compulsion to withhold the truth.

"If you call treatment being coerced to have sex or men pleasuring themselves by looking at my naked body, then no, it isn't helpful."

"What?" Dr. Rosenstern exclaimed, clearly shocked by her response. "I can't believe that. My ward staff would have apprised me of such aberrant practices. You must be imagining these things."

"I most certainly am not, doctor. And if your nurses haven't told you, then you would best reconsider the level of faith you place in them."

"Hallucinations and confabulation are not uncommon works of the Devil, Miss Ketchel. I fear the Prince of Darkness may have you in his grip causing your persecutory delusions."

"No, you don't understand," Hagatha began to protest, but Dr. Rosenstern quickly interrupted.

"Oh, I understand, Miss Ketchel. I understand only too well. But I don't want to dismiss your concerns out of hand. So let's go back to your ward. There, we can speak to the Head Nurse and clear things up. Shall we?"

Finally, Hagatha thought. Finally, she'd be able to tell him the truth and expose what the staff had obviously been hiding from him.

"I would appreciate that very much, doctor," she replied, getting up from her chair.

As they walked back to the ward, Hagatha knew that her ally, Maggie, could corroborate all that transpired if the Head Nurse balked at telling the truth. Maggie had threatened, more than once in the past, to go to Dr. Rosenstern. And today, she might just get her chance.

To Hagatha's surprise, Dr. Rosenstern escorted her through the Nursing Station, which was off-limits to patients. The Head Nurse was in her office and stood up from her desk when Dr. Rosenstern walked in with Hagatha.

"Please transfer this patient to the secure immersion ward immediately."

"Right away, doctor," she replied.

Hagatha didn't immediately understand what he had said. When she turned to ask him what he meant, two male orderlies, who had followed them to the office, grabbed her. She had been tricked, and she fought back like a wild animal – kicking, screaming, and trying to claw the orderlies.

"You bastard, you lied to me," she spat at Dr. Rosenstern as the orderlies took her to the ground and started putting her in a straitjacket.

"Miss Ketchel, if you persist with your wild accusations, you may spend the rest of your miserable life here," he said above her screams. "Clearly, you have not taken advantage of the treatment afforded you. You're obviously a very, very sick woman. I think you'll find our secure immersion ward a more therapeutic milieu."

Hagatha growled, and as Dr. Rosenstern started to leave, she cried out.

"A false witness shall not be unpunished, and he that speaketh lies shall perish, doctor. Did you hear me, you bastard? He that speaketh lies shall perish! You're going to die, so help me, God," her screams transforming into a sinister cackle that echoed through the ward.

Dr. Rosenstern paid Hagatha's threats no mind. He had been threatened by patients more times than he could count. All they were were the wild ravings of lunatics possessed by the Devil. And up until Hagatha Ketchel, perhaps he was correct. But Hagatha was no ordinary lunatic.

# CHAPTER 22

When Charles and Evelyn left the bakery, little did they know they were walking away from the best source of information concerning Dori's ancestry. Nevertheless, it was a visit and an interaction they would look back on fondly – amazed by the woman's generosity and how Dori had taken to her.

When they arrived at the Library, they didn't go in immediately. Choosing instead to take a seat on a bench outside to sample the box of goodies from the bakery. While Charles tried the Streuselkuchen, Evelyn selected a jam-filled, sugar-coated donut called a Berliner. At Dori's insistence, Evelyn gave her another Spritz cookie. And after Dori gave Dolly a make-believe taste, she dispatched it in three quick bites.

In the library, Evelyn and Dori went in search of the children's section. Charles went to ask the Librarian for archived copies of the local newspaper from 1894 – the year they presumed Dori was born. Fortunately, the Grand Rapids Herald was a weekly publication, making the research a bit easier. However, the paper didn't have a separate birth announcement section. The population of Grand Rapids was only about 1,500 residents, so births, deaths, anniversaries, and other events were all found in a section labeled "Happenings."

Charles quickly learned the futility of his research. Without knowing the parents' name, there was no way to determine which of the 38 baby girls born in 1894 was Dori. In addition, the April 1-7 edition of the newspaper was missing. Then Charles got a brilliant idea. He found the stack of 1895 papers and searched for the edition printed the week they had rescued Dori from drowning. Surely the newspaper would have reported on that event. And it did. It read, "A local woman tried to drown her baby in the Mississippi River. The baby was rescued by a young couple from Duluth. The local woman was apprehended by the police and transferred to the Fairdale Falls State Hospital." Thwarted, Charles suspended his research and went to collect Evelyn and Dori.

"Did you learn anything?" Evelyn asked.

"No. Nothing, I'm afraid," he replied. Unable to provide her more detail with Dori present. "Let's try the hospital."

They left the library, and before they got to the hospital, they saw the church.

"Let's go in here. No sense backtracking," Charles announced.

"Good morning. Welcome to St. Joseph's," an elderly priest greeted as they entered. "I'm Father Jorgensen. Are you new to town?"

"Good morning, Father. We're Charles and Evelyn Shepherd, and we're just visiting."

Evelyn recognized that Charles would not be able to talk openly to Father with Dori there. So she wandered off in the direction of a statue of St. Joseph at the front of the church that had caught Dori's eye. When they were out of earshot, Charles continued.

"Please excuse my wife for walking away. She's not trying to be rude. We're just looking for information that we don't want our daughter, Dori, to overhear."

"No offense taken. How can I help you, son?"

"We rescued Dori from being drowned in the river here last

year, and we were hoping to learn something about her parents. So we thought that maybe she was baptized here."

"Hilda Ketchel," Father stated out of the blue.

"I'm sorry? Hilda Ketchel?" Charles asked, thrown by Father's response.

"Yes, that's your daughter's original name. Her mother is Hagatha Ketchel, and her father is Enoch Slaughter, Mayor of Slaughter, Minnesota. It's about 12 miles northeast of here. Hilda's grandparents are Otto and Ursala Ketchel. They own a bakery here in town."

Charles was stunned.

"I'm sorry, I'm sure this must be a lot to take in. I should have been more circumspect."

"No, no, Father. That's quite all right. We want to know as much as possible. This Enoch Slaughter, what is he like?"

"I don't really know. Other than asking me to annul the marriage, he wasn't a regular church-goer. But, on the other hand, he lives in a mansion, so he must be fairly well-off financially."

"And Hagatha? I know she's in Fairdale Falls State Hospital now, but what was she like before that?"

"If you would have told me she would try to drown her child in the river, I would never have believed you. Hagatha was a beautiful, hard-working, conscientious, God-fearing young lady. Raised by principled parents who are pillars in the community. I still can't believe she tried to drown, Hilda. Or that she's in an insane asylum. It makes no sense."

"Do you happen to know Dori's, I mean, Hilda's actual birthday?" Charles asked.

"Not off the top of my head. But I'm sure the Baptismal record can tell us. Why don't you wait here, and I'll go look it up."

"Thank you, Father."

Father Jorgensen raced off on his mission as Charles took several long, slow breaths. He desperately wanted to tell Evelyn. But would have to wait until they got back to the hotel and Dori took her nap. Based on Evelyn's repeated glances back at him, he could tell that she was just as anxious to hear what he had learned from the priest.

Father Jorgensen returned.

"Her birthday is April 2, 1894."

"So she's actually 2 years and 4 months old," Charles said more to himself than for the priest's edification.

"Is there anything else I can help you with?"

"Maybe. How would you suggest we handle this with our daughter? We've been calling her Dori for over a year. And we celebrated her birthday yesterday."

"I can't imagine that she would notice if you started celebrating her birthday on April 2nd. Calling her something other than Dori may confuse her, however. You could keep Hilda as her official first name and make Dori her middle name."

"That's a good idea, Father. Thanks."

Charles didn't dare ask the priest about the more sticky topic of whether to visit Hilda's father. Nor did he divulge that they had just met their daughter's grandmother at the bakery unknowingly. Although the bakery box Evelyn was carrying was probably a dead giveaway. His head was spinning with the flood of information and the decisions he and Evelyn would have to make as a result. Not only in the short term but throughout their daughter's childhood.

"Are you all right, son? You're looking a bit peaked," the priest said, laying a hand on his shoulder.

The priest's question and compassion revived Charles. He took a deep breath and steeled himself against the deluge of questions swirling in his head.

"Thanks, Father. I'll be fine. I guess I just wasn't prepared to learn so much. Or the consequences of having this new knowledge."

Charles' response made Father think of a familiar Bible passage about the tree of knowledge. And Father, never one to miss an opportunity to preach, took the opening to try to weave a supportive reply.

"And the Lord God took the man, and put him into the garden of Eden to dress it and to keep it," he began, reciting a passage from Genesis.

Once again, Charles looked confused.

"Relax, my son. God has blessed you and your wife with the duty to care for this child. And while being a parent is a weighty matter, God is always with you. Seek your answers through Him. Do not make the mistake of Adam and Eve and eat from the tree of knowledge of good and evil. Instead, eat from the Lord God's tree of life. Seek His wisdom in all things. Now go. Go and collect your wife and your little one. And if you're still in town Sunday morning, you're welcome to come and help us worship our Creator."

"Thank you, Father," Charles replied, feeling an odd sense of calm come over him and observing his advice.

Evelyn could tell before Charles even opened his mouth that the enlightenment he received from Father Jorgensen made their planned trip to the hospital superfluous.

"I take it we don't have to visit the hospital?" she asked as he joined them.

"No, we don't," he replied simply.

Dori hadn't taken her eyes off the statue. Mesmerized by its depiction of Saint Joseph holding the Christ-child in one arm with a spray of three white lilies in the other.

"Then we should go back to the hotel and put Dori down for a nap," Evelyn suggested.

Hearing her name, Dori turned, pointed to the statue, and said, "Dada?"

"Yes, that's the baby Jesus's daddy – Saint Joseph," Evelyn replied.

"Saint Josup?" she said in response. Unable to replicate the f-sound.

"Yes, Saint Joseph," Evelyn repeated, emphasizing the correct pronunciation.

"Why do you suppose he's holding those flowers?" Charles asked.

"I don't know," Evelyn replied.

Father Jorgensen, who was tidying up the pews behind them, overheard the conversation and chimed in.

"Legend has it that Joseph was chosen to wed Mary when a walking stick given to him sprouted fragrant white lilies. White represents purity, and that there are three lilies symbolizes the Holy Trinity."

"Interesting. Thank you, Father," Charles replied.

Armed with all the information they needed, they thanked Father and made their way back to the hotel – at a decidedly faster pace. They passed Ketchel's Bakery on the way, with only Charles fully grasping how central it was to his daughter's ancestry. Dori cooperated and promptly fell asleep for her nap, allowing Charles the opportunity to finally spill his guts. Like her husband before her, Evelyn was shaken by the revelations and overwhelmed by the decisions before them.

While they could quickly agree to celebrate Dori's birthday on April 2$^{nd}$, all the other choices were much more difficult. Do we start calling her Hilda? Or do we adopt Father Jorgensen's suggestion? Why didn't her grandmother at the bakery say anything? Is there something wrong with Dori that she didn't want to acknowledge their relationship? Do we dare go back there and divulge that we know? Do we seek out Dori's father? Who, by all accounts, sounds like an upstanding and accomplished man. Is he looking for his daughter? And if not, why not? And what do we tell Dori? Do we let her know she's adopted? And, if so, when? What will we do if the mother or the father demand to have their child back at some point?

Charles and Evelyn had adopted Dori. However, their adoption was based solely on their desire to care for Dori in the absence of her parents or other family members willing to raise her. At the time, only Massachusetts and New York had legal processes to grant and recognize adoption. Without a legally binding adoption, Charles and Evelyn's status as Dori's parents was very tenuous.

That fact would color all of their decisions through the years. And the first and most urgent decision they made was to get the hell out of Grand Rapids and back to Duluth. Before Dori's grandparents or father potentially demanded that they return her to her rightful family.

# CHAPTER 23

The phrase "secure immersion ward" made it sound like a safe place where one would be deeply engaged in various therapeutic activities. Unfortunately, this was the furthest thing from the truth. While it was definitely locked, it wasn't necessarily safe. The patients on the ward were decidedly more deranged and dysfunctional. As for immersion, the only thing the patients seemed to be immersed in was a cacophony of chaos.

The ward consisted of two large rooms, one with 3 rows of 10 beds strung together head-to-toe, presumably for sleeping. There were no private bedrooms as in Hagatha's previous ward. The other room had 30 chairs arranged haphazardly throughout with no other furnishings – this room, she learned, was called the day room. Along the back wall of the ward were bathroom facilities, seclusion rooms, and the nursing station. Large wire-mesh-covered windows adorned the opposite wall, providing an abundance of sunshine to the rooms and a view out over Devil's Lake and the vast fields of wheat beyond that.

Hagatha was released from her straitjacket once she arrived. Although still incensed by Dr. Rosenstern's ruse, she resisted taking her anger out on the orderlies who had transported her. She knew the recipe for getting even with Dr. Rosenstern and was anxious to start the process. However, she was immediately accosted by an elderly woman who wanted to stroke her long blond hair and a middle-aged man who began stroking himself. Ward staff quickly intervened and shooed them back into their chairs with warnings of seclusion if they didn't remain seated.

"Thank you," she said to the orderlies upon their return. "Would it be possible to retrieve the Bible I had on the other ward, or do you have one I could use?"

"No. Reading material is not allowed," one of the orderlies replied.

"Then what am I to do?"

"Find a chair to sit in and don't cause any problems," the other orderly stated gruffly, then chuckling as he turned to go to the Nurses Station.

She found an empty chair and sat down. However, it was anything but relaxing as the patients around her let out a constant chorus of crying, screaming, moaning, and laughing – creating a symphony in the key of insanity. If that wasn't bad enough, the middle-aged man was staring at her from across the room. When her eyes happened to meet his, he let out a groan, releasing a geyser of ejaculate onto the floor in front of him. Drowning out the noise and the distractions were going to be a challenge. And without a Bible to consult, Hagatha would have to rely on her memory. Fortunately, she knew of a perfect mantra from the Book of James to make Dr. Rosenstern pay for deceiving her. She whispered to herself.

"But the tongue can no man tame. It is an unruly evil, full of deadly poison."

And despite the din and the disturbances all around her, she managed to work herself into a trance-like state. Her intense blue eyes staring out but seeing nothing but the image of Dr. Rosenstern drinking his morning coffee. Only to succumb to violent body spasms as the poison hit his bloodstream and coursed through him. Eventually cutting off his airway, causing him to fall out of his chair. Where he writhed briefly on the floor. Finally stilled from oxygen depletion.

She kept on silently repeating the line from the Book of James and rerunning the images of Dr. Rosenstern's last moments. Until an orderly shook her by the shoulder to bring her back to the here and now.

"Time to go to bed," he announced for the third time as Hagatha's eyes suddenly focused on his face.

"Bed?" she asked as if it was a foreign concept. Though her reaction was due more to her surprise at how many hours had passed. To Hagatha, it seemed like she had just sat down a minute ago.

"Yes, it's a metal frame with a mattress and pillow. You lay down on it, close your eyes, and sleep perchance to dream," the obviously learned and sarcastic orderly replied.

"Perchance to dream," she repeated, smiling. "Aren't you the quipster?" she laughed.

"Oh, you got that?" he asked, shocked at her response.

"Yes, why? Do you think I'm crazy as a loon or something?" she smiled, recognizing the irony in her response.

"Now, who's being the quipster?" the orderly responded. "Off to bed with you."

The orderly led her to an unoccupied bed in a row reserved for the female patients. A hospital-issued nightgown laid at the foot of the bed. After changing in the bathroom, she slipped into bed between two neighboring female patients. While the women had their own row of beds, they were only six feet removed from the nearest row of beds occupied by men. And despite orderlies strategically placed at the front and end of that divide, the potential for mischief was there. That fear and the scratchy material of the full-length gown with long sleeves made it impossible for Hagatha to sleep or, for that matter, to dream.

Instead, she resumed her previous reverie, silently repeating, "But the tongue can no man tame. It is an unruly evil, full of deadly poison." And visualizing Dr. Rosenstern's end-of-days over and over and over.

# CHAPTER 24

Otto came home to find Ursala sitting despondently on the living room couch, a handkerchief in one hand and a letter in the other. While she wasn't crying, her bloodshot eyes told him she had been.

"Ushi, what's the matter?" he asked, rushing to her side.

She didn't even react, her eyes locked in a thousand-yard stare.

"Ushi, please tell me what happened," he said.

To which she moved her hand that was holding the letter ever so slightly in his direction. He took it from her hand and read it.

"This can't be. What does he mean by insults to her emotional stability? And what prolonged and repeated destabilizing forces has she been exposed to? This makes no sense," he bellowed.

A tear came to Ursala's eye, and she dabbed at it with her kerchief.

"Our daughter had the most loving and stable upbringing a child could have," Otto protested. "And until she had that one indiscretion, her marriage seemed happy. Am I not right, Ushi?"

His words opening his wife's floodgates again, causing him

to put his arm around her.

"Oh, I'm sorry. I'm making you upset all over again. But this is an outrage. And we can't even visit her?"

This brought on a howl from Ursala, who turned, buried her head in Otto's shoulder, and disintegrated into tears. Otto put down the letter, suspended his anger, and wrapped his arms around his wife. Shooshing and rocking her gently until she regained her composure.

"What are we going to do, Otto?" she was finally able to ask.

"I don't know, Ushi. I have half a mind to go there and see her for myself. I just can't believe she is as sick as the doctor claims."

"But what if she is, and your visit makes things worse, as the doctor wrote?"

"Yes, that is what gives me pause. I just can't imagine what could have happened to our little girl in the two years she was married to Enoch."

"Maybe he was the source of her problems? Perhaps that is what drove our daughter into the arms of another man?"

"But wouldn't we have seen it? And wouldn't she have come to us if he wasn't treating her well?"

"Maybe she was too proud. Maybe she was trying to fix things herself."

"Perhaps," Otto acquiesced. "I guess we better not wait any longer to hire some help. It sounds like it might be a while before she's well," he concluded.

Both began to cry and console each other. Helpless in the face of the devastating emotional turmoil that had taken their daughter away from them. With no clues as to its genesis or its resolution.

"We must pray, Ushi. We must put this in God's hands," Otto said.

Ursala could only shake her head in agreement. Too distraught to utter a word.

# CHAPTER 25

Two years after Enoch Jr.'s birth, Enoch and Lila welcomed a second son, Esau, into the world. And a couple of years later, they were blessed with Ezra, the first Slaughter descendent born in the 20th century.

Enoch now had three sons, staking his claim as the winner in the race for most male offspring. A race that only he was running against his brothers. If nothing else, Enoch no longer resented his brothers. He even invited them up to the mansion from time to time.

Like Enoch's family, the town of Slaughter was also growing. The schools, which seemed extravagantly oversized when built, were quickly filling up. New homes were popping up, and new businesses were coming to town. Enoch leased portions of his land to the logging and iron ore industries, exponentially increasing his wealth and ensuring a steady income stream for years to come. The turn of the century seemed to bring with it a renewed optimism. And everything seemed to be working in Enoch's favor. His vision for his family and the future of his burgeoning town were coming to fruition.

As quick as Enoch could take credit for his successes, he was equally able to dismiss any perceived failures. And not just dismiss them, but completely erase them from his life – as if they never happened. The best example being his failed marriage with Hagatha and his unwanted daughter, now 7 years in the past. Those who knew about his previous union quickly learned it was not only fruitless to bring the topic up but suicidal to their social and professional lives if they did. Such was the case for one prominent shopkeeper in town who had the temerity to ask.

"Good morning, Mayor," greeted Torvold Finn, proprietor of Finn's Boots and Shoe store.

"Good morning, Tor," Enoch replied. "Get any new boots in lately? Winter's just around the corner."

"When isn't winter around the corner?" Tor laughed. "Yes, I have a few new selections. Take a seat, and I'll bring some out."

Enoch sat down and breathed in the fresh smell of leather. He wasn't much for clothing fashion, but footwear was a whole nother matter. In fact, he probably could have single-handedly kept the Swedish transplant's store profitable. Or should I say dual-footedly?

"I think you will like these," Tor announced, holding up a pair of boots upon his return. "Genuine seal skin. Much more comfortable and durable than leather boots."

As Enoch was trying on the boots, Tor made what he thought was small talk.

"So, Mayor, whatever became of your first wife, Hagatha, and your little girl, Hilda?"

At first, Enoch didn't even respond. Making Tor think the Mayor hadn't heard him. So he repeated the question.

"I don't know who you're talking about, Tor," he replied straight-faced as he was lacing up one of the boots. "Maybe ask me a different question," he added, as a look that could kill came across his face.

"Ah, ah, how do you like the boots?" Tor stammered, realizing that he must have crossed a boundary he shouldn't have.

"I like them just fine. And I heard they are free today,"

Enoch replied, with a look that dared Tor to tell him different.

"Why, why, of course, Mayor. You heard right," Tor said, starting to sweat.

"Then I'll take these and be on my way," Enoch said, removing the boot and handing it to Tor.

"Yes, of course. I'll box them up for you."

When Tor returned with the boxed-up boots, he attempted to make amends.

"I'm sorry, Mayor. Sometimes I ask too many questions. I hope you will forgive me."

Enoch just took the box from Tor and walked out without a word.

Shortly after that, dozens of townfolk descended upon Finn's. Having heard from the Mayor that he was offering free shoes and boots. He didn't dare disappoint them and considered it the cost of opening his big mouth. The next day, his store inventory nearly depleted, Torvold Finn received two devastating notices from the Mayor. The first notified him that his store's business tax had tripled and was due immediately. The second notice informed him that the property tax on his home had also tripled. Likewise, it was also due immediately.

Tor had a choice. He could either use all of his life's savings to pay the taxes, restore his inventory and hope to make a profit on sales despite the exorbitant tax. Or he could default on the taxes and pick up and find a new place to work and live. He chose the latter, recognizing that the town's most important and influential member would likely continue to punish him for his faux pas. So he packed up the remaining inventory from the store and his personal belongings and left town the next day. But not before warning several of his neighbors and fellow shop owners of the cost should they make a similar mistake.

# CHAPTER 26

When Dr. Rosenstern was found dead on the floor next to his desk, it was a shock to everyone except Hagatha. The same non-physician coroner who mistakenly ruled the patient's drowning in the lake due to a cramp now wrongly attributed Dr. Rosenstern's death to suffocation from an allergic reaction that closed his esophagus. The coroner surmised that it was hayfever since it was harvest time.

As you might expect, the coroner's conclusion had a chilling effect on the willingness of those assigned to harvest duty – patients and hospital employees alike. At the slightest sign of a sniffle, they would report to the infirmary, fearing imminent death. But, in the end, the wheat got harvested, and no one else succumbed to the same fate as Dr. Rosenstern.

Dr. Rosenstern's demise ushered in a new era for Fairdale Falls State Hospital. A new Chief Psychiatrist was hired, promising more humane and effective 20$^{th}$-century treatment. And an ambitious building project was initiated to expand the hospital's capacity from 400 to 1,000 patients over the next 5 years.

Hagatha, meanwhile, was showing the ill effects of her week-long trance. She had not slept or eaten for over a week, making her appearance absolutely skeletal. In addition to exhaustion, she complained of blurry vision, body soreness, and was bleeding in her mouth. Mentally she was confused, and when she attempted to talk, she could only babble incoherently. Finally, she was taken to the infirmary. Upon examination, she was found to have bleeding mouth ulcers, receding gums, and loose teeth. The doctor, thinking she may have some kind of parasitic infection, prescribed daily administration of Fowler's Solution – a tonic containing arsenic. For her vision, he had her try on spectacles from a box full of them – likely lost or left behind by previous patients. She found a pair of round wire-rimmed glasses, which eliminated her blurry vision.

It was fortunate that the orderly who had previously quoted Hamlet took an interest in her care. Although she tried to beg off eating as too painful, his insistence and obvious concern for her welfare convinced her to try. It probably saved her life. She didn't have a parasitic infection, and the daily arsenic tonics, if continued long-term, would have undoubtedly had a deleterious effect. What Hagatha was suffering from was scurvy – a relatively common condition in those days, confined primarily to sailors at sea for long periods and patients incarcerated in insane asylums. Unbeknownst at the time, scurvy was a function of a Vitamin C deficiency. And the meals offered at the hospital were fortuitously heavy in Vitamin C-rich vegetables like potatoes, cabbage, broccoli, and spinach. Within days, her symptoms disappeared, and the arsenic tonic was discontinued. The infirmary doctor would mistakenly attribute Hagatha's recovery to his astute diagnostic and treatment prowess.

In many respects, Hagatha dispensing with Dr. Rosenstern significantly improved the conditions for all the patients in the hospital. His replacement, Dr. Alexander Schmidt, had recently emigrated from Austria, where he had studied at Vienna University. He was introduced to Dr. Sigmund Freud, who gave weekly Saturday evening lectures at the psychiatric clinic. Consequently, adopting Freud's novel talking therapy approach. Never mind that there was no possible way Dr. Schmidt could apply this technique en masse to the growing numbers of patients. Or the simple fact that many of the patients were too deranged to talk coherently or understand the esoteric principles Dr. Schmidt spouted when plumbing the depths of their subconscious minds.

What Dr. Schmidt did do to improve patient's lives, however, was to outlaw forced labor. Under certain conditions, higher functioning patients could voluntarily request work in preparation for reintroduction into society. He also did away with Dr. Rosenstern's Catholic-based treatment. Eliminating the need to fast, abstain from certain foods, attend mass, read the Bible, or test patients' knowledge of scriptures. Bibles were taken out of patient rooms, and a proper library was established with a wide array of reading materials. The strict daily schedule of compulsory activities was replaced with a more leisurely calendar of optional activities. Seclusion and restraint were retained as interventions when patients were out of control. However, ice baths were eliminated.

You couldn't necessarily say it was a startling evolution in the effectiveness of mental health treatment. But it certainly decreased the more abusive aspects of Dr. Rosenstern's treatment philosophy. For example, whereas Dr. Rosenstern saw insanity as possession by the devil, Dr. Schmidt saw it as the failure of a patients' ego, id, or superego. Brought about by insults to these aspects of a person's personality, usually suffered in childhood, and typically attributable to the child's dysfunctional relationship with their mother.

For those select few patients who met with Dr. Schmidt for therapy sessions, it was relatively harmless. They would lay down on a couch and be encouraged to talk about anything they wished for 20 minutes while he sat out of view recording everything they said on a notepad. For the remaining 30 minutes, he would summarize the content of what they had said and launch into the psychoanalytic themes and conflicts he had deduced from what they shared. Unfortunately, a large proportion of patients would fall asleep during this portion of their session. Finding the couch, Dr. Schmidt's heavy Austrian accent and the unfathomable concepts he droned on about more effective as a lullaby than a source of enlightenment.

The Secure Immersion Ward was also closed, and patients returned to units equipped with private bedrooms. Hagatha felt fortunate to return to her original ward, where she was reunited with Maggie. However, the male orderly who saved her life was assigned to a unit in the new building.

For Hagatha, the downside of the less structured days gave her more time to ruminate. And when she did this, invariably, her mind would take her back to Slaughter. Reliving the pain and the anger anew of Enoch's rejection of her and their baby. She frequently pondered whether to aim the destructive powers she had cultivated on Enoch. Each time resolving not to do so in the hopes that eventually she would be released. At which time, she could go back to Slaughter and watch him suffer as she systematically destroyed all that he loved and cared about.

# CHAPTER 27

Dori Shepherd was now 9 years old and in the 4th grade. And besides her occasional bouts of night terrors, she was a bright, well-adjusted child. Charles and Evelyn's concerns that her birth parents might attempt to reclaim her were now a distant memory. While they did celebrate her birthdays each April 2nd, they decided not to change her name back to Hilda or divulge that she was adopted.

This didn't present any issues until one night when Dori woke up in terror from another nightmare – this one more vivid and disturbing than any previous.

"Oh, Dori, sweetheart. Did you have another nightmare?" Evelyn asked, wrapping her petrified daughter in her arms.

Dori shook her head affirmatively, too frightened to speak.

"Do you want to talk about it?"

Dori shook her head no.

"All right," her mother replied, continuing to hold and rock her gently.

"My name is Hilda, and you're not my mom," Dori exclaimed out of the blue, sobbing.

Evelyn was beyond shocked. She didn't even know how to assimilate her daughter's statement. How could she know? Who could have possibly told her? Surely, Charles wouldn't have said anything, would he have?

"Oh, honey, why do you say that?" she asked, holding Dori tight to her chest for fear she would be able to read the surprise on her face as confirmation.

"The scary lady told me. She told me she was my mom."

"Sweetheart, the scary lady is not real. How could she be your mommy?"

"But she seemed real," Dori protested.

"That's why nightmares are so scary. They seem real, but they're not. I'm your mom, and I always will be," she replied, looking Dori in the eyes, hoping her face would not betray her.

"Okay," Dori snuffled, burying her head back into Evelyn's chest and hugging her.

As much as Evelyn wished to know more about Dori's nightmare, she feared asking additional questions would just upset her daughter. And potentially perpetuate the nightmare's recurrence.

Eventually, Dori was able to get back to sleep, but the seed had been planted. It was a germ of an idea that she and the two people she called Mom and Dad weren't who she thought they were. A kernel that wouldn't erupt for a few more years, when the changes of adolescence would throw everything in her life into question and out of kilter.

# CHAPTER 28

Enoch was only too happy to invite his elderly parents, Elias and Ruth Slaughter, to move into the mansion from the Twin Cities. They had plenty of room, and he had the means to pay for the move. Lila also welcomed that their three sons, Enoch Jr., Esau, and Ezra, would have the opportunity to spend time with their grandparents. Not to mention occasionally relieve her of her parental duties. For Enoch, it was another way to demonstrate his primacy over his two younger brothers, Jeremiah and Abraham.

Enoch hadn't counted on his brothers deciding to move their families to Slaughter. When he found out, he was furious. Everything was copacetic between them when they lived at a distance. So much so that he'd even occasionally invite them for a visit. Now they wanted to ruin everything by moving to his town. And they didn't even have the decency to ask. His parents, Lila, and his boys, felt quite the opposite. They welcomed the Slaughter clan being united.

In many ways, Enoch was the victim of his own success and progress in the new century. Slaughter was a popular outpost for those who enjoyed living close, but not in, Grand Rapids. He had built a thriving and affordable community close to where most people worked – the logging and mining companies. In addition, the automobile age had begun, making transportation faster and more convenient.

Enoch was also the victim of his competitive fire. Ever since he was a child, everything was a competition. Not that his parents had raised him to be driven in that direction – quite the opposite. They espoused and encouraged cooperation, sharing, and humility. Qualities that his brothers embraced but which Enoch was never able to assimilate. He saw everything as a contest to be won. Enoch's confidence and drive could be quite attractive to people initially and in small doses. But his appeal suffered over the long term.

He was forever acting like an arrogant winner or a sore loser. Neither of which were endearing qualities. Any friendships he had growing up were usually short-lived, as they would tire of his constant one-upmanship. He would carry this trait into adulthood, which often found him at loggerheads with associates. Enoch's inflated opinion of himself and his faith that he was destined for greatness never waivered through it all. Leaving a wake of people in his past who would forever consider him to be nothing but a conceited jerk.

Nevertheless, this competitive spirit is something he tried to imbue in his children, despite Lila's opposition. Lila, much like Enoch's parents, valued cooperation and teamwork. The last thing she needed were the fierce fights, hurt feelings, and claims of cheating that would invariably ensue when the boys put Enoch's win-at-all-costs guidance into practice.

"Enoch, so help me, God, you need to quit filling these boys' heads with thinking everything is a game to be won. They're behaving like rambunctious little ruffians," Lila fumed after breaking up the latest battle between the siblings.

"So you'd rather they grow up to be little Nancy-boys? Maybe you should put them in dresses and give them dolls to play with."

"There you go again, misconstruing my words. Maybe if you had to watch over them all day while I cavorted around town acting all high and mighty like you do, you'd think different."

"Oh, that's what you think I do? Cavort?"

"Don't start with me, Enoch. I'm sure your job has its challenges, but I aim to raise proper boys who can behave appropriately when called upon. Not little varmints who run amok at every chance they get."

"I didn't get to where I am today by being a sucker, woman."

"Who said anything about being a sucker? I'm talking about simple decorum, Enoch. And if you can't get that through your thick head, perhaps you need to sleep in the Study tonight."

To which Enoch responded by storming off.

Lila just turned, smiled, and went about her business. She had played the trump card, and she knew that he'd eventually come crawling back all apologetic. Hoping to be welcomed back to their marital bed. Whoever said that the way to a man's heart is through his stomach was a little too far north in their anatomy.

# CHAPTER 29

Hagatha woke up in a cold sweat, her pillow and nightgown soaked. Once again, she was haunted by a dream of the child she thought she had drowned in the Mississippi River. But now, her child was no longer a baby.

As the years had passed, Hagatha would occasionally be haunted by dreams of Hilda. At first, she just wrote them off, thinking they'd eventually subside. Instead, they were becoming more frequent and vivid. If she had felt any remorse in drowning Hilda, she could have understood the source of her recurring visions. However, she hadn't felt guilt. She had felt relief. There was only one other possible explanation – Hilda must have survived. And if this were the case, Hagatha would see to it that Hilda didn't escape the torment she had caused her. In short, if Hilda could haunt Hagatha, she would do the same in return.

This revelation caused Hagatha to commit to weaving Hilda into her plan for destruction when she was discharged. Everything that had caused Hagatha turmoil would eventually be erased. In the meantime, she would do her best to make Hilda regret she survived her watery grave.

Hagatha had just sat down in her favorite chair with her Bible, anxious to ponder her grand scheme, when a well-dressed man she had never seen approached.

"Miss Ketchel, I apologize for interrupting your reading.

Allow me to introduce myself. I am Dr. Alexander Schmidt, Chief Psychiatrist."

"How did you know my name?" she asked, eyeing him with suspicion.

"One of the orderlies, I believe her name is Maggie, pointed you out to me. She thinks you'd be a good candidate for my psychotherapy sessions."

"And what exactly are psychotherapy sessions?"

"They're a time to talk about the things that are the source of your stay here, so we can potentially resolve them and return you to society."

"So if I go to these sessions, I might get out sooner?" she asked.

"That's definitely a possibility. But, of course, until I truly understand your issues, I can't say specifically how soon."

"And if I don't want to attend your sessions?"

"Well, if you don't attend my sessions, I'd say there is probably a greater chance you'll stay longer."

"When would they start?"

"They could start as soon as you'd like. Right now if you wish."

Hagatha was skeptical, having been duped by the previous Chief Psychiatrist. However, she was also anxious to get out. So she decided to take her chances. Knowing that the outcome would probably be worse for him than for her should she find he had led her astray.

"All right," she said, closing her Bible and getting up out of her chair.

"Wonderful. Follow me," Dr. Schmidt replied, turning and striding down the hall.

Except for the therapy couch and a tidier desk, everything about Dr. Schmidt's office was the same as it had been the last time Hagatha was there.

"Go ahead and make yourself comfortable on the couch. I'll be sitting right here, out of view, so as not to distract you."

Hagatha reclined on the couch and felt a bit self-conscious not being able to see Dr. Schmidt. And with good reason. Aberrant behavior by men while ogling her was more the rule than the exception. She waited for him to ask her questions, as Dr. Rosenstern had, but they didn't come. Not wanting to appear too anxious, she resisted saying anything a little longer. Finally, when she couldn't tolerate the prolonged silence any further, she spoke.

"Are you going to ask me questions?"

"No. Just say what's on your mind," he prompted.

This was not the response she expected. How could he expect her to just open up about what was on her mind without first building some kind of relationship or rapport? She didn't know anything about him other than his name and title. If it was Maggie sitting there, perhaps she'd feel more comfortable doing so, but that's because they had formed a level of trust over the years. How could this help? What if the thoughts in her head were just the random whimsical ponderings that occasionally danced in her head? She certainly wasn't going to divulge the dark and vengeful thoughts that predominantly occupied her brain. That would only extend her stay.

"I don't think I can do this," she said finally.

He didn't respond.

"Did you hear me? I said I don't think I can do this," she repeated a little more loudly.

Still no response.

"This is a waste of time. Can I go back to my unit?" she asked.

When she still didn't get a response, she got irritated.

"Can you at least have the decency to answer my questions? What kind of nonsense is this?"

This time when she didn't get a response, she acted.

"I'm done. I'm leaving," she said, getting up from the couch and striding towards the door.

She expected him to say something or stop her, but he didn't. She opened his office door and walked through the reception and waiting area. Then marched through the door that led to the hallway. Still with not so much as a word from Dr. Schmidt.

When she got to the unit door, she needed to knock to have someone let her in. Fortuitously, it was Maggie who opened the door.

"Next time Dr. Crackpot asks for recommendations for his supposed therapy sessions, kindly refrain from suggesting me!" she fumed, stomping past Maggie.

"Oh, Hagatha, what happened?" Maggie called after her.

"Nothing. Absolutely nothing. That's what happened," Hagatha replied, getting back to the dayroom only to see another patient occupying her favorite chair.

"Get the hell out of my chair," she screamed.

"I was here first," exclaimed the woman, perhaps 10 years Hagatha's senior and 50 pounds heavier.

Hagatha reached down and grabbed the woman by her hair. And in one smooth but violent move, pulled her out of the chair and threw her to the ground. The woman screaming and crying in pain all the way. When that wasn't enough, Hagatha started kicking her in the ribs and stomach. Male orderlies sprang to action, removing her from the dayroom, while Maggie attended to the injured woman.

Hagatha ended up in a straitjacket in the seclusion room. A place where she felt safe and did some of her best work.

# CHAPTER 30

Jeremiah and Abraham moved their families to Slaughter primarily to maintain their children's connection to their grandparents, Elias and Ruth Slaughter. They were wise to their older brother's ways. They knew that Enoch moving their parents to Slaughter was selfishly motivated more than anything else. They also knew that their decision to move to Slaughter without gaining his permission would irritate him. They didn't care. They were well beyond his pettiness and fed up with his competitiveness. What mattered was that their children grew up knowing and loving their grandparents and learning from their example.

Jeremiah, two years Enoch's junior, had married his high school sweetheart, Hannah, in 1887. They had two sons, Jacob, who was soon to turn 15 years old, and Jedidiah, who was currently 8. Enoch and Jeremiah were as different as night and day, except for naming their sons with the same first letter as their first names. Jeremiah was humble and unassuming, almost subservient to Hannah, who, much like Lila, was a confident and assertive woman who knew what she wanted and wasn't shy about going after it. As a matter of fact, had it been 100 years in the future, Jeremiah would likely have been the house-husband letting Hannah bring home the bacon. Instead, Jeremiah worked as a postal clerk. This was fortuitous because Slaughter's Post Office desperately needed additional clerks to keep up with the town's expansion.

New homes were being built as fast as possible in Slaughter to accommodate the unprecedented demand. Jeremiah and Hannah were delighted to find a 2-bedroom house on 100 Tailings Way. It was built on a spacious corner lot, perfect for their two growing and active boys. And as luck would have it, the house directly across the street at 101 Tailings Way was also for sale. Prompting Abraham, the youngest of Elias and Ruth Slaughter's boys, to buy it for his family.

Abraham, four years Enoch's junior, was married to Sarah, a quiet young woman and a deft seamstress. They had two children, Noah and Abigail – 11 and 6 years old, respectively. Abraham was a physical specimen who looked hewn out of stone. He had been a livery stable keeper in the Twin Cities, a job about to be made extinct by the automobile. Seeing the writing on the wall, Abraham had sold his business. Jobs as lumberjacks and mine workers in Slaughter were plentiful. Mainly because both were backbreaking work for low pay, often in an intemperate climate. But Abraham was built for such work and reveled in it. And with Sarah taking in a little extra money offering her seamstress services, they made ends meet.

Enoch didn't exactly roll out the welcome wagon for his siblings' arrival. In fact, if not for his parents and Lila, he would have been content to ignore and avoid them altogether. On the other end of the spectrum was the larger community of Slaughter residents, who gave them a hearty welcome and quickly assimilated them into the fold. In short, the town had outgrown Enoch's ability to exercise absolute control over it. And Lila and his parents were the effective governors preventing his desire to act inhospitably.

"Isn't it great to have the entire family together," remarked Elias, the family patriarch, at the dinner table one evening. "We should have a weekly family meal together. Heaven knows we have the room for it here," he exclaimed.

Enoch almost choked on the food he was chewing. Before he could recover and register his protest, Lila replied.

"That's a great idea, Dad! How about a Sunday brunch after church each week?" she proposed.

"Oh, I like that idea," Ruth said before her husband could reply. "Can you imagine seeing all the grandchildren together? Children, wouldn't you love to be able to play with your cousins each Sunday?"

Enoch Jr. and Esau, 6 and 4 years old at the time, voiced their enthusiastic support. But, of course, mentioning play at any time under any circumstance would have garnered a favorable response.

"It's settled then," Elias remarked. "Slaughter Sunday brunches."

"Don't I get a say in this? I mean, it is my house," Enoch asked, finally having swallowed his food and finding his voice.

"Why? Do you have another day in mind?" his father asked.

All those around the table turned their heads to stare at Enoch. His face went crimson, and while he opened his mouth to speak, no words came out. Instead, he threw down the fork and knife that were in his hands. The loud clatter as the utensils hit and broke some dinnerware startled baby Ezra, causing him to start crying. Enoch pushed his chair back from the table and stormed off.

"I guess I'll take that as a no," Elias said with a sly grin. "Lila and Ruth, can you see to it that Jeremiah and Abraham's families get invited to Sunday brunch for the foreseeable future?"

"We'll be happy to," Lila replied as she and Ruth returned broad smiles. Knowing they had shoe-horned Enoch into something he would never have suggested or approved.

# CHAPTER 31

A shaft of light blazed in, blinding Hagatha as the seclusion room door was opened. She had been in seclusion for three days. The straitjacket had been removed after day one. But she remained secluded an additional two days – primarily due to the damage she had done. The woman she had assaulted had three broken ribs and two bloody bald patches on her head where two shocks of hair had been pulled out.

"Dr. Schmidt has requested to see you," a muscular male orderly announced.

"Well, I don't want to see him," she replied, shielding her eyes.

"You don't have a choice," the orderly replied. "Now, do I have to drag you down there?"

"Only at your own peril," she threatened.

"What could a little wisp of a girl like you do to me?" he asked, laughing.

"You must be new."

"Yeah, so what?" he spat.

"You might want to consult your more experienced colleagues about what I can do. I'll give you a pass this time. But I warn you. Don't test me. Now get out of my way. I'll walk to

Dr. Crackpot's office under my own power."

The orderly stepped back and held his tongue. It wasn't her words as much as the fire in her eyes that convinced him to give her wide berth. Now fully acclimated to the light and wide open, her piercing blue eyes appeared to be rimmed with red and yellow flames. As if the fires of Hell danced in her eyes.

She walked down the hallway towards the door which led to Dr. Schmidt's office, as the male orderly followed at a safe distance behind.

"Do you want me to break this door down, or do you have a key?" she asked impatiently when she reached the door.

He raced to the door, unlocked it, and opened it for her.

"You might just be salvageable," she said, striding past him and down the hall. Again, stopping outside the door to Dr. Schmidt's reception area. This time he was Johnny on the spot and immediately opened the door for her.

"Your mother would be so proud," she cracked as she entered the reception area.

"Name?" asked Dr. Schmidt's receptionist, an attractive young woman about Hagatha's age.

"Yes, I have a name. Do you?" Hagatha replied sarcastically.

"I need to know your name to check and see if it's on Dr. Schmidt's schedule," she replied.

"And what if it's not? Will the world end? Don't bother me with such nonsense. We all know what Dr. Schmidt employs you for. And it's not to keep his schedule straight."

The receptionist was getting flustered, but before she could respond, Dr. Schmidt opened his office door.

"Oh, Hagatha. So good to see you. Please, please, come in."

Hagatha walked into his office without a word. While she had no difficulty making snarky comments towards the green orderly and Dr. Schmidt's nubile receptionist, she had nothing to say to him.

"Please, make yourself comfortable on the couch," he said.

Instead, Hagatha took a seat in the chair Dr. Schmidt sat in during her last visit.

"No, that's my seat. You need to lay on the couch," he said.

She didn't move and, instead, just gave him a look of defiance. As if challenging him to make her move.

"All right. I guess this just confirms my analysis from our first session. Tell me, was it your father or some other man in your life who caused your lack of trust and anger?" he asked, taking the chair across from her.

Hagatha didn't dignify his observation with a response. However, it did get her thinking about how he had gleaned that conclusion from their last session. A session in which she never talked and walked out shortly after it had commenced.

"Perhaps you resent your mother for taking something away from you that you thought was yours? Or maybe she prevented you from doing something you wished to do?"

Now Hagatha was really confused. How did he come up with that? At least his first comment had hit somewhat close to home. This one bore no such connection to her life or experience. She began to wonder if she had met with him after their first meeting and just forgot. Or maybe she was crazy and couldn't remember certain things.

"Did you walk out on him? Did you cheat on him, Hagatha? Have sexual congress with another man? Or perhaps with another woman?"

Now she was not so much confused as angry. He was clearly just grasping at straws. Or purposefully badgering her to get her to react. She would not be fooled into his sordid little game. To respond now, even if it was to protest, would make him think he struck close to the bone.

"Ah, now I'm beginning to understand. You're fixated in

the anal stage. Wanting to hold everything in. Your parents must have been very strict. Did they spank your little bottom when you had accidents? Did you learn to hold it in? Or did you put things in your anus as a child? Maybe you still like things inserted into your buttocks? Is that what it is, Hagatha? You want something long and hard inserted into your anus? You mustn't be embarrassed or disturbed by this desire. It's a common malady with the women I treat. Oh, yes, it's very treatable. And after a year or two of treatment, you could be freed of your fixation and living a normal life. Would you like that? Would you like me to treat you, Hagatha?"

"It sounds like the only one with an anal fixation is you, Dr. Schmidt. And no. No, I'm not interested in your treatment," Hagatha said, getting up from her chair and walking towards the door.

"May I remind you that the treatment I prescribe is not optional, Miss Ketchel. I can administer your treatment whether or not you consent to it. It's for your own good," he called after her.

Hagatha stopped and turned to face Dr. Schmidt.

"And if you know what's good for you, Doctor, you'll keep your treatment in your pants, or you will rue the day. You've been warned," she said, her eyes ablaze.

Turning and exiting the office, determined never to see the inside of Dr. Schmidt's office again.

# CHAPTER 32

Although Otto and Ursala Ketchel both came from hearty Germanic stock, the passage of time wore on them – more emotionally than physically. It had been 8 years since they had last seen their daughter. Both were approaching 60 years old, well beyond the average life expectancy of that day and age.

"Otto, I'm worried we may never see our daughter again," Ursala remarked. "We're not getting any younger."

"Ushi, we're both still healthy as horses. Besides, I can't imagine she won't be discharged from that hospital soon."

"That's what you said last year and the year before that! So I think we should go and visit her. We have reliable help at the store, and if we wait much longer, it will be winter."

"Why don't you try writing her again?" Otto suggested.

Ursala had tried sending Hagatha several letters over the years. In most cases, they came back undelivered. In some cases, they didn't get returned, but Hagatha hadn't replied. So she assumed that the letters were probably lost.

"I'm done writing letters, Otto. You know yourself that hasn't worked. Why are you so hesitant to go visit? Don't you want to see her?"

"Of course, I'd love to see her, Ushi. But, unfortunately, it's a long trip, and there are no guarantees that they will let us see her when we get there."

"I don't care. At least if we go, I know we will have tried. I just can't live with myself anymore, knowing that we haven't tried. We've prayed and prayed for her return. Maybe God is telling us to go. Just as He told us to come to America."

"All right, all right. We'll go," Otto relented, seeing his wife's dogged determination and frustration.

"You mean it? You really mean it?" Ursala asked with excited anticipation.

"Yes, I really mean it," Otto replied with a smile.

Ursala threw her arms around Otto and gave him a kiss.

"Oh, thank you, Otto. This means so much to me."

"To us. It means so much to us, bubala," he said, correcting her.

# CHAPTER 33

Hagatha returned to the ward from Dr. Schmidt's office, retrieved her Bible, and went to sit in her favorite chair. Ever since she had attacked that patient for sitting in it, no one dared occupy her chair.

Dr. Schmidt's words had disturbed her. And his threat to involuntarily treat her presumed anal fixation enraged her. She anxiously flipped through the pages of her Bible, seeking solace and a respite from the anger he had inspired. She was reading the Book of Matthew when two sets of hands grabbed her by the arms from behind. Lifting her out of her chair and sending her Bible flying.

"Unhand me," she screamed, her feet kicking wildly in the air.

"It's time for your treatment," the orderly on her left said.

"Doctor's orders," said the other orderly on her right, the one who had cautiously escorted her to Dr. Schmidt's office previously.

The last verse Hagatha had read sprang from her lips. "Give not that which is holy unto the dogs, neither cast ye your pearls before swine, lest they trample them under their feet, and turn again and rend you."

Which only made the orderlies chuckle. Thinking her religious babbling was an amusing symptom of her lunacy and inconsequential to their personal health.

"Back so soon, Miss Ketchel?" Dr. Schmidt smiled as the orderlies brought her into his office.

To which, Hagatha screamed, "You'll regret this day, doctor."

"Oh, I think not. On the contrary, I think I'm going to enjoy this very much. And I think you'll find that it, how should I put this, opens you up in ways you never could have imagined," he laughed.

"Bend her over the end of the therapy couch and strap her wrists to her ankles," he instructed the orderlies.

Hagatha fought hard, but the orderlies were too big and too strong. Before long, she was spent from the futile effort, and they had her in the compromising position.

"You may come back in an hour to retrieve Miss Ketchel after her therapy. Thank you, gentlemen."

The orderlies left, and Dr. Schmidt walked over beside the couch, running his hand over Hagatha's buttocks, still covered by the long gown she wore.

He started to undo his belt and take off his pants.

"You see, I'm committed to resolving your anal fixation, Hagatha. To not do so would compromise my obligation as a physician," he said as he took his place behind her.

He lifted her gown and pulled it up over her to reveal her backside and cover her head. Then, slapping her bottom still covered by an undergarment.

"Is that what Daddy used to do to you, Hagatha?" he laughed. Then, pulling her undergarment down and slapping her again with a resounding crack.

"You will suffer the vengeance of eternal fire for fornicating strange flesh," she said through clenched teeth.

"What was that? I didn't hear you, Miss Ketchel," he replied, slapping her ass again.

"You will suffer the vengeance of eternal fire for fornicating strange flesh," she screamed.

"Oh, there is nothing strange about your flesh, Miss Ketchel. And I'm going to get very well acquainted with it," he said, ramming his manhood into her.

The pain was so intense she nearly passed out. Dizzy and light-headed, she screamed as her skin progressively ripped from his brutal thrusts until blood from the lacerations provided some lubrication. Then, just as the pain was starting to decrease, his fingers started clawing at her vagina. Ultimately inserting and pistoning several fingers inside her, scratching and tearing the tender tissues further. She eventually fainted, only to wake up as the orderlies dragged her back to the ward and deposited her unceremoniously in the seclusion room.

# CHAPTER 34

The journey from Grand Rapids to Fairdale Falls State Hospital was only marginally less arduous than 8 years prior when Otto and Ursala first thought about going. A horse-driven carriage followed by a train ride was still the only way to get there. Only now, Otto and Ursala could travel south to catch the train in Aitkin instead of backtracking to Duluth. Cutting a half-day from what was formerly a two-day journey. While cars would eventually supplant horses and trains, they were still a few years off from becoming ubiquitous.

Otto and Ursala's carriage ride arrived in Aitkin a couple of hours before the train from Duluth would arrive. They took the opportunity to have lunch at the Foley Hotel, Aitkin's newest and fanciest.

"Oh, Otto, isn't this so exciting?" Ursala gushed. "Tomorrow, we get to see our daughter, finally."

"Tomorrow, we hope to see our daughter," Otto corrected, trying to tamp down his wife's expectations in case of disappointment.

"You must think positive, Otto. Negative thinking will jinx us."

"I'm not pessimistic. I'm trying to be realistic."

"Yes, well, was ich nicht weis, macht mich nicht heis," she

said in German, roughly meaning what I don't know, can't hurt me.

"Ja, ja, das stimmt," Otto replied, confirming the truth of the saying but now worried that she'd blame him if they didn't get to see their daughter.

They had a delicious lunch and vowed to perhaps spend an evening at the hotel on their return trip.

The walk from the hotel to the train depot was short, and they waited in restless anticipation for the train's arrival. When the scheduled time for the train's arrival came and went, Otto and Ursala grew concerned. Two characteristic traits of Germans were an intolerance for inefficiency and being late.

"Do you think we missed the train?" Ursala asked. Because a German's first thought is that maybe being 20 minutes early wasn't early enough.

"No, we would have heard and seen the train arriving from the restaurant," Otto replied.

"Then what do you think has happened? Maybe we should ask someone."

Which, of course, was Otto's cue to find that someone.

"I'll go ask," he replied, leaving the track-side platform to enter the depot and query the gentleman in the ticket booth.

"Excuse me. Might you know why the train is delayed?"

The station agent pulled out his pocket watch and consulted the time.

"I wouldn't worry about it. Sometimes it can be 15 to 20 minutes late. It should be here soon," he said optimistically.

Otto returned to the platform and reassured Ursala.

"That's the problem in America," Ursala complained. "No one respects schedules. Why even Father Jorgensen starts mass 5 minutes late! Is nothing sacred anymore? This wouldn't happen in our fatherland."

Otto just nodded and stared down the track hoping the train would make its appearance before his wife got any more irritated.

After 10 more minutes, Ursala started to pace up and down the platform with a disgusted look on her face. Then, when the train hadn't appeared 30 minutes after its scheduled arrival time, she erupted.

"This is all your fault, Otto Ketchel! Didn't I tell you your negativity would jinx us?"

"But bubala," he began, only to be interrupted by her tirade.

"Don't bubala me, mister. First, you hemmed and hawed about the trip being too long and tried to get me to write a letter instead. Then you had to jinx us by saying they might not let us see her. I'm beginning to wonder if you even want to see our daughter," she huffed.

Before Otto could respond and defend himself, she stormed off in the direction of the depot, shouting, "I'm going to give them a piece of my mind."

Otto didn't dare try to stop her or follow along. His presence would just make matters worse.

He could hear her animated voice crescendo from his place on the platform. He truly felt sorry for the poor station agent she was accosting. The usually meek and mild Ursala Ketchel had a long fuse, but when she blew, she really blew. Then suddenly, all was quiet. He was about to check on her when she came through the door, trudging trance-like. Her face, a mask of despair.

"Ushi, what happened?"

Her tear-filled eyes looked up at him, her lips trembling.

"Ushi, speak to me. What happened?"

"There was an accident. The train's not coming," she wailed, falling into Otto's arms.

He held and consoled her.

"Come bubala, we'll check into the hotel. Maybe we can catch a train tomorrow."

But the train had derailed, killing several people and injuring many. It would be days before they untangled the wreckage, recovered the bodies, cleared the tracks, and continued rail service. When they learned this the following morning, they had no choice but to return to Grand Rapids. Crestfallen, they boarded a carriage and returned home. Along the way, Ursala apologized to Otto.

"I'm sorry I blamed you for our misfortune, Otto. I was just upset that the train was late."

"I know, bubala. I just thank God we didn't travel to Duluth to catch the train. That could have been us dying or getting injured."

"Yes, a man's heart plans his way, but the Lord directs his steps," Ursala replied, quoting Proverbs. "We should be grateful."

"Yes, and we can try to go see her again next spring," he noted.

"Unless God willing, she comes home before then," Ursala added.

"Yes, God willing," Otto replied.

# CHAPTER 35

The pain between her legs was excruciating and radiated up into her abdomen. Hagatha had laid neglected in the dark seclusion room for over 24 hours. She needed to relieve herself but staved off doing so as long as she could. Knowing that it would bring about unbearable pain. When she finally urinated and defecated in the corner of the room, it was even worse than she imagined.

Maggie, back from two days off, immediately went to check on her. Upon opening the door, she was nearly overcome by the stench. Hagatha lay naked and unconscious, her nether region a swollen and inflamed mess of contusions and festering lacerations. An odoriferous stream of bloody pus draining from her vagina.

Maggie rushed her to the infirmary, where the doctor took quick action. Lancing the infected pustules allowing them to drain more rapidly. Hagatha came to, sat bolt upright, and screamed in agony when the doctor bathed the area in an iodine and bromine solution. Bromine was highly corrosive and painful. It was one of the few treatments available for infections at the time, as antibiotics would not be discovered for another 30 years. While bromine was reasonably effective in killing infected cells and tissue, it also damaged normal cells. In short, the scars from the doctor's treatment would follow Hagatha forever. However, it saved her life.

If not for Maggie's support and the solace Hagatha found reading and reciting from the Bible, she may not have made it through the painful recovery period. That, and the burning desire to avenge Dr. Schmidt's so-called treatment, drove her to persevere. So as she lay in bed recuperating, she repeatedly uttered the following phrase under her breath, "You will suffer the vengeance of eternal fire for fornicating strange flesh." And as she did, she focused singularly on Dr. Schmidt and the painful way she would commend him to Hell. She would deal with the orderlies in due time.

But beyond all of these things was one catalyzing moment. One experience so overwhelmingly inspiring that Hagatha knew she would be able to endure any pain, suffer any indignity, and survive any hardship. The event came in the form of a dream. A dream that gave her a vision of her future 50 or 60 years hence. Making her current trials and tribulations child's play in the grander scheme of things.

The vision occurred that night as her raging fever finally broke. In it, she sees herself as an old lady in a housedress in front of a small white house vigorously sweeping the sidewalk with a corn bristle broom. She goes back into her home to fix a cup of tea. But gets interrupted when a young woman in an unacceptably short dress gets out of a strange futuristic cream-colored 4-wheeled conveyance bearing the word "Falcon" on its side. She invites the young woman in. And recognizes she is her great-granddaughter, who has arrived to help her carry out her final plan – a plan to vanquish all the descendants of Enoch Slaughter. They share a cup of tea, and she puts her hand on her great-granddaughter's hand, passing her powers onto her. Powers her great-granddaughter will need to accomplish her mission.

Hagatha, despite lying in her sweat-soaked bed, wakes up healed, refreshed, and feeling invincible. Ready to face whatever hardships are necessary to get to that day, in the future, when her great-granddaughter comes to visit. In the meantime, she would set the stage for her arrival.

# CHAPTER 36

The extended Slaughter family now filled two pews on Sundays at St. Joseph's church. However, when it came time for the first Slaughter family Sunday brunch, Enoch predictably tried to weasel his way out of it. Claiming to have some critical mayoral duty after church to attend to.

"You go on ahead. I'll join you as soon as I can," Enoch said to the group while striding off hastily before anyone had the chance to interrogate him.

"Does he think we were born yesterday?" Lila exclaimed. "Who has business on a Sunday that can't wait until Monday?"

"I think I know where he might be going," Elias said. "You go and prepare the festivities, and I will deal with my son."

"Dad, do you want us to come with you?" Jeremiah asked, volunteering himself and his younger brother Abraham.

"No, you go on along. This is something just between your older brother and me."

They grudgingly cooperated and started to walk in the direction of the mansion as Elias turned to walk the way Enoch had gone, which was toward town.

Most of the stores in town were closed on Sunday, save for Loman's Grocery. Which wasn't truly a grocery store at all but a saloon in disguise. Stocking a few foodstuffs amongst the liquor bottles was how Loman's could skirt the State's blue laws.

Along with the Mayor's full approval, of course.

Suffice to say, when Elias opened the door of Loman's Grocery, Enoch and a handful of other men were not food shopping.

"You know, we have whiskey at the house," he announced, startling Enoch, whose back was to the door.

"Dad? What are you doing here? I told you I had some business to take care of."

"Yes, you did. And lying when you're in church is about as low as one can get."

"I wasn't lying," he protested his face flushing with embarrassment from being put on the spot.

"No, you're right, now you've lied twice. But, you know, for being my eldest son, you sure can act immature."

"Dad, let's continue this outside," Enoch pleaded, getting up from the barstool.

"No, you're going to listen to me, and if it embarrasses you, so be it. Maybe next time, you'll think twice about lying in front of God and your family. I don't value your wealth, title as Mayor, or your efforts to outshine your brothers at every turn. You can't even spend a couple hours with us as a family. That's what I value, and in that regard, you're a big disappointment. Now pay the proprietor what you owe him and get your sorry ass home," he said, skewering his son and turning to leave.

To hear his father, a God-fearing man, use profanity shocked Enoch. That alone emphasized how thoroughly he had angered and disappointed his father. He paid for his drink and those of the others at the bar. Hoping to regain some semblance of their goodwill, if not their respect. And rushed off to try to catch up to his father.

When he finally caught up to him, Enoch begged and pleaded for his father's forgiveness. He made lofty promises about changing his behavior towards his brothers and never disappointing his father again. Elias walked silently, stopping only when they arrived at the front door of the mansion.

"Your words mean nothing to me, son. You lost the privilege of my trust in your words by your bald-faced lies. The only thing that can mend that now is your actions. Not just today, but every day. Do you understand me?"

"Yes, father," he replied dejectedly.

And for a time, Enoch's actions made good on his word and promises to his father. The Slaughter family Sunday brunch became a tradition. And Enoch participated in them all and even appeared to enjoy them.

Ironically, Father Jorgensen's sermon the following Sunday was based on a verse from the Book of Jeremiah.

"Can the Ethiopian change his skin, or the leopard his spots?" he sang out from the pulpit. "Then may ye also do good that are accustomed to do evil," he paused dramatically. "My friends, what I believe Jeremiah is telling us, is that by accepting God into your life and letting him take the reins, you can cast off that which is evil in your nature."

Even if Enoch had been awake for that part of Father Jorgensen's sermon, his words would have been lost on him. For Enoch was a leopard whose spots would never change.

# CHAPTER 37

As a parent, you can convince a 9-year-old child to believe almost anything. And Evelyn and Charles had successfully hidden the near-tragic circumstances which caused them to rescue and adopt Dori. Not to mention, convince her that the scary lady in her recurring nightmares wasn't real.

But Dori, now 15 years old, wasn't so quick to buy into their stories. Then, of course, doubting one's parents in adolescence was the norm. But her doubt was based on a lifetime of nocturnal visitations by the lady who insisted she was her mother. Moreover, the nightmares had progressively grown more vivid. She was now subjected to images of the horrific deaths the lady caused and visions of her own future.

Evelyn and Charles nearly fell out of their bed when they were awakened by Dori's bloodcurdling scream.

"You will suffer the vengeance of eternal fire for fornicating strange flesh," Dori was repeating in a fever-pitched voice that was not her own.

She was sitting up in bed with her eyes open, but they didn't seem to be tracking things external to her. Instead, it appeared as if she was seeing things playing inside her head.

"Dori, wake up!" Evelyn shouted above her daughter's biblical utterances while grasping her daughter's shoulders and shaking her.

"You will suffer the vengeance of eternal fire for fornicating strange flesh," she kept repeating, her eyes now frantic as if she saw something terrifying.

When shaking her didn't bring her out of her trance-like state, Evelyn pinched her daughter's arm, hoping the pain would snap her out of the episode that had her so agitated.

"Oww," Dori howled, rubbing her arm with her hand where Evelyn had pinched her. "Did you pinch me?" she protested. Her gaze finally transitioned from a vacant stare to recognizing that her mother was sitting in front of her.

"I'm sorry, I had to, Dori. You seemed," she paused, unsure how to describe it. "Lost in some scary place that you couldn't escape. And you were saying something in a strange voice."

"What?" Dori asked in disbelief. "I had a nightmare, but I don't remember saying anything. What was I saying? And in whose voice?"

"Something about suffering from eternal fire," she paraphrased, not wanting to say the word fornicating to her teenage daughter. "And I didn't recognize the voice, but it sounded like an older woman.

"You mean my mom," Dori replied. "My mom was saying that and something about fornicating strange flesh."

"You saw me in your nightmare? Evelyn asked, once again trying to avoid the offensive phrase.

"No, not you. It was the lady who says she's my mother and that my name is Hilda."

"Oh, no, not that again. Honey, you know that lady isn't real."

"Then why do I keep seeing her? And why does she keep telling me she's my mother and that my name is Hilda?"

"I don't know, Dori," she answered simply. Hoping she'd let

it go.

"You adopted me, didn't you?" Dori said accusatorily. "You adopted me, and you don't want to tell me. Why don't you want to tell me? Shouldn't I know who my real mom is?"

"Oh, sweetie, no," she replied, tears welling in Evelyn's eyes. Unable to respond further to Dori's interrogation.

"I don't believe you!" Dori screamed. "My whole life, all I've seen is that same woman in my nightmares. And every time you'd tell me it's not real. So if she isn't real, why do I keep seeing her? And why do you call me Dori when my name is Hilda? Why are you lying to me?"

Charles, having heard his wife crying and the ongoing commotion entered the room.

"What's going on here?" he asked, seeing Evelyn sobbing. "And why is your mother crying?"

"She's not my mother, and you're not my Dad. I'm adopted, aren't I?" she blustered, catching Charles by surprise.

Evelyn wailed in response and fell into Charles's arms as he sat on the bed beside her.

"Come, Evelyn. You're upset," he said, stating the obvious and helping her up off the bed.

"Aren't you going to answer my question?" Dori protested.

"Can't you see your mother's upset? We will talk to you after she's calmed down."

"What about me? I'm upset too! And she's not my mother!" Dori shouted as they were exiting. Causing Evelyn to howl once more from the pain of Dori's words which cut into her as only the naked truth can.

"Go back to bed, Dori. We'll talk when it's not the middle of the night," Charles barked in response.

"My name is Hilda," she hollered back, needing to get in the last word.

Evelyn was an emotional wreck by the time Charles got her back to their bedroom. It would have been fruitless to talk, so he just helped her to bed and held her until her sobs became whimpers, and whimpers finally gave way to sleep. He knew they had some critical decisions to make, and he hoped that the answers would reveal themselves with the light of the new day.

# CHAPTER 38

Dr. Alexander Schmidt liked to take mid-day naps. But admitting such would have subjected him to ridicule as a hypocrite, as he had fired more than a few staff caught sleeping on the job. So instead, he took naps under the guise of requiring an hour each day to, as he put it, "ponder and untangle the psychodynamic puzzles his patients presented him." He would tell his receptionist not to disturb him, close and lock his office door, and recline on his therapy couch for a quick snooze.

For a time, his receptionist really believed he was engaged in the brilliant work of how to plumb the depths of the human psyche. That is until she heard him snoring. Not that she was going to do anything to get him in trouble. She needed the job. And besides, he would pay her a little extra when he asked her to use her mouth to "relieve his pent-up tension." He called it cathartic. She called it disgusting. But the money was good.

Then one day, during one of his naps, instead of snoring, she smelled smoke. At first, she thought it might be from a cigar, which he would occasionally smoke. When she heard his tortured howls and cries for help, she knew it wasn't a cigar. She fumbled with the office key, trying to unlock the door. When she finally got it open, the therapy couch was engulfed in flames. She couldn't even see Dr. Schmidt, but his screams told her he was caught amid the pyre.

Fire extinguishers at the time were heavy metal canisters filled with water. Before she could retrieve the fire extinguisher from her office and drag it into Dr. Schmidt's office, it was too late. The flames had already burned themselves out. All that was left lying on the smoldering couch were the charred remains of what used to be Dr. Schmidt. That the flames had not spread beyond the couch was an oddity that no one picked up on until the coroner raised the question.

"I do not see any water here. Did you use the fire extinguisher on the fire?" the coroner asked the receptionist.

"No. By the time I got it in here, the flames had died down," she said, regretting her choice of words.

"Well, that is strange," the coroner remarked. "This was obviously a very intense fire. I'm baffled at how the rest of the office didn't catch fire."

There was no such thing as a State Fire Marshal at the time. However, the unusual circumstances of the fire in a state facility would prompt the Minnesota State legislature to create such a position. But, of course, it was too late to investigate the fire that had consumed Dr. Schmidt by then. And even if such an expert had existed, they wouldn't have been able to explain it. It defied the laws of combustion and fire science.

Only one person knew what had led to the demise of the hospital's last two Chief Psychiatrists. And she wasn't talking. Well, she was talking, but no one mistook the biblical rants of a crazy lady who had been a patient there for 10 years as anything but what it looked like – sheer lunacy.

But Dr. Schmidt had died just as Hagatha had said repeatedly. "You will suffer the vengeance of eternal fire for fornicating strange flesh." And she looked upon her work and saw that it was good.

# CHAPTER 39

The Slaughter family Sunday Brunch tradition and Enoch's commitment to it lasted a little over three months. Both ended abruptly by his decree when his father, Elias Slaughter, contracted pneumonia and died. While the rest of his family mourned, Enoch wasted little time crowning himself the family patriarch.

"Enoch, think about your mother," Lila argued. "She is so distraught. And now you want to take away her weekly visits with the rest of the family?"

"What are you talking about? She'll still be living with us. And if my brothers want to see her, they know where to find her. Heck, if she wants to see them so badly, she can go live with them."

"Enoch, you know that's not possible. They don't have the room or the means to care for her."

"That's not my problem."

"And what about the kids. Our boys love playing with their cousins."

"They can see each other at school. We don't need them running around here. Besides, I think they're a bad influence on the boys."

"Bad influence? Where do you come up with these things? Their cousins are the most thoughtful, polite, and good-natured children they know. We should be so lucky to have our boys grow up to be like them."

"Oh, please, maybe if you want them to grow up to be little Nancy-boys!" he blustered.

"Enoch! What would your father think right now if he could hear you?"

"My father's dead, and I'll be damned if I go another week inviting those moochers to eat all my food, drink all my liquor, and have their little guttersnipes corrupt my sons."

"Enoch, they're your family! How can you talk about them in that way?"

"I never asked for them to move here. And they didn't even have the decency to ask if they could live in my town."

"Why should they have to ask? No one else who lives here has needed your permission." Lila fumed. "You're totally unreasonable right now."

"Well, you didn't have to grow up with my brothers."

"Well, if you ask me, they're the ones that grew up. You failed to, and now you're acting like a child."

"I don't need to take that from you," he yelled.

"Oh, you don't, do you. So what are you going to do about it, big man?" she asked defiantly.

"I have more important things to do than listen to your balderdash. I'm going into town," he said, storming off.

"Oh, what important things are those? Drinking at Loman's?"

"None of your business, woman," he shouted in response.

"And my side of the bed is none of your business, mister! So you can sleep on the couch tonight."

"Fine!" he shot back. Although it was not fine at all.

But for now, he was sticking to his guns. He had gone along

with getting along with his brothers just to appease his father. And now that he wasn't in the picture, he was going to end the charade.

# CHAPTER 40

Evelyn and Charles slept restlessly after being awakened by Dori's latest nightmare. The decision of what to tell her weighed heavily on them.

"I think it's time we told her the truth," Charles ventured.

"But then she'll know we lied to her all along. She'll never forgive us."

"Oh, she might be angry, but she'll get over it. We've done nothing wrong, Evelyn. We rescued her and raised her in a safe and loving home. Surely she'll understand why we waited until now to tell her the horrifying truth."

"I'm not so sure, Charles. And what if she wants us to call her Hilda?"

"Then we will call her Hilda."

"And what if she wants to know who her real mother and father are and wants to visit them?"

"We tell her who they are, and if she wants, she can write them a letter. Then, if they want to see her, we can make arrangements."

"But we don't even know where they're at or how to reach them."

"Exactly. She would need to do some research. We could help her, but she'll have to do the legwork if she's that curious."

"I don't know, Charles. Aren't you afraid she might meet them and want to live with them? Didn't you tell me her father was the Mayor of some town near Grand Rapids and lived in a mansion?"

"Yes, but don't you think that if they wanted to have their daughter back, they would have tracked us down by now? So I think it's more likely that they're happy not to have her. Besides, her mother may still be in the loony bin."

"I hope you're right. This isn't going to be an easy conversation."

"No, it won't. But when all is said and done, I think she'll realize that we've been her real parents all along."

Charles and Evelyn walked down the hall and knocked on Dori's bedroom door.

"Go away! I don't want to talk to you," she hollered, still angry and now also sleep-deprived.

"Dori, we're ready to talk now," Evelyn replied.

"My name is Hilda. And I'm tired of hearing all your lies," she responded acerbically.

"We're ready to tell you the truth," Charles said through the door.

Dori didn't respond, and for a moment, Evelyn and Charles thought she might have been ignoring them. But then, she suddenly opened her door.

"Really? You're not going to lie to me anymore?"

"No, Hilda. We think you're old enough now to know the truth," Evelyn replied.

The combination of calling her Hilda and admitting they had been withholding the truth came as a shock. So much so that her anger evaporated into tears, and she fell sobbing into Evelyn's arms. Charles joined the hug, sandwiching Hilda between them until she regained her composure. They retired to the living room couch, where Evelyn and Charles took up positions on either side of Hilda.

"So my name really is Hilda?" she snuffled, looking to Evelyn.

"Yes, dear. That was your given name. We learned that when you were 2 years old. By then, we had taught you that your name was Dori. We didn't want to confuse you by changing it. I hope you understand that."

Hilda nodded, but she had something more urgent on her mind.

"So that woman I've seen in my nightmares is really my mother?"

"That's hard to say, Dor," Evelyn started to say, then caught herself. "I mean, Hilda. I'm sorry, it's going to take a while for me to get used to calling you that."

"I understand. But why is it hard to say?"

"Well, we really didn't get a good look at your mother. We were too busy," she paused and looked to Charles.

"What she's trying to say, Hilda is that we were too busy rescuing you. We know she had long blond hair, but otherwise, our focus was saving you."

"The lady in my nightmares has long blond hair and blue eyes, just like mine. You saved me from what?"

Charles and Evelyn looked at each other. Both knowing what they had to do but fearful of how their adopted daughter would react.

"This is difficult for us, Dori. I mean Hilda," Charles began. "Your mother tried to drown you in the Mississippi River. We don't know why. But I dove into the river and saved you."

He stopped. Not wanting to overwhelm her with all the information they had been withholding.

"Drown me? Didn't she want me? Didn't she love me?"

"We don't know, sweetheart," Evelyn chimed in. "All we know is that the police found her and took her to a hospital."

"A hospital? Was she hurt or sick?" Hilda asked.

"Not that kind of hospital," Charles intoned. "A hospital for people with problems in their heads," he said, trying to avoid the shock and the stigma of calling Hilda's mother insane. But Hilda was far too wise.

"An insane asylum? My mother's insane? Does that mean I'm going to go insane?" she asked frantically as tears returned.

"No, no, that's not what it means," Charles responded quickly, although he had no basis upon which to be so confident.

In fact, he and Evelyn had often wondered that same thing. Given the prevailing wisdom at the time, Hilda was the victim of a triple whammy – the offspring of a lunatic mother who was orphaned and subsequently adopted. All three circumstances were high on people's list for medical complications, lunacy, and deviant behavior.

"We don't even know how long she might have stayed there. It could have just been a temporary thing," Evelyn added, hoping to minimize the damage but inadvertently painting herself into a corner.

"But if it was temporary, why hasn't she looked for me? Is there something wrong with me? And what about my Dad? Who is my Dad?"

Hilda became more distraught and distressed. Evelyn and Charles both started to doubt the wisdom of telling their daughter the unvarnished truth.

"We don't know who your Dad is," Charles lied. "And there's nothing wrong with you. Maybe your mother is still in the hospital."

"Honey, we've raised you over the past 14 years, and you're perfectly normal. In fact, we think you're exceptional. There's nothing wrong with you," Evelyn added.

"It's normal to have nightmares all your life about your mother and how she's killing people?" Hilda replied, divulging for the first time the details of some of her most recent visions.

"Killing people? You never told us that you saw her killing people," Evelyn exclaimed, horrified.

Evelyn's shocked response only communicated what Hilda feared. She was not at all normal or exceptional. Instead, she was crazy, just like her mother. She decompensated before Evelyn and Charles's eyes. All they could do was hold her and look at each other, wondering whether they had forever scarred their little girl.

# CHAPTER 41

In 1912, Minnesota was in the midst of America's Progressive Era. Brought on by the automobile, the telephone, and developments in manufacturing which made travel, communication, and construction faster and easier.

Despite the untimely deaths of their Chief Psychiatrists, Fairdale Falls State Hospital grew exponentially. The patient population had tripled from 400 to 1,200. The hospital now included six 3-story patient wings to accommodate this growth. Three patient wings on either side of an impressive central Administrative Building with one 6-story tower flanked by two smaller 4-story turrets.

However, the Progressive Era did not have much to offer in the way of advanced treatment for the insane. Some would even say that treatment entered its Regressive Era. Lobotomies were becoming increasingly popular. And just the challenge of too few staff trying to care for so many patients filled seclusion rooms. When they ran out of seclusion rooms and straitjackets, the hospital employed chained restraints. The treatment philosophy wasn't treatment at all. But rather an out of sight, out of mind approach. And woe to the patient who became too unmanageable. They became immediate candidates for having a scalpel inserted through their eye socket, severing the connections in their prefrontal cortex. A procedure that resulted in one of two outcomes – a mute and docile patient oblivious to everything or an even more agitated patient subject to epileptic seizures occasionally resulting in death.

Fortunately, Hagatha Ketchel's days of acting out were long past, and she was content to while away the hours in her favorite chair with her Bible. In her 17 years there, she had honed her skills of visiting calamity on those who dared cross her. Except for dispatching with the occasional staff member or patient who irritated her, most of her time was spent planning. The calm before the storm, you might say.

Most people in Hagatha's shoes would have chosen to move on from the sentinel event that enflamed her vengeance. Just forget about Enoch Slaughter, move somewhere else, and start a new life. But this was an impossibility for Hagatha. In addition to her powers to cobble together destructive spells, she was tormented by visions of the progression and success of Enoch's empire. So even if she wanted to move on, she couldn't. It galled her. Her only choice was to take note and wait for the day that she could begin to make inroads disassembling and destroying it.

Knowing that she would ultimately meet her great-granddaughter to pass along her powers, Hagatha knew this would be her life's work. But her most pressing need was to ensure that the daughter she almost drowned would now meet a man to begin the life cycle necessary to make that future come to fruition. In essence, Hagatha was playing God. Giving life where necessary to ensure her ultimate destiny. And eventually, raining down terror on anyone born with the surname of Slaughter. How poetic it was going to be to slaughter the Slaughters, she thought.

When Hagatha was not babbling biblical phrases, she could be seen with a wry smile on her face. Whispering "Slaughter the Slaughters" under her breath repeatedly. Staff and patients alike thought this was a threat – a harbinger of a violent outburst brewing. They were right. They just didn't know that it would need to ferment for several more years before it bubbled over. People watched her like she was a volcano, long overdue to erupt. But as they say, a watched pot never boils. And eventually, she blended into the woodwork of lunacy as more and more patients filled the hospital's wards to overflowing.

The three-word mantra of slaughter the Slaughters was her way of slipping into a trance-like state where she could discern the future. She would see her daughter Hilda and the couple who had saved and raised her. She would see her parents. Slightly older but still at the bakery. These visions were comforting.

On the other hand, she frequently saw Enoch's brothers and their families, as well as Lila, the woman he had married, who had given him three sons. However, she never saw Enoch, which perhaps was more disturbing than if she could have seen him. He was the central object of her fury and the one individual for whom she reserved her most devious scheme and agonizing demise. That he could hide from her extraordinary precognitive powers enraged and frustrated her.

"For nothing is secret, that will not be revealed, nor anything hidden that will not be known and come to light," she quoted from the Book of Luke. "I will find you, Enoch Slaughter. And when I do, you will pay dearly for casting me aside."

# CHAPTER 42

Enoch slept on the couch for two nights, thinking that Lila would eventually invite him back to their marital bed. When it appeared as though he would be spending a third night on the sofa, he cracked.

"I'm sorry," he said to Lila from the doorway of their bedroom.

"For what?" she asked, turning the page of the book she was reading in bed.

"Come on, you're not going to make me do this, are you?"

"Do what? I haven't the slightest idea what you're apologizing for," she replied naively, despite knowing full well.

Lila was no fool. She knew she had the upper hand. She was going to make sure this interaction was as painful to Enoch's overinflated ego as possible. Enoch momentarily considered whether to sleep another night on the couch. Then, finally, breathed a heavy sigh of resignation.

"I'm sorry for ending our Slaughter family Sunday brunch. We can have them once a month," he announced.

"Then you're not sorry enough. Good night, Enoch," she replied, closing her book, turning off the bedside lamp, and rolling over to go to sleep.

"Twice a month?" he asked lamely.

When Lila didn't respond, he had no choice.

"All right, every week," he relented.

"And you have to apologize to your brothers and your mother," Lila added.

"Yes, dear," he said, sounding defeated. "Now, can I come to bed?"

"Yes, you may."

Enoch excitedly got out of his clothes and into his nightshirt. Joining Lila in bed in anticipation of a blissful reconciliation. Only to be thwarted when he realized she was wearing her menstrual belt. He let out a frustrated groan.

"Maybe tomorrow night, dear," Lila said, turning away and smiling.

# CHAPTER 43

Hilda eventually recovered from the shock of learning about how she came to be raised by Evelyn and Charles Shepherd. Of course, it helped that she hadn't experienced any nightmares for almost a year. And while she still had questions about her biological parents, they took a backseat to more typical adolescent concerns and motivations – like boys. Or, in Hilda's case, a man.

Hilda loved music and dance. So much so that she would save up her allowance to see productions at the Superior Dance Theatre in town. Evelyn and Charles were happy to support this interest – it being one of the few things that genuinely made their daughter happy. Just the anticipation of going brightened her mood for days in advance. And the afterglow of the performance would shine on her countenance for days following.

Cyril Frost was a dashing 21-year old who danced and acted at the Superior Dance Theatre. His dream was to eventually move to New York City and act and dance on Broadway. And he may have had the chops to do just that had he not spied Hilda in the audience during one of the theatre's productions. It was one of those moments that changes your life. Just a glance, and the universe is forever altered. And in this case, lightning struck twice. Hilda was as smitten by Cyril as he was enamored with her.

After the performance, she waited in the lobby. Hoping that she hadn't just imagined the moment they had shared. Hopeful, he would think to find her waiting there. After 15 minutes, she was the only person in the lobby. She began to have her doubts.

"Oh, what was I thinking," she said to herself. "I'm just 16. He was probably looking at someone else behind me or beside me."

She started heading for the exit only to stop short when she heard a door open behind her, and he walked into the lobby. Their eyes met. And without a word between them, she ran and jumped into his arms. Like two magnets, they came together. It was highly inappropriate and intensely passionate. He took her to his apartment. Along the way, they talked as if they were long-lost friends desperate to tell each other everything about their lives apart. When she finally left his apartment to go home, they knew each other in mind, body, and soul. Convinced they had found their other half and determined to spend the rest of their lives together.

Suddenly, Hilda's ancestry was not as crucial as her destiny. She walked into the house and announced she was moving out and going to live with Cyril. As you can imagine, this was not met with joyful exuberance by Evelyn and Charles. In fact, they grounded her to her room for coming home late and forbid her from ever going to the theatre or seeing Cyril again. To their surprise, she accepted her punishment and went to her room without argument. Only to check on her 30 minutes later and find that she had climbed out of her window. They combed the streets looking for her to no avail. The next day, when the theatre opened, they were able to learn where Cyril lived. But when they got to his apartment, there was no one there.

"Did you happen to see a young girl leave this apartment today? She's blond with blue eyes," Evelyn asked the next-door neighbor lady who was coming out of her apartment.

"Oh, yes, pretty girl. And what a cute couple. I'm afraid you missed them. They were catching a plane to New York."

"New York!" she exclaimed.

"Yes, they said they were going to see some shows on Broadway. It must be nice to have that kind of money. I'm not surprised though, he's quite the talent. Is she your daughter?"

"Yes, she is," Charles replied.

Evelyn was about to launch into a fit of hysterics only to be interrupted by the neighbor lady who seemed impervious to her distress.

"Oh, you must be so happy. Cyril is such a gentleman and successful to boot. Count your blessings. My daughter ran off with some no-account good for nothin'. And now I'm left to take care of the baby. He ran off and left her, and she has to work to make ends meet."

As if choreographed, the cries of a baby rang out from inside her apartment.

"Oh, that would be Madeline. Probably needs changing. Duty calls!" she announced. "Congratulations on your daughter's good fortune," she said as she disappeared back into her apartment.

It was probably fortuitous that the chatty neighbor lady had made her high opinion of Cyril known. Otherwise, Evelyn and Charles's fears would have increased exponentially. Even before they visited the theatre, they had debated going to the police to report Hilda missing. Now, the neighbor lady's characterization of Cyril gave them pause. That and the fact they didn't have any legal proof that she was their adopted daughter, should the police request such.

In the end, they chose to hope and pray that she would come back safe and sound. Until then, they waited anxiously. Hoping to God that Cyril was the fine upstanding gentleman the lady claimed.

# CHAPTER 44

You couldn't have conceived of a worse place to be than Fairdale Falls State Hospital in 1918. Not only was the hospital bursting at the seams with over 1,600 patients – 400 more than the hospital was equipped to safely manage. But an infectious scourge was killing people worldwide – the Spanish Flu. The most susceptible to succumb to this pandemic were those in large congregated living quarters where the virus could spread unabated.

I suppose you could say, and some people did, that this was nature's way of thinning the herd of the weak and infirm. But the reality was that the Spanish Flu didn't confine itself to the frail and elderly. In fact, healthy children and young adults had the highest mortality rates.

Deaths from the virus temporarily relieved the overcrowding pressures on the hospital. However, the aftermath of the pandemic combined with American soldiers coming back traumatized from the Great War in Europe caused a new wave of patients. And by early 1919, the patient population had ballooned to over 2,000 patients.

It was a hospital in name only. There was no way to provide anything resembling humane treatment or a therapeutic milieu. It would have been better classified as a warehouse for the dregs of society – a place where the rest of humanity could store, hide, and forget about the embarrassing, the dangerous, and decrepit souls. Those subhumans they didn't want haunting their perfect little neighborhoods and towns.

Living and working at the hospital was more akin to a survival challenge. Not unlike the war to end all wars from which some of the patients had fought. There were daily skirmishes and more than a few deaths – some from assaults, others by their own hand. And probably even more from abject neglect.

Through it all, Hagatha soldiered on. Her favorite chair had long been disposed of. In fact, the activity room no longer had any furniture. It took up too much space and posed a threat to be used as a weapon. Consequently, patients were forced to sit on the floor. The prime sitting areas being those against the walls so one could sit and have a backrest. Every day there would be a chaotic frenzy to claim a prime sitting area. And every day, several patients would be taken to the infirmary, having lost in their bid to secure a valued spot. Once a prime sitting spot was obtained, you dared not leave it. This became a problem for when nature called. And many patients just chose to sit in their own urine and feces rather than go to the bathroom and give up their spot.

This was not a problem for Hagatha. Not that staff noticed, but she never ate. Except for an occasional cup of lukewarm tea, she no longer required the typical sustenance from food and drink. And thus, normal human eliminatory functions were not something she had to contend with anymore. Somehow, through the 24 years of her incarceration, she had developed a way to sustain herself through her trance-like hibernations. Consequently, she never left her little corner. She even slept there, finding it more conducive than her bedroom, which now held three additional cots for other patients.

The doors to the patient rooms had been removed ostensively for patient safety. But there was nothing safe about open bedrooms. There wasn't enough staff to supervise the patients and not enough seclusion rooms or restraints to prevent daily assaults, rapes, or self-harm. Most of the ward staff chose not to intervene in patient conflicts unless they felt it was manageable or had adequate back-up – which was rarely the case.

This was not true of Maggie, who, through the years, somehow continued to show the compassion which Hagatha had found so endearing. So much so that Hagatha would interrupt her daily reveries to talk with her. Maggie was the one true fixture in her life. Her only real connection to the here and now.

"Good morning, Hagatha," she greeted, sitting down on the floor in front of her.

"Good morning, Maggie. How are you?"

"Hey, isn't that the question I should be asking you?" Maggie laughed. "I'm doing fine, Hagatha. Thank you. But I have some news for you."

"Oh, what's that?" Hagatha asked.

"Well, I'm afraid this might be a little difficult for you to hear. So I'm sorry if what I'm about to say upsets you," she said, pausing.

Hagatha's face communicated her confusion. Maggie had never done anything to upset her. What could she possibly say that would change that?

"I'm retiring next week," Maggie said, reaching out and putting her hand on Hagatha's arm.

"Retiring?" Hagatha said in astonishment.

"Yes. I'm getting too old for this. But I want you to know, I've put in a request to have the hospital administration consider discharging you."

"Really? Do you think they'll listen to you?"

"Yes, I do. As a matter of fact, they asked the staff to recommend patients we thought were safe to discharge. They need to reduce the number of patients and are going to select from those we nominate. I've known you for 24 years. And for the life of me, I don't know why you're still here. Would you be happy to be discharged? I mean, would you feel safe?"

"Yes!" Hagatha answered enthusiastically.

"Yes, you'd be happy, or yes, you'd feel safe?" Maggie chuckled.

"Both," Hagatha exclaimed as a rare but genuine smile blossomed on her face. "Thank you, Maggie."

"It's the least I could do. I'm going to miss you. Where do you think you'd go if you were discharged."

This was a loaded question for Hagatha. And while she felt she could trust Maggie, she didn't want to tell her the truth.

"Oh, I don't know. Maybe someplace warm. I don't even want to think about it. In case I'm not selected."

"Someplace warm sounds nice. And I'll keep pushing them to discharge you while I'm still here."

"Thank you again, Maggie."

"You're welcome. I better get back to the other patients," she said, giving Hagatha a hug.

"Don't you dare leave next week without saying goodbye to me," Hagatha called as Maggie got up from the floor.

"With any luck, you might leave before me. In any case, we'll have a chance to say our goodbyes."

And just like that, Hagatha could finally see the light at the end of the tunnel.

# CHAPTER 45

Evelyn and Charles's fears about Cyril were put to rest shortly after their daughters' return from New York City. Everything the neighbor lady had claimed Cyril to be was borne out. Moreover, it was immediately apparent that Cyril and their daughter had an uncommon and extraordinary bond. They were clearly made for each other.

While Evelyn and Charles approved of their relationship, they vehemently opposed their living together outside of marriage. It was considered socially unacceptable, morally bereft, and an outright embarrassment. Hilda and Cyril, however, were about 50 years ahead of their time. They were forerunners to the hippies, the women's libbers, and the overall anti-establishment sentiment of the 1960s.

Eventually, in 1917, Hilda and Cyril made it official and got married. A year later, they announced Hilda was pregnant. Usually, pregnancy was an occasion for celebration. However, the timing of Hilda's pregnancy couldn't have been worse. The influenza pandemic had claimed millions of lives, many of those babies and young children. Evelyn and Charles were more than a little concerned. However, it was Hilda's strength and faith at this time that helped reassure her parents.

"I defied death when you lovingly saved me," she told them. "And our baby will defy death by the love Cyril and I provide."

It was hard to argue with her reasoning or her unshakable confidence. Their daughter had grown up to be a strong, fiercely independent young woman who wasn't afraid to test boundaries. What parent wouldn't be happy and proud of that? Especially given the challenges she had faced surviving her childhood.

But ultimately, the birth of Hilda and Cyril's daughter, Elsa, would be a bittersweet event. Two weeks shy of her birth, Charles contracted the flu and died. Evelyn, fearful she might come down with the flu, didn't dare visit her granddaughter until Elsa was nearly 3 months old.

If not for Elsa and Cyril, Charles's death would have likely put Hilda into a tailspin. He was her savior. Without his quick, unselfish actions, she would have perished. To think that Elsa would grow up without him in her life was too painful to bear. So instead, she would make sure that Elsa knew him and why her life was as dependent upon him as Hilda's life was. It was the only way she could think of to fill the deep, dark, and excruciating void his passing had created in Hilda's soul.

It was Cyril's idea to have Evelyn move in with them. It was a generous offer that Evelyn couldn't refuse. Now, instead of being all alone in a big empty house, she could help raise her granddaughter. It sparked renewed purpose in her life and helped Hilda cope with the loss and with first-time motherhood. In time, having Evelyn there to care for Elsa would allow Cyril and Hilda to go out dancing and take occasional trips to Broadway.

# CHAPTER 46

Enoch's intention all along was to have his eldest son Enoch Jr. succeed him as Mayor of Slaughter. In preparation, he named him Town Manager at the tender age of 16. Hoping that in a year or two, he'd have the requisite experience to allow Enoch to hand the reins over and finally get to enjoy the fruits of his labors and a life of luxury. But when Enoch Jr. turned 18, President Woodrow Wilson had other plans for him. And the President's plan, codified under the Selective Service Act of 1917, took precedence over Enoch's. As a result, Enoch Jr. was drafted into the army and sent to Europe to fight in World War I.

Enoch was livid and railed against the President's actions, which ran counter to his reelection campaign promises to stay out of the war. But, in truth, Enoch's anger at the President just masked the real reason he was upset. Not only did it short-circuit his retirement plan, but it put his namesake in harm's way.

That Enoch Jr. was Enoch's favored son was no secret. Much like Enoch's relationship with his brothers, Enoch Jr. had distinguished himself from his siblings. And like his father, Enoch Jr. was ruthlessly competitive with more than a hint of a superiority complex. Enoch Jr. was his only choice to supersede him and carry on the Slaughter legacy in his father's eyes. In truth, Enoch would have happily sent his two younger sons into battle to save Enoch Jr. from going if that had been an option.

Fortunately, Enoch Jr. survived the war and came home to a hero's welcome – serving to significantly elevate Slaughter residents' opinions of him. Shortly after his return, however, he had no choice but to seize the Mayoral reins. Enoch Slaughter died. Another sad statistic in the devastating Spanish Flu pandemic.

Enoch was 53 years old when the virus cut him down. While his personality hadn't endeared him to many, his sudden death sent shockwaves through the community. Town folk may not have liked him, but they recognized and appreciated his accomplishments. And his death bred uncertainty about Slaughter's future.

It was Lila, more than anything or anyone else, that restored the town's faith that Slaughter would survive and thrive following Enoch's passing. In true Lila fashion, she bloomed rather than wilted in the face of Enoch's tragic death. She organized and funded a week-long community-wide celebration of Enoch's life. Commissioning an artist to create a sculpture of Slaughter's founder. And authorizing the creation of a recreational area that was christened Enoch Slaughter Park.

If that day and age weren't so culturally blind to women as leaders, Lila would have been the best choice to become Slaughter's Mayor. But women still couldn't vote, let alone hold office. Consequently, Enoch Jr. stepped forward to become Slaughter's mayor, cut from the same cloth as his father.

Although Enoch didn't know it, his premature death granted him a reprieve from what he would have endured had he lived to see Hagatha's return to town. Instead, he died with the knowledge that his namesake would carry on his legacy. Shortly before the end, he penned his dying wishes. Ensuring that when the time came, Enoch Jr. would be granted the keys to the Slaughter kingdom. It sat like a divisive time bomb that wouldn't explode for another 20 years. Tick, tick, tick.

# CHAPTER 47

Ever since Maggie told Hagatha about nominating her for discharge, she suspended her reverie of terror. Instead, she recited a different kind of mantra – one aimed at making her release a reality.

"And ye shall know the truth, and the truth shall make you free," she now repeated incessantly from the Book of John.

Staff and patients noticed the shift away from the dark and disturbing slaughter the Slaughters. Some were unable to help themselves from commenting.

"The only truth is we ain't ever going to be free," said another patient who was chained to the wall within earshot of Hagatha.

But Hagatha took no notice. Once in a trance, very few things could sway her attention away from what she was experiencing internally. All but the sight of Maggie walking towards her wearing a broad smile and carrying a cardboard box.

"Are you leaving?" Hagatha asked, terrified she may have been in a trance all of Maggie's last week on the job.

"No, but you are," she beamed. "Now get up and follow me. I have something to give you."

Hagatha did as instructed, and Maggie led her to a private office behind the nursing station. Ironically, the same office where Dr. Rosenstern had deceived her and had her transferred to the secure immersion ward. Hagatha hesitated to follow Maggie in.

"What's the matter?" Maggie asked, putting the box down on a table in the office.

"The last time I was in there, it didn't end well," Hagatha said as the memory haunted her.

"You have nothing to worry about, Hagatha. This is my office now, and today is a day to celebrate."

"Your office? You're the Head Nurse?"

"Yes, until a few days from now when I retire. Now get in here," she said, motioning for Hagatha to come in.

Hagatha entered as Maggie started pulling clothes out of the box.

"I've bought you a few things to tide you over until you can do some clothes shopping," she said, displaying a floral print house dress. "Nothing fancy, but comfortable."

"You bought this for me?" Hagatha said, astonished to see the bounty of house dresses, undergarments, and a sturdy pair of brown boots.

"Well, you don't want to wear that hospital gown when you leave today, do you?" Maggie chuckled. "Try this on," she said, handing the housedress to Hagatha as she closed the office door for privacy.

Hagatha got out of the hospital gown and into the housedress. Unlike the scratchy gown, the dress was soft against her skin.

"This is so," Hagatha began but stopped and began to cry – overcome by Maggie's generosity.

"Oh, there, there," Maggie said, giving Hagatha a hug. "No crying allowed," she said as tears came to her own eyes. "Now, see, you've started me crying."

They held each other, recognizing that their time together

was coming to an end. Then, Maggie packed up the rest of the clothes, along with Hagatha's well-worn Bible, placing them in a carpetbag and sending Hagatha on her way.

Maggie had been Hagatha's one and only connection to sanity. For some reason, when Hagatha was with Maggie, it quieted the demons in her head. Maggie thought Hagatha's normalcy was the result of her extended stay and treatment at the hospital. But Hagatha knew better. She knew that the moment she left Maggie and walked out the door of the hospital, all reasoning, lucidity, and judgment would be lost – forever.

# CHAPTER 48

Even the most well-adjusted individual would have had severe culture shock when reintroduced into society after 24 years away. Arriving at the hospital in 1895 and walking out of it in 1919 was like entering an entirely different world. Transportation, previously reliant on horses, had given way to automobiles and trucks. Dirt roads were now paved. Roadside billboards and automobile service stations dotted the countryside. There was more of everything – more buildings, more people, and more noise. Even people's clothes had undergone a significant shift from drab ultra-conservative to bold, colorful, and innovative styling.

Hagatha's journey from the hospital to Grand Rapids still entailed a train ride from Pelican Rapids to Aitkin. However, her trip's first and last legs were now accomplished in a Ford automobile rather than a horse-and-buggy.

Her head was spinning when she stepped out of the automobile in Grand Rapids. Her excited anticipation to see her parents suddenly shattered. What used to be Ketchel's Bakery was now a barbershop. She tried to tell herself that maybe they had sold the bakery and retired. Then, in disbelief, she started walking in the direction of her childhood home. When she got there and saw a pedal car and a doggy pull toy on the walkway, her heart sank.

She knocked on the door. A harried young woman with a

baby on her hip and a young boy at her side answered the door.

"If you're selling something, I'm not interested," the woman said, seeing the carpetbag in Hagatha's hand.

Tears came to Hagatha's eyes, and without saying a word, she turned and walked away – now fearing the worst.

Hagatha no longer recognized Grand Rapids and had no idea how to learn what became of her parents. So she wandered aimlessly, progressively growing more anxious, overwhelmed, and untethered. Finally ending up on a street corner, paralyzed by the masses of unfamiliar faces, the cacophony of cars, and her relentless grief.

"Mutti, Papa," she yelled as tears streamed down her face. "Wo bist du? Gib mir eine Antwort," she repeatedly said in German, asking her parents where they were and beckoning them to answer her.

It didn't take long for the police to arrive and escort her to the station. She was cooperative but distraught. Fortunately, there was someone at the station who spoke German.

"Kann ich Ihnen helfen?" he said, asking her how he could help.

"I'm looking for my mother and father," Hagatha replied.

"Oh, you speak English," the officer replied in shock.

"Of course, I do. I was born here," Hagatha answered, not realizing she had been speaking German.

"What are their names?" he asked.

"Otto and Ursala Ketchel. I'm Hagatha Ketchel, their daughter," she replied.

The officer's face grew sullen. He recognized the name because he used to frequent the bakery for free pastries.

"I'm sorry to have to tell you this," he began, as tears once again welled up in Hagatha's eyes, knowing what he was about to say. "They died last year from the flu."

Hagatha wailed. The police officer offered her a handkerchief, which she accepted. He sat with her until she pulled herself together.

"What do I do now?" she asked.

The police officer wondered why she didn't know what happened to her parents. However, he didn't know how to ask without sounding indelicate.

"You should go to the Town Office. The County had to sell the bakery and their house. If you're next of kin, I'm sure they can tell you more."

"The Town Office? Where is that?" she asked.

"I'll take you there," he said, recognizing her dilemma.

Hagatha anticipated having to walk, but he led her to an automobile and opened the door for her.

"So you said you were born here?" the officer asked over the din of the engine. Hoping his gentle foray might shed some light on why she didn't know of her parent's deaths.

"Yes, but I've been away for a long time. I don't even recognize it anymore."

All the police officers who would have been familiar with Hagatha's story had either moved on, retired, or died.

"Yes, lots has changed here," he said, prefacing his next question. "Where do you live now?"

"I'm actually moving back," she said.

"To Grand Rapids?" the officer asked.

Hagatha was starting to get suspicious of his questions and decided their little chit-chat had gone far enough.

"Yes, to Grand Rapids," she lied.

"Well, welcome back then. I'm sorry it's under such distressing circumstances."

Hagatha didn't respond.

"Here we are," the officer announced. "Would you like me to escort you in?"

"No, thank you, officer. I think I can manage from here," she said, opening the door and stepping out.

"All right. I guess I'll probably see you again, then. Let me know if there's anything else I can do to help," he called after her.

Hagatha didn't reply and just continued to walk into the Town Office. There, she learned a bit of good news. Her parents had named her sole beneficiary. She was paid $8,500 from the sale of their home and the bakery equipment. She also learned that her parents were buried at St. Joseph's Church Cemetery.

Abhorring the infernal four-wheeled noise machines, Hagatha walked from the Town Office to the cemetery. Finding her parent's grave marker in the shade of an oak tree, she sat down on the grass. Tracing her finger along the letters and numbers carved into the granite headstone. Unable to fathom the loss or put her grief into words. Finally, uttering the words her mother used to say to her at bedtime, "Schlaf gut." Sleep well.

From the cemetery, she walked to a hotel. The same hotel where she and Enoch had their first dinner date over 25 years earlier. But she didn't choose the hotel for that reason. She picked it because it looked familiar. And right now, she needed familiar.

# CHAPTER 49

You would have thought that the luxurious hotel accommodations would have been a welcome reprieve for Hagatha after years of enduring the hospital's austere and inhospitable conditions. But, instead, it turned out to be Hagatha's private little hell.

When you're used to living in chaos and cruelty, comfort and quiet are nearly intolerable. She couldn't sleep in the soft bed with its fine linen sheets and eiderdown duvet. Eventually, throwing back the floor rug so she could sleep on the hard, unforgiving wooden floor. But even with that, sleep didn't come easy. And when it did, it was abbreviated by a disturbing nightmare.

She saw herself in a small, white house at night under attack by an army of Slaughter family members. Enoch led them, his face and hands stripped of their skin, bloody and boiling with crawling maggots. The throng was carrying torches, pick-axes, and guns. They were casting stones at the house, breaking windows, and shouting threats. She was cowering inside, screaming, "Go away. Leave me alone." All to no avail as they pushed down the small fence that had been holding them out. Advancing on the house and now beating on the door. Hagatha, knowing the door would not hold, ran to a back bedroom and hid in a closet. She heard the door splinter and the horde march into her house. Coming closer.

Suddenly, all was silent. Had they left? She waited for a couple of minutes before cautiously opening the closet door. Only to have Enoch pull it open violently. Now standing in front of her, his body naked and crawling with vermin.

"I will fill you with my seed, and you will bear me a male child," he roared, advancing on her and grabbing her arm.

She screamed as he flung her onto the bed, where members of the threatening mass held her down and tore at her garments. She struggled under their firm grip as she was laid bare. Enoch climbed onto the bed between her outspread legs, his bloody body covered in larvae, now moving to mount her.

Suddenly, Hagatha erupted with a stream of words.

"And they shall go forth, and look upon the carcasses of the men that have transgressed against me: for their worm shall not die, neither shall their fire be quenched; and they shall be an abhorring unto all flesh."

And with this, Enoch and all the Slaughter family horde burst into flames, allowing Hagatha to escape. The bodies burned until there was nothing left but ash heaps throughout the house. But, somehow, only their bodies burned. Leaving the house undamaged.

She saw herself sweeping out the ashes from the little white house using a corn bristle broom and then awoke with a start.

It was the middle of the night, but she wasn't going to spend another minute in that room or hotel. So she packed up her things and began to walk to Slaughter. Knowing there was a little white house there that she needed to buy.

# CHAPTER 50

The Slaughter family had grown to quite a crowd, numbering more than two dozen when Hagatha strode into town in the late summer of 1919. Enoch's two brothers and their spouses accounted for 4 children, all of whom were now adults. They, in turn, were married and, to date, had produced six grandchildren. Add to that Enoch's three boys approaching marrying age, and the prospects for growing the Slaughter family legacy looked bright.

Hagatha walked into Slaughter in the predawn hours on a mission – to find her home. She wandered up and down the streets of Slaughter, taken aback by how the small town she left had grown. Then, finally, coming to Tailings Way and spying the little white house she had seen in her nightmare. She didn't know the first thing about how to buy a home, so it was fortunate that the house had a "For Sale" sign out front, guiding her to a real estate office on Main Street. She arrived at the office just as it was opening.

"Good morning, how may I help you?" asked a middle-aged man dressed in a suit.

"I'm here to buy the white house on Tailings Way," she announced.

"Certainly, I can show you the property. Let me get the key, and we can take a drive over there," he said, getting up and going to a cabinet where a collection of house keys was kept.

"I don't need to see it. I just want to buy it," Hagatha said.

The man turned back, astonished. "You don't want to see it?"

"No, I'm quite certain it will be just fine. Now how much does it cost?"

"I feel I need to warn you. The home doesn't have electricity or phone service."

"That's fine. I don't need them. Now, are you going to tell me what it costs?" she asked, getting irritated.

"Yes, yes, of course," he said, fumbling with a logbook in which he kept home prices. "Let's see here, that's 33 Tailings Way. The price is $3,500."

"Very well. I'll take it," she said, reaching for her bag.

"You will need to make a down payment of $350. There's a bank down the street where you can apply for a mortgage. Once I get confirmation from the bank that financing is in order," he said, launching into his usual spiel. Only to stop short, when Hagatha removed a stack of $100 bills from her bag.

"I'll just pay it all right now. Is that satisfactory?"

"You, you, you want to pay it all?" he stammered.

"Yes. Why? Is that not allowed?" she asked, looking confused and moving to put the stack of bills back into her bag.

"No, no. It's just fine," he said. "I'll be happy to have you pay in full."

"And I require the house immediately. Is that understood?" she asked as she started to count out the bills.

"Yes, yes, it's yours. It's been vacant for some time. I'm afraid it might be a bit dusty in the house. But, I can go over and clean it for you before you move in if you'd like," he offered.

"That won't be necessary. I can take care of it myself," she said, handing over the money. "I trust you will get me any necessary paperwork to show that I am the rightful owner."

"Of course, of course. I will put the particulars in your mailbox. Will that do?"

"It will. Now may I have the key?"

"Oh, yes, of course," he said, jumping up from his desk, grabbing the key from the cabinet, and handing it to her. "Thank you very much, Mrs.," he said, pausing as he realized he hadn't gotten her name.

"Miss Ketchel. Miss Hagatha Ketchel," she replied, getting up from the chair and marching out the door.

Hagatha stopped in at McInerney's Mercantile on her way home to pick up the one and only thing she needed. There, she was greeted by Seth McInerney, one of Lila Slaughter's older brothers.

"How can I help you today, ma'am," he greeted.

"I need a broom," she said, looking around the store with its vast array of products.

"Floor broom or whisk broom?" he asked.

"Floor."

He strode off to the back half of the store and quickly returned with a broom in hand.

"How is this?" he asked, handing it to her.

She looked it over. Then gave it a few sweeps on the floor to test it. "This is acceptable."

"What else can I get for you?"

"That will be all," she said.

"Are you sure? We have an end-of-season sale on some seeds for planting."

Initially, Hagatha felt annoyed by his blatant salesmanship but then softened.

"Maybe," she replied tentatively. "Show me."

"Right this way."

She followed him to a display case with packets of various seeds for vegetables, herbs, and flowers. She selected a few envelopes of herbs, including mint, lavender, and rosemary.

"You'll want to start those off indoors and transplant outdoors next spring. I'll throw in some pots and soil for you."

"That's kind of you," Hagatha replied.

"And here's a little secret. Soak the seeds in water for a day before you plant them. They'll grow better."

Hagatha hadn't expected she'd enjoy her little shopping adventure.

"Thank you. I'll do that. By the way, do you have a tea kettle and tea?" Hagatha asked, thinking about how she used to enjoy drinking tea at the hospital.

"We do. Follow me."

She finished shopping and eyed her purchases.

"Oh, my, I didn't anticipate buying so much. I guess I will have to make two trips to get it all home," she lamented.

"Nonsense," replied Seth. "I'll deliver it to your home later this afternoon."

"That would be delightful."

"Where do you live?" he asked.

"33 Tailings Way. Can I take my broom with me, though?"

"Of course, you can. You bought it!" he chuckled. "I'll see you later then."

Hagatha was quite the sight to see striding down the street in her floral housedress and army boots, carrying her carpetbag and broom. Her graying hair blowing wildly in the wind. You might have thought she looked like a witch. And perhaps, you wouldn't have been wrong.

While Hagatha was shopping, the real estate agent was

busy spreading the news around town about his good fortune. You couldn't really blame him. It wasn't every day that someone walks in off the street and pays cash for the entire cost of a house sight unseen. But the last thing Hagatha needed was a bunch of lookie-loos descending upon her little white house, hoping to catch a glimpse of Slaughter's newest resident. Especially after her recent nightmare.

So when she saw a gaggle of people convened in front of her house, her response was, you might say, not very neighborly. Incensed, she wielded her broom like a baseball bat and ran towards the crowd. Swinging it wildly and bellowing at the top of her lungs a verse from the Book of Deuteronomy,

"The Lord shall smite thee with a consumption, and with a fever, and with an inflammation, and with an extreme burning, and with the sword, and with blasting, and with mildew. And they shall pursue thee until thou perish."

The group scattered in every direction, narrowly avoiding Hagatha's broom but not her wrath. Suffice to say, Hagatha guaranteed she wouldn't be receiving any plates of baked cookies welcoming her to the neighborhood.

# CHAPTER 51

To Hagatha's surprise, whoever lived in her house previously, left some things behind. There was a small table and two chairs in the kitchen. And the kitchen cabinets contained some dishware and cookware. An oversized, stuffed chair sat in the living room. And one of the bedrooms had a small cot and a dresser in which she found blankets and towels. She unpacked her housedresses and undergarments and placed them in one of the dresser's empty drawers.

Hagatha's first priority was cleaning the house. She was busily breaking in her broom, sweeping the actual dust and the imaginary human ashes from her home, when someone knocked on her door. It startled her initially, but then she relaxed, thinking it must be Seth from McInerney's Mercantile delivering her purchases. However, when she opened the door, she was taken aback by a young man with an angry scowl on his face.

"Miss Hagatha Ketchel?"

"Who's asking?" she replied suspiciously.

"I'm Mayor Enoch Slaughter Jr.," he said. "I don't usually welcome new residents to my town, but I've received complaints from your neighbors."

"Oh, you have, have you? If you're talking about those miscreants trespassing on my property that I shooed off, then you're wasting your breath, Mayor."

"No need to be surly with me, Miss Ketchel. I'll have you know that you may own this home, but the property upon which it sits is mine. You'll understand that more acutely when you get your annual property tax assessment. And if you want to continue living here affordably, I'd suggest you be a little more neighborly. My father, God rest his soul, founded this town. And I'll be damned if I'm going to let you terrorize the good people who were just trying to welcome you."

His words stopped Hagatha in her tracks. Not because she respected his authority or feared him raising her property taxes. She was stunned by the news that Enoch was dead. Now she suddenly realized why she could never see him in her visions of the future. While a small part of her was ecstatic, a more significant part of her was disappointed. She so wanted to slowly torture him with her systematic destruction of his family and town.

"My apologies, Mayor. You'll get no more complaints. Moving has been more stressful than I had anticipated."

"I'm glad you've taken my words to heart. Good day, Miss Ketchel," he said and turned to leave.

"And good day to you too," she said under her breath as she closed the front door. "It may be the last good day you have, Mayor!"

Hagatha was furious. She was so looking forward to seeing the look on Enoch's face when he discovered she was back in town. Now his little wet behind the ears son was trying to boss her around. Well, she was going to show him who was boss. After sweeping the house and the walkway, she went to consult her trusty Bible.

"I'll cook you up a spell Mayor Enoch Jr.," she cackled. "You will regret you ever darkened my doorway."

But before she could devote herself to the business of

punishing Enoch's firstborn, there was another knock on her door. This time it was a more welcome interruption as Seth delivered her supplies and diverted her attention away from more calamitous pursuits.

She fixed herself a cup of tea and set the herb seeds to soak as Seth had advised. The Chamomile tea, the effects of a long, emotional day, and sitting in her one comfy chair made her drowsy. Finally, she drifted off to sleep but was haunted by a vision for the second day in a row.

She saw Enoch Jr. as an elderly man standing at the head of a long dinner table. Behind him, on the wall, was a portrait of Enoch, seeming to be looking down approvingly on the gathering. Enoch Jr. had his hand raised in a toast. At least a dozen people sat around the table. All with glasses lifted toward a young couple. Hagatha didn't recognize any people around the table or the young man looking lovingly into the young woman's eyes. But the young woman, to her surprise, was definitely her great-granddaughter.

"To my grandson and his lovely bride. Congratulations on being in a family way. We look forward to welcoming my great-grandson Enoch V into our family," Enoch Jr. toasted.

"Here, here," rose the chorus of cheers from around the table as all drank. Followed by the young couple kissing to the delight of the onlookers.

It was a brief but disturbing revelation that made Hagatha completely rethink the destructive plan she had envisioned. While she knew that her great-granddaughter would eventually join her in her deadly crusade, this vision threw a different light on how the battle would be won. Hagatha couldn't indiscriminately cast a spell on Enoch Jr. as she had intended without compromising what needed to occur in the future. Now, Enoch Jr. had to survive and thrive to ensure her great-granddaughter could eventually embed herself into the Slaughter family. And in this way, destroy the Slaughter family legacy from the inside out.

So Enoch Jr. needed to have a son, who needed to have a son, who would meet and fall in love with her great-granddaughter. This placed a new and unique burden on Hagatha, who wasn't used to protecting the family she sought to eliminate. She would have to choreograph the family's demise judiciously and systematically. Harnessing her unbridled and uncontrollable fury was going to be a challenge. Fortunately, there were plenty of other Slaughter family members at her disposal.

# CHAPTER 52

It wasn't just Enoch Slaughter's side of the family that had a penchant for politics. Jeremiah and Hannah Slaughter's first son, Jacob, had run and won election to Minnesota's House of Representatives 8th District in 1918. He won primarily on a platform that opposed prohibition – a proposal gaining strength due to the efforts of Congressman Andrew Volstead from the neighboring 7th District. Jacob took after his fiery and boundary-pushing mother more so than his milquetoast father. This made for some epic exchanges between Jacob and Andrew Volstead when debating the pros and cons of prohibition.

Jacob had married his college sweetheart, Lucille, in 1908. They subsequently had two boys, Matthew and Mark, who were now 10 and 8 years old. Matthew and Mark's daily walk to and from school took them past Hagatha's home. Which had already earned the reputation as a danger zone to be avoided. Consequently, they usually would cross the street when they approached her house. But children can never be counted on to follow prudent practices. Eventually, like a moth to a flame, they are drawn in. Compelled by some rebel instinct.

"Why do we always have to cross the street here?" Mark whined.

"You know why. The old lady that lives there eats children," Matthew replied.

This is how the story of Hagatha's broom-swinging tirade evolved. Each successive retelling of the tale, embellishing the facts until they bore no resemblance to the actual event.

"But how could that be? Wouldn't she be arrested?" Mark asked.

"Maybe she did it a long time ago."

"I think it's just a story someone made up. Tomorrow we should walk past the house and see what happens."

"I don't know if that's a good idea," Matthew counseled.

"If she comes out, we run. She can't be faster than you or me."

That's all it took to plant the seed that would compromise Matthew's better judgment. The next day, they walked past the house. Only to have Hagatha burst through the front door with her broom in hand. They were fortunate. They ran and escaped her clutches.

Had they stopped there, perhaps they wouldn't have attracted Hagatha's unwelcome attention. But they didn't. The next day, Mark dared his older brother to throw a rock and see if he could break one of her windows. Matthew was a pitcher on the school's baseball team. And while he was generally a respectful, law-abiding child, his pride at throwing accurately got the better of him. He shattered the window, and once again, they escaped. Or so they thought.

That evening, Hagatha put her considerable powers of perception to work. Reciting a verse from Deuteronomy and falling into a trance.

"Then shalt thou bring forth that man or that woman, which have committed that wicked thing, unto thy gates, and shalt stone them with stones, till they die."

And in a vision, she saw the boys and their parents. And when she came out of her reverie, she knew they were descended from Jeremiah Slaughter, Enoch's brother. Wasting no time, she cast a spell.

"You are no consequence to my future," she cackled. "You will rise up on eagles wings, only to perish in hell's fire."

The following week, Jacob and his family were invited to take a plane trip. The owner and manufacturer of the plane was a very well-heeled and influential businessman in Duluth. Plane travel was becoming increasingly popular. And the manufacturing of passenger planes was seen as the next big economic opportunity. Courting favor with Jacob was a thinly-veiled effort to ensure the Congressman would support legislation advantageous to the businessman's company.

So on one bright sunny morning at the airport in Duluth, Jacob, Lucille, Matthew, and Mark joined the businessman and his family on a 10-passenger plane for a scenic flight over Lake Superior. The plane barrelled down the runway, the occupants abuzz with excited anticipation. The aircraft lifted off the tarmac and not 30 feet in the air, clipped an elm tree, and crashed into an empty field, erupting into a fireball. There were no survivors.

Back in Slaughter, Hagatha sat sipping her tea. Then, words suddenly spilling from her mouth, "And he said unto me, it is done. I am Alpha and Omega, the beginning and the end."

Neighbors didn't hear what she said, but they did hear the gales of demonic laughter that followed for minutes afterward. They didn't dare investigate or complain. Which was wise from the perspective of self-preservation.

# CHAPTER 53

News of the plane crash that killed Congressman Jacob Slaughter and his family spread quickly. From a political perspective, it helped clear the path for ratification of the National Prohibition Act, which came to be known as the Volstead Act. On a local level, it was devastating news to the townfolk of Slaughter and the Slaughter family.

All, but perhaps Enoch Jr., who always felt upstaged by Jacob both politically and personally. Like his father, Enoch Jr. saw his relationship with his brothers and cousins as a competition. His brothers, Esau and Ezra, did not concern him. They were younger, and his military service and duties as Mayor placed him head and shoulders above them. But this was not the case with his cousins. They were several years older than him, and all were married with school-age children. In short, all Enoch Jr. could hear was his father's voice from the grave. And it was berating him for failing in his duty to ensure his side of the family was preeminent in all things, and especially in expanding the Slaughter family's legacy.

So it was not surprising that Enoch Jr. saw Jacob and his family's demise as an opportunity to make up some ground. While the rest of the family mourned, he was busy pursuing a pretty high school girl named Mary Becker. But Mary already had a boyfriend, a high school senior named Wayne who worked part-time at her father's sawmill. So Mary wasn't interested in the Mayor's attention. But Enoch Jr. was accustomed to getting his way, and he would go to great lengths to do so.

His first step was to instruct his Chief of Police to keep an eye on Wayne and charge him with any infraction he might commit. His first citation was for spitting in public. A few days later, he was cited and fined for being out after curfew – a legal statute never previously enforced. Wayne's third strike was public indecency which landed him briefly in jail when he and Mary were caught kissing in Enoch Slaughter Park.

But this strategy didn't work. As a matter of fact, it backfired. Mary found she was turned on by Wayne's bad-boy image, and with each new infraction, she grew more enamored with him. So Enoch Jr. nixed that tactic.

Enoch Jr.'s next act was to double the property tax on the home and business of Wayne's family, hoping they would move – and they did. However, Enoch Jr. didn't count on a friend of Wayne's inviting him to stay with his family so Wayne could continue to see Mary and graduate with his friends.

Frustrated, Enoch Jr. took a more direct approach. He invited Mary's father out for a drink at Loman's. Getting a personal invitation to meet with the Mayor was a rare opportunity in itself. And having a drink on the Mayor's dime was even more extraordinary given prohibition.

Enoch Jr. was not a fan of prohibition and had no intention of enforcing it in Slaughter. This didn't exempt Slaughter, however, from a possible investigation. The State Police and agents of the Bureau of Prohibition were known to descend on unsuspecting towns to investigate and bust illegal distilleries or drinking establishments. As a result, Loman's had literally gone underground. A sliding shelving unit now hid the basement door to the speakeasy.

"Mr. Becker," Enoch Jr. began. "I have a proposition for you," pausing to down his whiskey.

"I'm all ears, Mr. Mayor," he replied, throwing back his glass and draining it.

Enoch Jr. motioned for another round and continued.

"Let me get to the point. I fancy your daughter, and I wish to make her my bride."

Mr. Becker nearly fell off his chair. Not because he was upset or shocked by the Mayor's pronouncement. It was more like he was ecstatic and recognized that his daughter's social and financial status would greatly improve if this came to pass.

"I'm honored to hear that, Mr. Mayor. You have my blessing."

"Well, thank you. But with all due respect, it's not your blessing that I need."

Mr. Becker could have taken offense at this but didn't. He knew he was looking a gift horse in the mouth.

"Then what is it you need from me?"

"I want you to get her boyfriend out of the picture and get her to see me instead."

"You don't mean out of the picture like out of the picture, do you?" he asked, his hand forming an imaginary gun as he extended his index finger and raised his thumb.

"Whatever it takes. You do what you have to do. If your daughter marries me, you'll never pay another cent of property tax on your home or your sawmill business."

"Never?" Mr. Becker asked in disbelief.

"Yes, never!" he replied.

The bartender delivered their second round of drinks just in time for Mr. Becker to propose a toast.

"To getting my Mary to marry you," he said, raising his glass with a smile.

"To marrying Mary," Enoch Jr. replied, clinking his glass enthusiastically with Mr. Becker's.

Mr. Becker lost sleep that evening, toiling over how to dispense with Wayne. First, he considered trying to discourage his daughter from seeing him. But knew that probably wouldn't fly as he had previously spoken glowingly about Wayne's work at the sawmill. Then he contemplated hiring someone to make Wayne disappear. But didn't know how to go about finding a hitman and remaining anonymous while doing so. Next, he toyed with the idea of inviting Wayne out to go deer hunting and having an unfortunate accident. However, he didn't think he could stomach going through with it. Finally, as dawn was breaking, he had a revelation.

Steam-powered sawmills were inherently noisy and dangerous. One misstep could easily result in injury or death. However, Mr. Becker's sawmill had a perfect safety record. This was unique in the industry and a source of great pride. It also allowed Mr. Becker the opportunity he needed to fulfill Enoch Jr.'s request without getting blood on his hands, so to speak.

Wayne was a good worker but not experienced working in proximity to the vertical saws that transformed two-ton logs into lumber planks and beams. He typically just hauled carts filled with sawdust to the boiler and fed the fire that produced the steam for the sawmill. Wayne had been asking to do more meaningful jobs, but up until now, Mr. Becker had been hesitant to let him do so. So when Mr. Becker asked Wayne to man the position of sawyer, cutting logs using the vertical saw, Wayne jumped at the chance. Unfortunately, he was jumping into the most dangerous job. And saw blades don't discriminate between wood or flesh. With enthusiasm minus proper training, Wayne unknowingly stepped into the path of the hydraulic carriage propelling him into the twin saw blades and cutting him in half before he knew what happened.

Mr. Becker voluntarily reported the unfortunate accident

to authorities, saying Wayne had manned the vertical saws without his knowledge, proper training, or authorization. Investigators learned of Wayne's recent run-ins with the law, which only served to give credence to Mr. Becker's claim that Wayne had acted irresponsibly. Since this was the first and only blemish on the sawmill's record, authorities didn't find any negligence on Mr. Becker's part.

Mary, of course, was devastated by the news. Cloistering herself in her room for days. Mr. Becker was only too happy to allow Enoch Jr. to visit his distraught daughter. Much to his wife's surprise, as she couldn't understand why the Mayor was taking such a personal interest.

Paralyzed with grief, Mary couldn't protest Enoch Jr.'s visits or resist his attempts to console her. Which had more to do with resolving his sexual desires than alleviating her sorrow. Slowly, over months of his regaling her with gifts and professing his love, he started to grow on her. The fact that she missed her period also helped convince her to finally accept his umpteenth marriage proposal.

You would have found it difficult to determine who was happier by her decision, Enoch Jr. or Mr. Becker. Which made Mrs. Becker suspicious. Because the only thing that ever made her husband that ecstatic was a financial windfall. Nevertheless, Enoch Jr. got what he wanted. And now, he could only hope that Mary was carrying his hope for the future – Enoch III.

# CHAPTER 54

If it had been up to Hagatha, she would have liked to have dispensed with the entire Slaughter clan in one fell swoop. But she kept on having dreams disclosing that her reign of destruction would be achieved over decades instead of days.

Her most recent vision foretold the circumstances that would bring her great-granddaughter to Slaughter. However, Hagatha's joy that she would see her great-granddaughter was tempered by knowing some of the Slaughter family would have to survive well into the 20$^{th}$ century. And ironically, she might have to protect some Slaughter family members from harm for her master plan of their extinction to come to fruition.

Such was the case for Abraham and Sarah Slaughter's daughter, Abigail, and their granddaughter, Kathleen, currently 6 years old. Abigail had married Finn Flanagan in 1913, giving birth to Kathleen two years later. In her dream, she sees Abigail and Finn raising Kathleen, who ultimately becomes Slaughter Elementary School's 7$^{th}$-grade teacher. Kathleen never marries but teaches at the school for over 30 years until she dies of natural causes. It is then that Hagatha's great-granddaughter applies for and gets hired for the Elementary School's teaching vacancy. So any of Hagatha's thoughts of a scorched earth approach were out the window. Instead, she needed to ensure that Abigail and Finn Flanagan and their daughter, Kathleen, lived long and healthy lives.

The one silver lining in Hagatha's dream is that she sees herself laying her hand on a young boy's shoulder and casting a spell. He's one of Enoch's great-grandsons. And in the dream, she hears the boys' friends calling him Bobby. Her curse causes Bobby and his parents to become gravely ill and leave Slaughter. Which, in turn, vacates the house her great-granddaughter then occupies.

The intricacy of what needed to transpire over the next few decades was overwhelming to Hagatha. Realizing that if she indiscriminately wreaked havoc on the Slaughter family, she could compromise her long-term goal. Invariably, at these times, she would turn to the one thing that hadn't failed her – her Bible. So, flipping to the Book of Ecclesiastes, she read.

"To everything, there is a season and a time to every purpose under the heaven. A time to be born and a time to die. A time to plant and a time to pluck up that which is planted. A time to kill and a time to heal. A time to break down, and a time to build up."

Reciting these verses repeatedly gave her some solace. And often led to revelations of those family members who weren't included in her dreams as needing protection. Those for whom you might say it was a time to kill.

# CHAPTER 55

Hilda and Cyril's marriage seemed like a perpetual honeymoon. Their love seemed limitless and new, despite the passage of time. Another blessing was that Hilda hadn't experienced any night terrors or visitations from her biological mother for 8 years. She thought that finally, she had outgrown them. Elsa also proved to be an exceptionally easy child to raise. And she flourished under the love and attention given by Cyril, Hilda, and her Grandma Evelyn.

Once a year, Hilda and Cyril would take off on a jaunt to New York City to see all the most popular theatre productions. They'd wine, dine and dance to their heart's content. But that all changed in 1925 when Evelyn fell ill.

It was first just a fever and night sweats. But then progressed to a cough, which became more persistent. By the time she went to a doctor, she had lost considerable weight and was coughing up blood. She was subsequently diagnosed with tuberculosis and admitted to a sanatorium.

Tuberculosis treatment in the mid-1920s was little more than confinement, bed rest, and getting fresh air. In Duluth, Minnesota, this meant sanatorium staff wheeled Evelyn outside periodically to breathe in the brisk air coming off Lake Superior. As invigorating as the winds off Lake Superior are, they didn't have the power to cure Evelyn. Her TB killed her, as it had so many others without more effective treatments, which wouldn't become available until the 1940s.

For five-year-old Elsa, Grandma Evelyn's passing was her first true experience of loss and grief. And at that age, there is nothing more shattering or confusing as the finality of death. For Hilda, it signaled a crossroads. The two people she thought of as her real parents were now gone. And the two people responsible for her existence were probably still out there. As much as she tried to deny or forget it, they were always that little niggling thought that wore on her. Like water that slowly eats away at the rocks until it carves a path through them. Now the dam that had held the reality of her life at bay was breeched. Her tears were as much for the rejection by her biological parents as they were for losing her adopted mother.

But humans have a tremendous ability to suppress a truth that they do not wish to acknowledge. They bury it deep in some subconscious subterranean vault, thinking it will never see the light of day. Only to be mortified when it reveals itself in a most unusual and usually painful way. So after Hilda got through mourning, she pushed her demons away, anxious to continue the idyllic life she had led since meeting Cyril.

Now that Elsa was older, Hilda and Cyril began taking her on their trips to New York City. The first time was in 1927, which Hilda and Cyril christened as their "second honeymoon." Eight-year-old Elsa was no stranger to theatre. She had seen her father perform in Duluth, and their phonograph always seemed to be playing music. But New York City and the Belasco Theatre were beyond anything Elsa could have imagined. They went to see a musical called Hit the Deck and the show tune "Nothing Could Be Sweeter" became an instant favorite. Growing up, one of Elsa's enduring memories was of her parents putting that song on the phonograph and dancing in the living room.

It was heady times, but they and few others could have

anticipated the dark and dismal days of the Depression just around the corner.

# CHAPTER 56

Noah Slaughter, Abraham Slaughter's only son, worked for the Fullmore Brush Company as a door-to-door salesman. Most of the residents of Slaughter and the surrounding towns didn't mind when Noah came to their home peddling Fullmore's wide variety of brushes, mops, and brooms. They liked the convenience of shopping in the comfort of their home, where Noah was only too happy to demonstrate the wonders of the company's products.

Such was not the case with Hagatha, who more than once shooed him away. But Noah was nothing if not persistent. And while this was a valued quality in a salesman, it was a dangerous trait when applied to Hagatha Ketchel.

"You know, a Fullmore broom would do a better job in half the time," he called to Hagatha, who was so enthralled in sweeping her walkway she hadn't noticed him approach.

"I thought I told you last time what you could do with your brooms," she barked.

"Oh, yes, that was very colorful indeed, ma'am. But I see you out here every day toiling away when your time could be better spent relaxing or tending to that garden you have there."

"Maybe I find this relaxing. And what about my garden doesn't appear well-tended, Mr.," she paused, realizing she didn't know his name.

"Mr. Noah Slaughter at your service," he said, holding up a Fullmore broom. "Let me show you just how much better this works," he said, unlatching the gate.

"And if you walk through that gate, Mr. Slaughter, I'll show you just how well this broom works!" she replied, raising it up and gripping it like a baseball bat.

"Just five minutes of your time, and I promise, you'll be thanking me," he persisted, taking a step through the open gate.

"Mr. Slaughter, you are dust, and to dust, you shall return," she menaced and started towards him, swinging her broom with a whoosh that narrowly missed his head.

Noah had the sense to high-tail it out of there, but the damage had been done. He had aroused Hagatha's ire, and she was going to make sure she would never see him again.

Hagatha went back into her house, randomly cracked open her Bible, and read a passage from Jeremiah.

"For behold, I will send serpents among you. Vipers which cannot be charmed. And they shall bite you."

For two days, Hagatha focused on Noah and repeated this verse non-stop. As in the past, this exercise produced visions of what would happen. And since she didn't get any signals that Noah needed saving, he was expendable.

Noah Slaughter was named after the biblical ark-builder. While he didn't have an ark, like many Minnesotans, he owned a small boat. When he wasn't hawking brushes, brooms, and mops, you could often find him fishing on one of the many lakes or rivers in the area.

On this particular Saturday, he and his 10-year-old son Luke were fishing for walleyes near the Prairie River Dam. The day started out clear and sunny. But as is the case in northern Minnesota, wait 10 minutes, and things can change rapidly. The wind kicked up, causing just tiny ripples in the water at first. Then, ominous steel gray thunderheads blossomed on the horizon, and the ripples became waves. Noah was about to suggest that they make their way to shore when Luke got a heavy strike on his line.

"Jeez, Dad, it's a big one. Get the net," Luke yelled, struggling to keep a grip on the rod.

As Noah was retrieving the net and cautiously navigating his way towards his son, the wind and the waves grew more intense. The little boat rocked precariously as white caps repeatedly hit the side of the vessel, soaking Noah and Luke in the process.

"Luke, this is too dangerous. We should cut the line and head in," Noah called above the howling wind and the rumble of thunder in the distance.

"No, Dad. I've almost got him," Luke protested, standing up in the boat and giving a mighty pull in hopes of dragging the leviathan to the surface.

Suddenly, the line snapped, sending Luke tumbling off the opposite side of the boat and into the water. The abrupt shift in weight aided by an enormous wave served to flip the vessel over, tossing Noah into the drink with his son. Fortunately, Luke and Noah could cling to the overturned boat, now being pushed towards a cove by the wind and the waves.

Noah began to relax as they floated into the calmer waters of the cove. The storm was still bearing down on them. However, based on the time between lightning strikes and thunderclaps, he calculated the worst of the tempest was over a mile away. As they approached land, Noah saw strange ripples in the water that appeared to be closing in on them from the shoreline. It almost looked like the water was boiling. As the undulating waters grew closer, Noah thought he must be hallucinating. It looked like hundreds of snakes slithering their way towards them.

"Get up on the hull of the boat," Noah commanded Luke.

"Why? We're almost to shore," Luke replied, not seeing the impending danger.

"Just do as I say," Noah shouted, just before the snakes struck, biting his head and arms that were out of the water and his torso and legs underwater. He flailed at the snakes, trying to ward them off, but they were too numerous. Venom was coursing through his veins, paralyzing his body as he struggled to keep his head above water.

Meanwhile, Luke's legs were still in the water as he tried to pull himself onto the boat hull. Giving the snakes easy targets as they attacked, wrapping themselves around his legs and sinking their fangs into him. He screamed as if a hundred burning hot pokers were impaling him. Then, finally, slid back into the water, a sitting duck for the hundreds of ferocious vipers roiling around him.

Noah and Luke's bloated and bitten bodies were discovered on the shore hours later. Authorities were baffled by the snake bites. The only snakes prevalent in that area were the garter snake, the eastern hog-nosed snake, and the red-bellied snake. All non-venomous and harmless.

In his grief, Abraham Slaughter demanded a full investigation and autopsy of his deceased son and grandson. It didn't take the coroner long to discover the cause of death. As he removed the organs to weigh and examine them, an eastern massasauga snake slithered out of Noah's stomach, nearly biting the coroner. The eastern massasauga is one of only two venomous snakes in Minnesota - both only found in the southeast corner of the state – 250 miles away. Based on the number of bite marks, and the level of venom in Noah and Luke's blood, the coroner estimated that dozens of snakes must have bitten them.

This finding caused a swift but panicked response in the community. Search parties were organized to find and exterminate the horde of deadly eastern massasauga snakes. But after weeks of hunting, no venomous snakes were found. Of course, in the search parties' zeal and paranoia, many garter snakes and eastern hog-nosed snakes were sacrificed.

Meanwhile, Hagatha just kept sweeping her walkway, comforted by the knowledge that she wouldn't be interrupted by some pushy salesman.

"For behold, I will send serpents among you. Vipers which cannot be charmed. And they shall bite you," she said with a grin.

# CHAPTER 57

Much like his father, Enoch Jr. was just lucky when it came to financial matters. Whereas his father had literally fallen off a horse to discover iron ore, Enoch Jr. kept the family's wealth in cash in a secure basement room of the Slaughter mansion. Thus, shunning the advice of so-called financial experts to save his money in a bank and invest in the stock market. In short, Enoch Jr.'s paranoia made him look like the smartest man alive when the stock market crashed on October 29, 1929, and banks subsequently began to fail.

Nonetheless, the Great Depression and a severe worldwide economic crisis made for hard times for Slaughter residents. The lumber and mining industries, which were the foundation of the area's economic engine, ground to a halt. If not for the foresight and generosity of Lila, the family's matriarch, it's doubtful the town of Slaughter would have survived. Not that Enoch Jr. hadn't protested vehemently against her kindness.

"Are you crazy, mother? We cannot have a moratorium on collecting property and business taxes."

"Oh yes, we can. And that's not all. We're not going to collect leasing fees from the timber and mining companies either."

"What? That's our most significant source of income!" he blustered.

"Don't you understand, son? No one can afford to pay us right now. If we demand payment, not only will they not be able to pay, but we will run them off. So we can stand a little pain now for continued profits in the future."

"Father would never have agreed to this. So I don't know why I should," he argued.

"Then you didn't know your father. He may have objected to my suggestions and stormed off, but in the end, he always understood that I was the one with the business sense. Your father was lucky to come into his fortune. Whereas I grew up in a family that had to fight tooth and nail for our success. So you best listen to me. Otherwise, you'll find yourself penniless, and I won't be around to help you."

"Don't talk that way, mother."

"I'm 51 years old, son. I'm not going to live forever."

Fortunately, Enoch Jr. took his mother's advice. And even followed her recommendation to invest some of the family's wealth in the stock market a couple of years later. Investing in industries for which they had a vested interest, like wood, paper, and mining. Investments that would pay off handsomely in the future.

Yes, Enoch Jr. was lucky. Lucky to have a mother who knew how to manage a son who was a daily reminder of her narcissistic, arrogant, and selfish husband.

# CHAPTER 58

Hagatha didn't always have to rely on her evil spells to hasten the planned extermination of the Slaughter family. The natural aging process also played a part. Enoch's two brothers, both in their 60s, died in the early 1930s – Jeremiah from heart disease and Abraham from pneumonia. The only male descendants left from their sides of the family were Jeremiah's youngest son, Jedidiah, and Jedi's teenage son, Edward.

Meanwhile, to Hagatha's vexation, Enoch's side of the family was flourishing. Enoch Jr. and his two brothers, Esau and Ezra, were all married, and their wives were popping out babies like there was no tomorrow. So by 1933, they had nine Slaughter descendants between them – five boys and four girls. It rankled Hagatha not to be able to put a stop to it. Knowing that if she didn't, like rabbits, they'd multiply. However, each time she devised a sinister plot for the demise of a Slaughter heir, she'd have a dream or a vision that would dissuade her from carrying it out. If it wasn't for the triumphant victory that would be achieved in the future through her partnership with her great-granddaughter, she would have ignored the signals to wait.

Instead, she bided her time taking what she could get. And on one rainy April day in 1933, two Slaughter children meandered past her house on their way to school. One was Enoch

Jr.'s firstborn, Enoch III, who she knew was off-limits. She knew that 10-year-old Enoch III needed to grow up to have a son, Enoch IV, who would eventually marry and impregnate Hagatha's great-granddaughter. The other child was Enoch Jr.'s second son, 7-year-old Eben Slaughter. And to Hagatha's delight, she couldn't recall having a vision of Eben's future. Finally, she would get some retribution on her ex-husband's namesake. She took out her Bible and prepared for when little Eben would walk past her house on his way home.

She was sweeping her walkway when Eben and Enoch III approached that afternoon. They were with a few other snot-nosed kids Hagatha recognized as responsible for previous taunts and rock-throwing incidents. It was tempting to go after the little scoundrels, but her focus was on Eben. Innocent little Eben, whose only fault was being born a Slaughter.

So when all the kids, including Enoch III, started to run as Hagatha approached, Eben was late in recognizing the danger. He fell behind the pack, and like baby wildebeest being chased by a cheetah, Hagatha had him in her clutches. She smelled of death, and her face was contorted with rage. And from her lips came an other-worldly cry.

"Behold, the scab spreadeth in the skin," she shrieked. "Now go, never to return."

Upon which she let Eben go. He had pissed his pants, and he thought his heart was going to explode. But, when he caught up with his older brother and the others, they just laughed at his soiled pants.

"It's not funny," he protested, starting to cry.

"Oh, don't be a cry baby. She let you go. You'll live," Enoch III replied nonchalantly.

Enoch III didn't know how wrong he was. He hadn't heard what Hagatha had said to Eben. And Eben couldn't remember what she said. Not that he would have told anyone. Eben was too embarrassed. So he had no problem when his older brother demanded that nothing be said about the incident to their parents.

Meanwhile, in the middle of the night, Hilda and 13-year-old Elsa awoke terrified by simultaneous nightmares. When Hilda recovered enough to console her daughter, they learned that they had seen the same images. A horrified little boy in the grasp of Hilda's mother. And when she releases him, ulcers and boils erupt all over his face and hands. And before their eyes, he starts to decompose and shrivel up until he's just a pile of ashes that blows away with the wind.

It wasn't the first time or the last time they'd have simultaneous nightmares. Hilda learned that Elsa had also dreamt of the horrific plane crash that claimed Congressman Jacob Slaughter's family and of the snake attack that killed Noah and Luke Slaughter. It was Hagatha's way of staying connected to her daughter and granddaughter. A way to ensure that her great-granddaughter would be infected with the powers she would need to carry out her master plan when the time came. Of course, Eben didn't exactly shrivel up and become a pile of ashes. That was poetic license Hagatha used to make sure her daughter and granddaughter respected her powers.

However, a few days later, Eben fell ill and suffered from a bizarre set of symptoms. He lost his eyebrows, and his skin was covered in discolored patches. His face was swollen and misshapen by lumps. And there were ulcers on his feet. He didn't complain of pain, but he looked hideous.

Enoch Jr. took him to a doctor in Grand Rapids who was baffled. The doctor called in several of his colleagues, who were equally puzzled after examining Eben. They recommended he be seen at a specialty hospital south of the Twin Cities. There, he was diagnosed with leprosy. They gave him chaulmoogra oil injections, the recommended treatment for leprosy in that day and age. It failed. Parts of Eben's body started to reabsorb or crust over and fall off. He eventually succumbed to his consumptive condition.

It was only then that Enoch III told his parents about the incident with the old lady on Tailings Way. Claiming she was responsible for Eben's death. But Enoch Jr. and his wife Mary were too distraught, and their son's tale too unbelievable to merit their consideration. Enoch III would try to swallow the guilt he felt for not protecting his little brother. But it would forever haunt him. Eventually morphing into the need to be all things to all people. Which subsequently required him to avoid accountability and appear faultless at any cost. Characteristics well-suited for flip-flopping politicians and maniacal leaders who hid their divisiveness behind messages of unification and goodwill. Traits that 35 years later he would employ when the mantle of Mayor was passed down to him by his father.

# CHAPTER 59

By 1938, the United States and Slaughter Minnesota were well on their way towards recovering from the effects of the Great Depression. The mining and lumber industries, as Lila had predicted, had survived the economic downturn and were once again healthy contributors to the area's fiscal revival. But there were storm clouds on the horizon. In Germany, an angry little man with a funny mustache named Adolf Hitler had self-appointed himself Führer and making waves with his neighbors. If he didn't pipe down, America would likely be thrust into war.

But far and away, the more imminent threat to Slaughter and the Slaughter family was Lila's health. She had suddenly grown weak, her body racked with muscle pain and weakness. She had fallen a couple of times when her legs inexplicably gave out on her. A few days later, she was confined to her bed, finding it hard to breathe and unable to move her legs.

Enoch Jr. called in a team of doctors, who diagnosed Lila as having Polio. The diagnosis was devastating. Polio was one of the select few diseases for which no effective treatments existed. Progressively destroying the nerves until complete paralysis rendered them unable to breathe.

Undaunted, Enoch Jr. spared no expense. He purchased an Iron Lung, which was beyond the financial reach of 99% of the population. But laying in an air-tight tube for weeks, if not permanently, with only one's head exposed, was no way to live.

"Get me out of this infernal thing," Lila protested after several days.

"No, mother. The doctors said it takes 1 to 2 weeks before most people get better," Enoch replied.

In actuality, the doctors had said some people get better, but Enoch Jr. wasn't about to give up hope. He pressed the doctors to do more. But other than an experimental vaccine, there was nothing more they could do.

"Then give my mother the vaccine," Enoch Jr. demanded.

"It's not that easy. There are protocols that need to be followed. Criteria that have to be met," the doctor replied.

"Will $2,000 satisfy your protocols and criteria, doctor?" Enoch Jr. asked, not above bribery.

The doctor paused as if considering his offer.

"$3,000?" Enoch Jr. offered.

"Yes, I'm sure we can make that work," the doctor replied.

While that may not sound like much money, $3,000 in 1938 was the average doctor's income for an entire year. But, unfortunately, experimental vaccines are called experimental for a reason. And in Lila's case, it didn't work. In fact, it probably hastened her demise. Not that the doctor would admit it. So while Lila's death was a devastating blow to the family, Enoch Jr. at least felt redeemed in the fact that he had done everything possible to save her.

And, for this, he was ultimately rewarded. When Lila's last will and testament were read, Enoch Jr. made out considerably better than his two younger brothers. This is because Lila's will had incorporated Enoch's wishes. And Enoch had always shown favoritism towards his eldest son. While the family's monetary wealth was equally apportioned between Enoch Jr., Esau, and Ezra, Enoch Jr. was willed the Slaughter mansion and the deed to the 320 acres of property. Thus, Enoch Jr. was the sole beneficiary of the income produced from all the business leases, including the lucrative logging and mining company agreements.

As you can imagine, this inequity didn't sit well with Esau and Ezra. While they had always tolerated Enoch Jr.'s competitiveness and one-upmanship, this changed the entire dynamic between the brothers. Now Esau and Ezra felt like they needed to compete against each other for Enoch Jr.'s favor.

Enoch Jr. was either blind to the inequity, or more likely, felt he deserved it. Consequently, he did nothing to remedy it. And Esau and Ezra didn't dare complain to him. Each was now unwilling to do something that might irritate him and endear him to the other. Lila's death and the apportionment of the family's riches drove a stake between the three brothers. In short, the Slaughter family became a house divided.

This division would translate to subsequent generations, primarily concerning the social circles they moved in. Descendants of Enoch Jr. would move in decidedly more exclusive and privileged circles to those of Esau and Ezra. And communication between the brothers and their family's nearly ceased. Only dire circumstances compelling them to come together or speak with one another.

Not that they knew, but the fact that Hagatha Ketchel existed guaranteed that dire circumstances were on the horizon. Who do you think was behind Lila's sudden health crisis and demise?

Envy is a powerful emotion. Capable of stealing one's desire to live because of their perpetual feelings of inadequacy. Or, as in Hagatha's case, capable of ending the life of the source of your jealousy. And thereby breeding animosity and chaos between the members of the family you wish to destroy.

# CHAPTER 60

Hagatha's visions increasingly shifted from the chaos she could create in the present to her role in ensuring the future played out as necessary. That her powers could be used for constructive purposes was new to her and not nearly as satisfying. Instead, she preferred the immediate gratification and finality of her destructive capabilities. Even though they seemed to drain her more so than her future-oriented spells.

She would often need to hibernate for weeks at a time after casting a catastrophic curse. It was somewhat similar to what the farmers had to do with their fields. Allowing them to lay fallow for a season so that they could rest and regenerate.

Most of her dreams now involved Elsa and ensuring she would meet the right man to bear the great-granddaughter Hagatha required to carry out her master plan. But Hagatha was restless and often interrupted her more constructive reveries to consider what pandemonium she could produce.

On a lark, she spent a couple of days casting a future-oriented spell on Etan, the 10-year-old firstborn of Esau and Roberta Slaughter. Esau, like any father, had high hopes for his eldest son. And, as all Slaughter men were conditioned, foremost was the expectation of adding more male heirs. But Hagatha had other plans. As she was hesitant to cast any spell that might dispose of a Slaughter heir crucial to the future, she devised a curse she thought was deviously elegant. Accomplishing her desire to slow the growth of the Slaughter family without killing anyone. She recited a verse from Leviticus and set the clock for her spell to be fulfilled when Etan turned 13.

"If a man lies with a male, as he lies with a woman, both of them have committed an abomination."

But Hagatha wasn't happy that she'd have to wait 3 years before her spell on Etan revealed itself. So she didn't stop there. She then thought of an equally clever spell she could cast on Edward Slaughter, the last remaining male descendant of Jedidiah and Charlotte Slaughter.

Edward was a rugged and handsome man who cut an impressive figure from his years working as a lumberjack. He was a man's man whose prowess wielding an ax and manning a saw was legendary. Edward was engaged to be married, and Hagatha meant to put a crimp in those plans. So she recited a verse from Deuteronomy, explicitly reserved for Edward.

"A woman shall not wear anything that pertains to a man, nor shall a man put on a woman's garment, for all who do so are an abomination."

Imagine the scene when Edward showed up at his worksite with his ax in hand wearing one of his fiances' dresses. Never mind that his muscular frame had torn some of the seams of the dress. At first, his fellow lumberjacks thought it must be a joke and laughed nervously.

"Nice dress, Edward. Are you wearing Melissa's knickers too?" one lumberman wise-cracked.

When the laughter died down, Edward responded.

"Oh, yes. See?" Edward said triumphantly, lifting the dress to reveal Melissa's frilly and dainty underwear stretched beyond its limits.

This act elicited groans of disgust.

"Okay, the joke has gone far enough, Edward. Go and

change into your real clothes. We have trees to fell."

"This isn't a joke. These are my real clothes," he replied in all seriousness.

Suffice to say, Edward was invited to leave the worksite. Had Edward seen fit to go back home and change clothes, perhaps his job and engagement could have been salvaged. But instead, he went to Loman's in hopes of having a drink. Only guaranteeing that everyone in town, including Melissa, would learn of Edward's cross-dressing. She broke off the engagement. And Jedidiah and Charlotte Slaughter were mortified.

"What were you thinking? Was this some kind of sick joke?" his father spat.

"No, I just like to wear pretty dresses."

"Since when? You never wore them before. You need to stop this. It's embarrassing."

"Why? It feels right to me. And they're comfortable. You should try it."

"I'm not some Nancy-boy," Jedidiah exploded. "And neither are you. Now stop this nonsense and come to your senses."

But Edward couldn't control his proclivity for ladies' clothing. The final straw was when he tried to buy dresses and undergarments in a local clothing store. The proprietor called his parents, who gave him the ultimatum – leave town, or they'd commit him to a mental institution.

Edward left town and moved to the Twin Cities. Getting a job as a female impersonator at a cabaret in Minneapolis and changing his name to Edwina Starr. Not that his parents cared or even acknowledged he existed, but he made quite a name for himself. Eventually, moving to Chicago and then to New York City.

# CHAPTER 61

As Hagatha had arranged in a vision, her 19-year old granddaughter Elsa moved from Duluth to Minneapolis for her appointed date with destiny. Hilda had encouraged her to stay in Duluth but fully understood when her daughter said she needed to strike out on her own, just as she had as a teenager.

Elsa had secured a job as a secretary at a large insurance company in Minneapolis. But it was the big city's active nightlife that really appealed to her. She had been raised to appreciate music and dance, and the Twin Cities had no shortages of clubs. So as often as she could afford, she would convince her girlfriends to go out on the town.

Klaus Garber was a tool and diemaker who emigrated from Dresden, Germany, to Minneapolis in 1938. He was 5 foot 6 and 150 pounds with wavy black hair with soft brown eyes. When Klaus wasn't working, he enjoyed rowing and dancing. Although he could drink beer prodigiously, he preferred moderation and dancing with as many women as possible. And there was usually no shortage. Women thought he was handsome and found his broken and heavily-accented English cute. It also didn't hurt that he was light on his feet on the dance floor.

"Vant you to tanzen?" he asked Elsa, who had just sat down at a table with a couple of her girlfriends.

"What?" she asked with a confused looked.

"Tanzen," he repeated, mimicking as if he was dancing.

"Oh, you want me to dance with you?" she asked.

"Ja," he nodded his head and held out his hand.

She put her hand in his, and moments later, they were floating across the dance floor as in a dream. Something akin to what had happened when her mother and father's eyes had met in the theatre now occurred to them on that dance floor. Their connection was electric. And when she finally stepped off the dance floor, she knew he was the man she would marry.

But the little man with the funny mustache who couldn't get along with his neighbors intervened. And while Klaus was a German, he enlisted in the U.S. Army. You see, he and his parents had fled their homeland for fear of what that little man would do. Klaus's father was Catholic, but his mother was Jewish. And in the eyes of the Nazi's that made him and his mother targets. So, fortuitously, they left Germany for America just a few months before Kristallnacht. Otherwise, Elsa wouldn't have met Klaus. Which was necessary for the cascade of things that needed to happen to ensure Karen Garber's birth in 1946.

Of course, Elsa didn't know that their future was predestined. So when Klaus was whisked off to some undisclosed training facility, she mourned and worried that she'd never see him again.

It just so happened that the U.S. Army was recruiting German Jews for a secret operation to intercept, gather, and transmit Nazi combat intelligence. Ironically, Klaus found himself back in Germany, interrogating prisoners of war, mixing in with the locals, and giving valuable information to the U.S. Army and its allies. It was dangerous, and Klaus feared every day that his real identity would be discovered. And while there were several close-calls along the way, he survived. And Klaus and the special band of brothers with whom he trained provided an immeasurable amount of intelligence in aiding the successful war effort. Causing the cowardly little man with the funny mustache to kill himself before he could be held accountable for the atrocities he had committed.

# CHAPTER 62

While Klaus Garber bravely went off to war, Enoch Jr. was busy trying to find a way for 18-year-old Enoch III to avoid serving. While Enoch Jr. was a decorated WWI vet, the last thing he wanted was to have his only male heir go off to war. Claiming to be a conscientious objector was not an option. They had to find a reason for deferment that was honorable and served to elevate the Slaughter family name. The only two options that fit these criteria were being an elected public official or a minister.

Enoch III was not religiously inclined, and even Slaughter's Mayor wasn't an elected position. So Enoch Jr. got creative. While Slaughter had a volunteer fire department, they didn't have a Fire Chief. So, with the powers vested in his position as Mayor, he decreed that the town would conduct its first election for the post of Slaughter Fire Chief. His announcement generated a fair amount of excitement and interest. That is until townfolk learned two things - the position was an uncompensated 10-year term, and Enoch III had thrown his hat into the arena.

Consequently, Enoch III ran unopposed and garnered all 1,423 votes, constituting 95% of the eligible voters in Slaughter. This was incredible since barely 10% of the eligible voters actually showed up at the high school auditorium to vote. Nonetheless, Enoch III was now the duly-elected Slaughter Fire

Chief and subsequently received a Class 4-B deferment.

This, in turn, made Enoch III the only eligible bachelor in town as all the rest of Slaughter's young men went off to war. He had his pick of dozens of eligible young women. Some who all but threw themselves at him and others who, missing their boyfriends, could probably be had with just a little consoling. However, he rejected what he considered easy pickings. Reasoning that if they were worth it, their boyfriends would have married them before they went off to war. Instead, he set his sights on Margaret Urlauben. A 15-year-old virgin with an hourglass figure. Unspoiled primarily because of her strict German parents, who, for good reason, rarely let her out of their sight.

When Margaret wasn't at school, she was working in her parent's Pharmacy. Her father often relegating her to duties in the back office to discourage male callers who were more interested in flirting with Margaret than having prescriptions filled. Or, as he put it, "Jemandem Honig um den Mund schmieren," a German saying for trying to butter her up. Which literally translated to someone who smears honey on your mouth.

But when you live in Slaughter, Minnesota, and someone with the last name of Slaughter makes a request, even the most overly protective parent makes compromises. And Enoch III didn't waste any time courting the pure and zaftig daughter of the town's Pharmacist. So while many young American men were dying making incursions on Nazi forces, Enoch III made less risky and more pleasurable incursions on Margaret.

Margaret may have been a bit naïve, but this didn't make her a pushover. She had principles. And regardless of Enoch III's last name, she wasn't about to compromise them. At any other time, Enoch III may have balked at having to slow-play a relationship. However, since there was no competition, he did his best to observe her restrictions. It wasn't easy. And he would often try to push the boundaries. Only to make slow and painful progress. But, by the end of the war, they were engaged to be married.

# CHAPTER 63

Given the secrecy of Klaus's assignment, Elsa didn't have the opportunity to send or receive letters or get updates on his whereabouts or health. If not for the metaphysical connection they shared, their years apart would have been unbearable. Even given this connection, there were times when Elsa's spirit would flag, and doubt and fear would creep in. At these times, two things would buoy her outlook – visits to or from her parents and reassuring dreams.

Elsa thought at first that the dreams were generated by Klaus, somewhere halfway around the world, sending her comforting messages. Until that is, she spoke to her mother and learned that she too was having similar dreams.

"Do you think that Hagatha's responsible for our dreams?" Elsa asked.

"I don't know anyone else who has haunted us," Hilda replied.

"But these are so different. They're," Elsa paused, trying to find the words.

"Happy, not horrific?" Hilda ventured.

"Yes. What do you think it means?

"I haven't a clue. But at least we're not waking up screaming in a cold sweat."

"Unless she's just giving me false assurances. Do you think she's that evil?"

Hilda hesitated to answer her daughter. Fearing that Hagatha was indeed that evil, if not more so.

"Oh, I don't think so, honey," she said, not having the heart to extinguish the hope the dream had provided.

"Maybe she's getting nicer in her old age," Elsa speculated.

Hilda bit her tongue and let her daughter's statement go without a comment.

"Maybe we should visit her. Maybe she's sending us comforting visions because she feels bad about all the scary nightmares she gave us."

"Oh, I don't know if that's a good idea, sweetheart. We don't even know where she lives. Or if she's even alive. She'd have to be close to 70 years old now."

"Well, whatever or whoever is doing this, I'm thankful. It gives me hope. Just when I needed it most."

"Yes, dear. That's what is important. Stay hopeful," Hilda replied, while in the back of her mind, she didn't trust that Hagatha could have a benevolent bone in her body. There had to be an ulterior motive. But what that could be was anyone's guess.

Elsa's suggestion that they visit Hagatha had planted a seed in Hilda's head. A seed she wasn't sure she wanted to feed or germinate.

# CHAPTER 64

Margaret Urlauben and Enoch III were married shortly after World War II ended. And a year later, Margaret gave birth to a baby boy, christened Enoch IV. While Margaret stayed home with the baby, Enoch III was forced to finally make a living. He had lived off of his parent's generosity for 25 years. So long that the thought of toiling in some job to make money was anathema to him. Then he got a bright idea.

Most of Slaughter's townfolks knew Enoch III's position as Fire Chief was a ruse for him to avoid the draft. And during the war years, except for the most cursory and irregular fire inspections, he rarely exercised his authority. But that all changed, now that he had a family and needed to earn a wage.

He started making regular inspections of the businesses in town. And flexing his Fire Chief muscles when he found it advantageous or when he had an ax to grind with a particular proprietor. Although the position was uncompensated, Enoch III began assessing and pocketing fines for fire safety infractions – some real, but most just made up. For the most part, the business owners didn't protest. Knowing the futility of complaining to the Mayor and recognizing that Enoch III's term as Fire Chief would be up in 2 years. It was the price of doing business in Slaughter. And a small price to pay compared to the costly and heavy-handed mob-run operations in other cities and towns.

Meanwhile, on Tailings Way, Hagatha continued weaving together the circumstances that would eventually bring Enoch IV and her great-granddaughter together. She hadn't done anything in years to slow the growth of the Slaughter family. Stopped at every turn by visions that required the next generation of Slaughter heirs to be born unfettered by any of her deadly interventions. She couldn't help but feel she was losing ground. And the thought of her moratorium on slaughtering Slaughters extending another 20 years was nearly unfathomable.

The only recent victory she could claim was Etan Slaughter. She had cast a future-oriented spell on him when he was 10. Three years later, at the appointed time she had scheduled, Etan was in his Physical Education class when something unexpected happened. He was wrestling another boy and became aroused – and not in an aggressive I want to kick your ass kind of arousal. He broke off their clinch before the boy or anyone noticed and ran off, claiming he needed to use the bathroom. He wrote it off as an idiosyncratic reaction. But when the boys hit the shower room after class, he couldn't help but become aroused again when seeing his classmates' naked bodies. He escaped again without notice, but the die was cast – he was a homosexual.

But the price of being a homosexual in those days was severe. So he tried to hide it. He forced himself to ask girls out all through high school, even though he fantasized about boys. Due to his age, he avoided being drafted for the war. Which was fortuitous, as being in close quarters with other young men would have made it difficult, if not impossible, to hide the truth.

But Etan couldn't restrain himself forever, and one evening he went to a bar in Grand Rapids and met another man similarly inclined. They spent the night together, and Etan knew he couldn't continue to hide his true nature. He also knew that no one in Slaughter would accept him, least of all his father,

Esau Slaughter. So the next day, he left a note for his mother, divulging his secret. By the time she read it, he was well on his way to the only place he knew that would accept him – San Francisco.

# CHAPTER 65

Hilda couldn't get her last conversation with her daughter out of her head. Specifically, Elsa's suggestion that they visit Hagatha. Hilda thought she had made her peace with never having to meet her biological mother. But now, her daughter had reopened that possibility, and it was staring her in the face. Just as Hagatha's face had terrorized her in nightmares when she was a child. Every time she would try to whisk the thought away, back it came. "Why not visit her?" she said to herself.

It didn't help that Cyril was in Chicago performing in a play. Otherwise, he may have been able to talk some sense into her. So, against her better judgment, she began the process of trying to track down the woman who had tried to drown her in the Mississippi River some 50 years ago. With little information to go on, she jumped in her car and headed towards Grand Rapids. Seeking answers to questions, she didn't know if she really wanted.

However, before she got to Grand Rapids, a road sign for Slaughter, Minnesota caught her eye. She knew that her biological father's name was Enoch Slaughter and that he had been the Mayor of a town outside of Grand Rapids. So, it stood to reason that Slaughter must be that town.

As she approached downtown, she spied a giant bronze statue of a man at the entrance to a park. She pulled over, got out of her car, and approached the sculpture. At the foot of the statue was a plaque, which read, “Enoch Slaughter, 1865 – 1918, Founder and Mayor of Slaughter, Minnesota.” It was her father, and she waited for emotions that never came. The image and the information conveyed were just that – information. A part of history that didn’t seem to have any connection to her, even though he obviously did. She got back in her car, thinking that maybe her parents were both dead. Now actually hoping that Hagatha was also deceased. So she could finally stop wondering. Perhaps that is why she and Elsa hadn’t experienced any nightmares for years, she thought.

Assuming no statues had been erected for her mother, she knew that the most reliable place to get information in a small town was at the local diner. So, Hilda pulled up outside the Downtown Diner. However, the thought of eating made her stomach lurch as it was already aflutter from anticipation.

“Excuse me,” Hagatha said to the hostess. “I’m from out of town and was wondering, do you know of a Hagatha Ketchel who lives here?”

The moments between finishing her question and the hostess’s answer seemed to stretch on forever. Meanwhile, Hilda prayed she would receive a negative response or information confirming her mother was dead.

Then with a look as if the hostess wondered why in the world anyone would want this information, she replied.

“Oh, yes. She lives on Tailings Way in a little white house. You can’t miss it.”

The hostess thought about asking if she knew Old Lady Ketchel. And then considered at least warning her that Hagatha didn’t react well to visitors. But ultimately, decided to mind her own business and just held her tongue.

“And how do I best get to Tailings Way?”

“Just continue down Main Street and take a right on Taconite Avenue. Follow it for about a mile. Tailings Way will be on the right."

"Thank you. You've been most helpful," Hilda replied, despite a churning in her stomach that made her feel she might throw up.

"My pleasure," said the hostess, who then called to a couple standing behind Hilda. "Your usual table, Mr. and Mrs. Erickson?"

Hilda managed to get back to her car on wobbly legs. However, she didn't immediately start on her way, unsure whether she had the desire or fortitude to meet her mother.

What would she say? "Hi, Mom, remember me?" Or maybe "Hi mother. I was just in the area and was wondering if you wanted to go swimming with me in the River?"

This was a bad idea, she thought. But now that she was here and knew her mother was still alive, what else could she do? If she just left without seeing her, she'd continue to have questions swirl in her head. Maybe she'd finally get some answers. Maybe Elsa was right. Perhaps the comforting dreams they were experiencing were her mothers' way of making amends for the past. She took in several long, slow, deep breaths. Steeling herself against the war taking place in her stomach. She started the car and followed the directions she was given.

As the hostess had predicted, the small white house on Tailings Way stood out. She parked on the street in front of it and took a few more deep breaths before getting out. She opened the small gate and was about halfway up the walkway when Hagatha burst through the door screaming, broom in hand.

Hilda raised her hands in surrender, hoping this would stop her mother's charge. When it didn't, she turned and ran back the way she came. Once outside the gate, she screamed, "Stop, I'm Hilda, your daughter!"

Hagatha stopped dead in her tracks. Her face grew dark with eyes aflame in rage.

"I have no daughter. Depart from me, you cursed, into the everlasting fire prepared for the devil and his angels."

Hilda wasn't about to argue. She was terrified. All she could imagine was Hagatha casting a spell on her and dying an ugly death. Just like that little boy in the nightmare she and Elsa shared many years ago.

She got in her car and didn't stop until she was safely back in Duluth. Vowing never again to set foot in Slaughter. All her questions had been answered. Her father was dead. And while her mother was alive, she denied having a daughter. So much for the theory that Hagatha was planting favorable dreams to reconcile terrorizing them in the past. No, she was pure evil. And all Hilda could do was hope that her visit wouldn't set off a catastrophic response.

# CHAPTER 66

Elsa and Klaus's reunion following the war was nothing short of white-hot. Their years apart had done nothing to compromise what was a magical connection. In fact, the separation had probably only stoked the flames. Within weeks they were married.

For their honeymoon, they rented a remote cabin on a lake in the Northwoods of Minnesota. Anxious to get away from the hustle and bustle of the city and indulge in each other's company. There they drank in the peace and quiet, broken only by the sounds of nature and their own cries of ecstasy. On their last evening there, lying tangled up in each other by the fireplace, Elsa fell asleep and dreamt. When she awoke, Elsa knew three things – she was pregnant, she would have a baby girl, and they would name her Karen.

"Klaus, I had the most incredible dream," she exclaimed when he stirred in her arms and woke up.

"That you woke up in the arms of a handsome naked man?" he joked.

"Oh, yes, that's incredible too, but no. I dreamt that I was pregnant and that we'd have a baby girl we'd name Karen."

"Well, after this week, I would be surprised if you weren't pregnant," he said smiling.

"What do you think of the name Karen?" she asked excitedly.

"It's very American. I like it. Our German names aren't very popular these days. We will name her Karen if your dream comes true," he replied.

"WHEN OUR dream comes true," she responded, correcting him.

"Yes, you're right. When our dream comes true. Ich liebe dich mein schatz," he said, giving her a kiss.

"I love you too, Klaus," she replied, her eyes brimming with tears of joy.

And nine months later, it came to pass. Elsa delivered a bouncing baby girl who they christened Karen Hilda Garber. In keeping with her dream and a nod to the baby's grandmother and her German heritage.

Elsa and Klaus couldn't have been any happier. So too was the baby's great-grandmother, who from afar smiled and exclaimed, "This is the beginning of the end. We will one day form our alliance. And things that are not yet done will be done. And my counsel shall stand, and I will do all that I intend."

# CHAPTER 67

The Slaughter family was not exempt from the baby boom era. Despite the loss of Eben and the defection of Etan to San Francisco, nine Slaughter heirs were born between 1946 and 1960.

On Enoch Jr.'s side of the family, Enoch III and Margaret gave Enoch IV a baby sister, Anna, in 1951. While Enoch Jr.'s daughter, Eve, married Carl Dinkeldorf and had Alan in 1955.

Esau's daughter, Ester, married Ian Brandon, and she had a son named Lee in 1956. Meanwhile, Esau's only straight son, Eli, married Anika, and they had two sons – Soren in 1958 and Erik in 1960.

Ezra's eldest son, Elijah, married Sonja, who gave birth to Sigmar in 1953. His daughter, Elizabeth, married Adolf Altemeyer, and the two were blessed with Paul in 1956. Finally, Ezra's youngest daughter, Edith, married Earl Briars, and they had a son Robert in 1958, who became known as Bobby.

All told, the families of Enoch Slaughter now numbered 30. Thirty souls Hagatha had to watch as they fulfilled her ex-husband's dream of building a lasting legacy. Of these thirty, 8 were male descendants capable of further expanding on that heritage. By now, Hagatha had made peace with the continued growth of the Slaughter clan. Knowing that not until Bobby Briars grew up and made the mistake of letting her catch him would the dominoes begin to fall in her favor.

In the meantime, she continued to satisfy herself by cobbling together the plan she would eventually unleash. A deadly blueprint whose inception would ironically begin in what would become known as the "Summer of Love."

For sport, Hagatha continued to wield her broom and chase school kids who loitered on her property. And she would occasionally invite some calamity upon the little delinquents that threw rocks at her house or purposefully littered her yard. But for the most part, she isolated herself in her home, pouring over the Bible. Ensuring that those who were players in her final act safely navigated the vagaries of life. On more than one occasion, she had to intervene to save lives, not take them.

Like the time Enoch IV got a severe case of measles complicated by pneumonia when he was 3. The doctor feared the infections might take him despite giving him penicillin which had recently been developed and was being touted as a miracle drug. The doctors' message to Enoch III and Margaret was dire when the penicillin didn't appear to help. But Enoch IV recovered, and his parents sang the praises of penicillin. However, it was Hagatha who saved him from the brink of disaster with a verse from Isaiah.

"I have seen his ways and will heal him. I will also lead him and restore comforts to him and to his mourners."

Then there was the time, as a 12-year-old, that Enoch IV convinced an older boy to let him drive his motorcycle. Enoch IV had always had a fascination for motorbikes. However, his parents were deadset against letting him ride until he was older. Had Hagatha not cast a spell, causing a logging truck to break down short of a curve in the road, the outcome of Enoch IV's ride would have been fatal. He was going too fast when he reached the bend, causing him to drift into the oncoming lane. Fortunately, the logging truck wasn't there, and Enoch IV once again cheated death.

But perhaps the most ironic of interventions that Hagatha made in service to the future was rescuing baby Karen when she was 2. Elsa and Klaus had joined the 1940s and 1950s boom of moving to suburbia. They owned a home just south of Minneapolis in the upper-middle-class neighborhood of Richfield. Karen's personality as an adventurous, free-spirit revealed itself early. The moment she could walk was the moment she felt liberated to explore wherever and whenever she desired. Keeping tabs on her was a full-time job. And Elsa and Klaus did a commendable job, most of the time.

But just before dawn one morning, as Klaus and Elsa slept, Karen escaped from her crib on a mission. It was summer, and something in the neighbor's yard had attracted her interest. You would have thought that the front door would have thwarted her getaway, but Karen was resourceful. First, she pushed an ottoman to the door and clambered up it to be able to reach the doorknob. Then, using her two little hands, managed to turn the knob and disengage the latch. Finally climbing down from her perch, moving the ottoman, and pulling open the door to freedom. Had Klaus or Elsa locked the front door, it may have stopped her. But no one locked their doors in the 1940s.

Likewise, no one in that neighborhood fenced in their yards. Everyone knew their neighbors and property lines were either non-existent or demarcated by a driveway or hedges. So little Karen had no trouble getting to the object of her fascination – an above-ground pool. Her first obstacle was a ladder, which for her was no obstacle at all. Her climbing skills had earned her the nickname "Monkey" from her father. Swimming in 4-feet deep water was an entirely different matter.

Karen fell into the pool with a splash without the faintest clue of how to swim. Immediately, she sank below the surface and swallowed water. She should have died and would have, if not for Hagatha. Who, ever vigilant, cast a spell using another verse from Isaiah.

"When you pass through the waters, I will be with you. And through the rivers, they shall not overflow you. When you walk through the fire, you shall not be burned. Nor shall the flame scorch you."

And miraculously, Karen started flailing her arms and legs until her body rose up off the bottom of the pool and her head broke the surface. Coughing, she clung to the side of the pool until her lungs were clear. And then commenced to swim and splash in the pool until her cries of glee woke the neighbors. To Karen's vehement objections, they extracted her from her watery playground and alerted her parents.

Klaus and Elsa were mortified that she had escaped without their notice but forever grateful that she had somehow survived. Years later, they would tell the story as a source of pride in how precocious and accomplished their daughter was.

Little did they know that Karen's seemingly superhuman abilities emanated from a destructive force. A vicious old woman who had almost made Elsa and Karen's existence impossible many years ago. They say that God works in mysterious ways. However, there was nothing godly about Hagatha Ketchel. And God couldn't be a party to this insanity. No matter how much she read and recited that Bible. She was the Devil incarnate, and to think anything else was pure madness.

# CHAPTER 68

Cyril never realized his childhood dream of acting on Broadway. Instead, he was content to continue his career at the Theatre in Duluth, where he had met Hilda. However, he would occasionally accept invitations to perform in theatre productions in the Twin Cities and Chicago. Hilda often accompanying him on these occasions. This was especially the case with his guest appearances in the Twin Cities. Allowing Hilda to spend time with Elsa, Klaus, and most importantly, her granddaughter, Karen. And, of course, Cyril and Hilda continued to make their annual treks to New York City.

Anyone who knew Hilda and Cyril would agree that their's was a fairytale romance. However, that was about to change. As he had done countless times before, Cyril was walking to the theatre to prepare for an evening production. It was a cold and blustery winter day, which was more the rule than the exception for the season. Unfortunately, on this occasion, Cyril slipped on a patch of ice partially covered by snow. His hip and his head hit the sidewalk with a resounding crack. It was fortunate that someone witnessed his fall and called for help.

Hilda heard the ambulance siren but thought nothing of it. Instead, she put on her favorite phonograph record and started to clean the house. She was dancing to her favorite song, "Nothing Could Be Sweeter," while dusting the furniture when the phone rang.

"Mrs. Frost, we have your husband here at the hospital. Unfortunately, he had a fall, and it would be best for you to come quickly."

The last word in her sentence is what paralyzed Hilda with fear. Not just come to the hospital, but come quickly. She somehow got in the car and drove to the hospital. Although, to this day, she doesn't even recall how she got there.

When she got to the hospital, it was too late. Hilda didn't hear anything after the doctor said, "I'm sorry, Mrs. Frost, but." The ground seemed to disappear under her feet as she crumbled to the floor in tears. Her beloved partner of 43 years was gone. Leaving a chasm in her chest where once her heart had been.

Cyril died of an intracranial hemorrhage, not that it mattered to Hilda. After Cyril died, it was as if Hilda died too. Nothing mattered anymore. She didn't play her music, didn't dance, didn't eat, didn't leave the house, and didn't even answer the phone. It was for this reason that Elsa and Karen showed up on her doorstep one day. They were lucky she even answered the door.

"Mother, you look awful. Why haven't you been answering your phone? I've tried to call you at least a dozen times," Elsa chided when her mother opened the door.

Hilda didn't even respond. She just turned and trudged back into the house.

"Aren't you even going to talk to me?" Elsa asked, following her into the house.

"Why?"

"Why? Because I'm your daughter and your granddaughter is here too. We've been worried sick about you. Haven't we, dear?" Elsa said, looking to Karen, who nodded in agreement.

"What's the use? My life is over. You both have something to live for. I don't."

"Don't be ridiculous, mother. I know you miss him, but what about us?"

"Miss him? Is that what you think this is? That I just miss him? You have no idea what he meant to me."

"Of course I don't, mother. But I bet you mean as much to your granddaughter and me as he meant to you," Elsa countered.

"Yeah, I want to grow up and be just like you, Grams," Karen added.

"Oh, don't talk nonsense, child. Why would you want to grow up like me?"

"Because you're groovy. Everybody my age talks about being free, loving who they want to love, and doing whatever they want to do. And you've done it. You and Grandpa traveled all over the place, and you two were always singing and dancing. I never saw you like this. You were always so happy."

"I'm groovy, huh? Well, that's a new one on me. Your Grandpa used to say I was the bee's knees back in the 1920s."

"See," Karen replied. "Even he knew you were groovy way back then. So please don't be sad, Grams."

"It's hard not to be sad, dear. We were together for so long, and I never even got to say goodbye. I didn't get there in time, and he died alone."

"I'm sure he didn't feel alone. He was thinking of you, Grams," Karen replied. "When was Grandpa not thinking of you? He knows you were with him. You were always with him."

"You know, for a 14-year-old kid, you're pretty smart," Hilda responded as a tear escaped down her cheek. Then wiped it away and wrapped her arms around Karen. "I'm pretty lucky to have a granddaughter like you."

"Thanks, Grams," Karen blushed.

And that interaction and visit helped pull Hilda out of her dark place and back into the light. Elsa went grocery shopping, and Karen helped Hilda start to make a dent in cleaning the house that had been neglected for weeks. At one point, Karen turned on the phonograph and played the record that was on the turntable. As the music began to play, Hilda came out of the next room in tears.

"What's the matter, Grams? I thought this would help cheer you up," Karen said innocently above the music.

"That's the record that was playing when I got the call about Grandpa, honey. It was our favorite record. We used to dance to it all the time," she sniffled.

"I'm sorry. I didn't know," she replied as tears came to her eyes.

"Oh, don't you start crying now. Come on, let's dance," Hilda said, putting down her dust rag.

And the two danced until their tears were transformed into laughter. It was a special moment. One Karen would recall nearly 10 years later that would help convince her to accept a job at Slaughter Elementary. But now, it just served to strengthen their connection and pull Hilda out of the quagmire of despair she was wallowing in.

Yes, it was another moment that was manufactured by Hagatha Ketchel. A despicably tender and poignant moment that was necessary to ensure the death and destruction to come. Lending a whole new meaning to the Devil's in the details.

# CHAPTER 69

Elsa also had a moment with her mother during their visit to pull her out of her doldrums. This over coffee the following morning while Karen slept in until noon as teens are apt to do.

"Have you had any bad dreams?" Elsa asked, stirring creamer into her coffee.

"You mean, other than waking up in an empty bed?" Hilda replied.

"You know what I mean, Mother. Has Hagatha been haunting you?"

"No, surprisingly. Have you had any nightmares?"

"No, I haven't."

"Well, thank God. That's the last thing we need. Has Karen ever had any nightmares?"

"No, but I'm almost too frightened to admit that or think she won't ever have them. Like if I do, I'll jinx her."

"I understand. But I can't even remember the last nightmare I had. Can you?"

"Hmm, no, it's been a while."

"Oh, now I remember," Hilda exclaimed after a moment. "It was that little boy who she caught that turned into ashes."

"Yes, I think you're right. Maybe she got tired of scaring us with her crazy, gruesome made-up stories."

"I'm not sure they were made-up, but I'm glad we haven't had any."

"You actually think that some of those were real events?" Elsa asked incredulously.

"Well, it's not like we've researched them. Who knows?" Hilda replied.

And once again, one of their conversations planted a seed in Hilda's head that would ultimately sprout. Compelling her to determine if their nightmares had any basis in fact.

Two weeks later, after many internal battles weighing the pros and cons of investigating their nightmares, Hilda got into her car and drove to Grand Rapids. Her only misgiving was the fear of learning that their nightmares were actual events perpetrated by her mother. But the pull of the possibility that they were fictional was too strong. Knowing they were made-up horror stories would put her mind at ease.

The only nightmare to which Hilda could affix a date with any specificity was of the little boy who disintegrated after being in Hagatha's clutches. Elsa was 13, meaning it was 1933 when they had this nightmare. Even if Slaughter, Minnesota, had records from 1933, Hilda was not about to risk going back there. Instead, her destination was the Grand Rapids Public Library to review archived copies of the local newspaper – the Grand Rapids Herald.

Little did Hilda know that she was reprising what Charles Shepherd, her adoptive father, had done 65 years earlier. He had researched archived copies of the newspaper to learn the identity of Hilda's biological parents. Although she was known as Dori then. That effort had failed but ultimately led Charles and Evelyn to St. Joseph's Church, where they found the answers they were looking for.

Sitting in almost the same spot as Charles had, Hilda

combed through the obituaries of 1933, looking for any young male child that had died of strange circumstances. While libraries in the Twin Cities and Duluth had started to microfilm newspapers and other old records, such was not the case at the Grand Rapids Library. Consequently, it was slow going as Hilda had to go through archived copies of the actual newspaper.

Unfortunately, she started reviewing newspaper editions from the end of 1933 backward in time. Had she chosen to start from the beginning of the year on, she would have found her answer more quickly. Thus, she was only through the last half of the year with no results when the Librarian informed her it was closing time. She hadn't anticipated staying overnight but took a hotel room, hoping to get an early start the next day.

But morning didn't come quickly. Hilda was awakened in the night by a brief but startling vision. She saw Hagatha's face, and all she said was, "O you of little faith, why did you doubt?" But it was enough to keep Hilda from going back to sleep. Suddenly, she was worried that digging into the past and her close proximity to Hagatha had reawakened her haunting ways. She forced herself to wait until daybreak to call Elsa. When she answered, Hilda could tell by her daughter's voice that something was not right.

"Elsa, is something wrong?" she asked, hoping that maybe she had just woken her up.

"You had the nightmare too, didn't you? That's why you're calling me, isn't it?"

"I'm sorry. I think I may have caused it," Hilda replied.

"What did you do?"

"I'm in Grand Rapids researching whether that little boy we saw die was real."

"Mother, you should have left well enough alone."

"I know, I know, but our conversation a couple of weeks ago got me thinking."

"That was your first mistake. What do you think it means? You of little faith," Elsa asked.

"I have no idea. But how can she think I should have faith in her when all she's ever done is try to drown me and plague me with nightmares? I have every reason to doubt her!"

"That's for sure. Have you learned anything yet from your research?" Elsa asked, shifting the conversation.

"Nothing yet. I'm going back to the library soon."

"Are you sure that's a good idea?"

"No, but if I've stirred up the hornet's nest already, there's no reason not to finish what I started."

"Well, I hope you're right. Let me know what you find. And be careful!"

"I will."

Hilda got to the library just as it was opening and commenced her search. When review of the June and May obituaries produced nothing of note, doubt crept in. When it did, all she could think about were the words Hagatha had uttered, "O you of little faith, why did you doubt?" Surely the nightmare couldn't have been a foreshadowing of the doubt she now felt, could it?

She tried to erase the image of Hagatha and the words echoing in her head and continued on. Until that is, she got to Thursday, April 20, 1933. There in black and white read, "Eben Slaughter, 7-years-old, son of Enoch Jr. and Mary Slaughter. Succumbed to leprosy." Hilda didn't know much about leprosy, except that it was rare, caused growths on the skin, and ultimately the reabsorption or shedding of body parts. In other words, almost exactly what they saw in the nightmare. Eben's skin erupting in ulcers and boils and disintegrating before their eyes.

Forcing Hilda to wrestle with a horrific truth – her mother was more evil than she imagined. And that her little research junket to Grand Rapids had reawakened Hagatha's visitations in the night only made this horrific truth more terrifying.

She didn't even take the time to call Elsa about her findings until she was back in Duluth. So intent was Hilda to put greater distance between her and the malicious she-devil. But no expanse away from Hagatha was far enough. If Hagatha could conjure you up, you were within easy reach.

# CHAPTER 70

Karen played a pivotal role in helping Grandma Hilda recover from her loss, but that is not to say she didn't suffer the typical turbulence of being a teenager. Combine that adolescent angst with one of the most tumultuous and consequential decades in U.S. history, and you have a potent recipe for producing behavior that didn't just push the boundaries. It obliterated them.

How could anyone, especially an impressionable and idealistic young woman, not be influenced by the era of rock-and-roll, the Vietnam War, hippies, drugs, civil rights, sit-ins, flower power, race riots, free love, Woodstock, women's liberation, the space race, and the assassinations of John and Bobby Kennedy, and Martin Luther King, Jr.? It was as if the country was experiencing its own adolescent rebellion along with Karen. And both were happy to give the finger to anything that had to do with maintaining the status quo.

When Elsa and Klaus's efforts to keep tight reins on Karen failed, and she threatened to run away and join a commune, they were forced to adjust their parenting strategy. Subsequently giving their daughter more latitude than was comfortable so as not to lose her altogether.

As it turns out, giving Karen more freedom didn't result in the catastrophe that Elsa and Klaus feared. Oh, they had more than their fair share of hand-wringing sleepless nights.

But, when faced with responsibility for her own actions, rather than reacting to her parents' prohibitions, it regulated just how far she was willing to go. That is not to say she didn't drink alcohol, experiment with drugs, participate in civil disobedience, or have sex – she did. And some nights, she didn't even come home. But, whether it was the values her parents had instilled, Hagatha's protective oversight, or dumb luck, Karen survived her most egregious and high-risk behaviors. Then again, what teen who survived the 1960s doesn't occasionally look back and say to themselves, "I'm lucky I'm alive."

Karen wore hip-hugger bell-bottom jeans, tie-dye shirts, mini-skirts, and go-go boots, as was the fashion of the day. Marijuana would usually make her reflective and philosophical. Drinking alcohol would make her promiscuous, sad, and sick in that order. Neither she nor her sexual partners used protection, and somehow she avoided getting pregnant. She had a lesbian encounter when she and her best friend tried some magic mushrooms. They never talked about it afterward, both not sure if it had been real or imagined, despite waking up naked in bed together the following morning.

And somehow, amid all of this personal and societal upheaval, Karen managed to be one of the top students in her high school class. When it came to answering the age-old question of "What do you want to be when you grow up?" she surprised everyone, including herself.

"I want to be a teacher," she replied to her guidance counselor. Not sure how those words had spilled out from her mouth.

"Really?" the guidance counselor asked. "I would have thought you'd want to be more of a trailblazer, like a doctor or a lawyer, for example. You have the smarts and the grades to get into the best colleges. Are you sure you want to be a teacher?"

"Yes, I'm positive," she countered. Once again, feeling like she wasn't in command of what she verbalized but oddly at ease with it.

Nothing in Karen's past would have given anyone a clue she had an interest or aptitude for teaching. In fact, it was precisely the type of career that she had protested against as society's way of keeping women in thankless, low-paying jobs. While men were offered more prestigious, high-paying positions.

But there was a power at work that superseded any of Karen's principles or desires concerning her future. The future, in fact, was not hers to dictate. Hagatha had been piloting Karen's course for nearly two decades. And now she was on final approach, and Hagatha was determined to land her in Slaughter, Minnesota, at the appointed arrival date and time.

# CHAPTER 71

Slaughter, Minnesota, and most of its residents, including Enoch IV, were somewhat insulated from the societal and cultural upheavals of the 1960s. Sure, a few kids grew their hair longer and adopted some of the vernacular of the time. And you couldn't prevent the rock-and-roll that played on the radio stations. But unless you did your clothes shopping in Duluth or the Twin Cities, it was nearly impossible to lay your hands on the so-called trendy 60s fashions. And the news of the war, protests, and riots were obviously topics of discussion. But most often talked about in terms of how fortunate Slaughter was not to be a party to the demise of good, old-fashioned conservative values.

However, Enoch IV, now a teenager, had grown into a rebel and a risk-taker. It was almost as if surviving death as a child made him feel invincible. He sought out dangerous things to do, just to feel alive. One day it would be diving off a cliff into a lake. Another day it would be surreptitiously riding a friends' motorcycle at top speed. He even played fast and loose with the girls that struck his fancy. Dating several girls at a time and somehow managing to keep them all satisfied and at bay while he continued to play the field. In short, he was Hagatha's worst nightmare. Demanding so much of her attention that she wondered if she would ever be able to get him to that fateful day when he would meet her great-granddaughter.

And when it came time to get a job, Enoch IV was torn between the two most dangerous occupations in the area – logging and mining. Eventually settling on mining, not so much for the risks but for the opportunity to operate the heavy equipment. Approaching his birthday, he begged and pleaded for his parents to buy him a motorcycle. Reasoning that he needed to have a way to get to work.

"What are you going to do in the winter?" his father, Enoch III, asked, finding the flaw in his son's logic.

"I'll save up and buy a car or a truck by winter," he argued.

"How about we buy you a car, and you save up for a motorcycle?" Enoch III countered.

"What kind of car?"

"What do you want?" Enoch III asked, thinking any car was better and safer than a motorcycle.

"I want that new Ford sportscar?"

"The Ford Mustang?" Enoch III asked incredulously.

"Yeah, the fastback," his son replied. "Red," he added.

Enoch III hadn't counted on his son knowing about the V-8, 225-horse power muscle car priced at $2,700. But, now backed into a corner, he had no choice but to fulfill his son's wishes. Which wasn't surprising. All of Enoch's namesakes down through the years were spoiled and got preferential treatment.

How Enoch IV drove his new car made it marginally safer than driving a motorcycle. But it was pedestrians crossing the streets who were most in danger as he tore around town. Fortunately, he eventually modified the muffler, giving the car a distinct and loud growl, which gave people fair warning of his approach so they could clear the streets.

He was working at the Taconite Plant in Hibbing, a good 45-minute drive from Slaughter. Which made U.S. Highway 169 to and from work his racetrack. Each trip became an exciting opportunity to set a new personal best for speed and time. The two-lane highway was lightly traveled in the early morning, making his trip to Hibbing generally faster than the return trip in the late afternoons. However, Enoch IV liked the exhilaration of passing vehicles while dodging the oncoming traffic. More than a few times, Hagatha had to intervene to ensure he narrowly avoided head-on collisions. But instead of discouraging him, these close calls only amped up his adrenaline and made him bolder. Add a couple of speeding citations from the State Highway Patrol, and now the challenge grew even more exciting.

But Hagatha was not going to stand for this day-in, day-out recklessness. So on one of his return trips, she produced a brief but blinding snow squall as he rounded a bend at breakneck speed. Besides being unable to see the road, controlling the rear-wheel-drive Mustang was virtually impossible as it hit a patch of snow and ice. It did a 360 before launching off the road, narrowly missing the guard rail and clipping some trees before crashing into Snowball Lake. Enoch IV got away with minor injuries, but his Mustang was a total loss.

This time Enoch III put his foot down and, without consulting his son, bought him a used 1963 Chevy K10 Pickup in Brigade Blue. Fast it was not, but because it was a 4-wheel-drive, it could conquer anything the Minnesota winters threw at it. Enoch IV wasn't happy, but he wasn't in a position to argue.

Suffice to say, Enoch IV now drove a safer vehicle, and Hagatha didn't have to be quite as vigilant.

# CHAPTER 72

Elsa and Klaus were delighted when their daughter informed them that she would be attending the University of Minnesota to pursue her teaching certification. Which was a far cry from the previous callings she expressed interest in that horrified her parents, like joining the Peace Corp and working in a third-world country. Or moving to California and living in a commune to "find herself," as she had put it.

"That's wonderful, honey," Elsa gushed, biting her tongue to keep from disparaging her daughter's earlier life plans. "It will be nice having you home for a few more years."

"Oh, I'm not staying here. I'm going to stay on campus."

"Why would you do that when you have a perfectly nice place here and can stay for free?"

"No offense, Mom, but I want to be closer to where the action is," Karen exclaimed.

"Action? What action?"

"Clubs, concerts, hanging out with classmates. You know, like having fun."

All Elsa could picture was her daughter amid wild orgies and drug-addled concert-goers, but she had learned the hard way. Every time she expressed her fears and misgivings, she got the same reaction. First, the eye-roll, followed by, "Oh,

Mom. You worry too much." So she settled on the next best thing she could think of that hopefully wouldn't trigger an exasperated reaction from her daughter.

"Well, don't forget you're there to get an education and become a teacher."

"I know, Mom," Karen replied, only moderately annoyed.

So Sanford Hall on the University of Minnesota's campus became Karen's new abode that September – her and about 400 other first-year students. To Elsa, Karen's 133-square foot room without a private bathroom looked like a prison cell. And the community bathroom shared by 11 other students seemed unconscionable. But to Karen, the room felt like a cozy little haven amid a world of possibilities.

"I can't believe you'd want to live here instead of at home," Elsa lamented.

"Oh, Mom, it's not so bad. It's just a place to sleep. There are lounges, study rooms, a dining hall, a laundry room, and even a game room. What more do I need?"

"Yes, but you have to share them with hundreds of other people you don't even know."

"It will be fine, Mom. It will make it easier to make friends."

"If you say so. Just know you can come home anytime you want."

"Thanks, Mom. Don't worry. If this was as bad as you make it out to be, all these kids wouldn't be here. This is what college is all about," she replied as if she was already a grizzled college veteran.

"I wouldn't know, and I'm glad I never had to find out," her mother said with a look of disgust.

"Oh, Mom, don't be such a downer. This is going to be a blast."

But Sanford Hall wasn't what had Karen so upbeat. It was

what lay outside the walls of the residence that held all the mystery and wonder. So after her mother left and she was settled into her room, she intended to go exploring. Apparently, some of her neighbors were similarly inclined.

"Hi, I'm Molly," called a tall, skinny blond girl who was standing in the hall outside Karen's room. "A couple of us are going to bug out to Dinkytown. Do you want to hang with us?"

"Dinkytown?" Karen asked, confused.

"Yeah, it's fab. Come with us. You'll dig it."

"Okay, cool. Thanks. I'm Karen."

And just like that, Karen was on her way to making friends. And uncovering the mysteries of a unique little corner of the world named Dinkytown. Passing by coffee shops and a bookstore before browsing through a record store and a couple of shops selling everything from vintage clothing to hippy-chic. There was even an incense and smoke shop – supposedly selling paraphernalia for discriminating tobacco-smokers. Finally, they ended up at The Scholar, a little café with a small stage where mostly wannabe musicians performed with the occasional notable artist making an appearance.

"Did you know that Bob Dylan played here?" Molly asked, flipping her long blond hair out of her face.

"Far out, that must have been boss," replied a short and sturdy young lady named Doris with mousey brown hair.

"How did you know about Dinkytown?" Karen asked.

"Oh, I grew up here," Molly replied. "Well, in St. Paul, actually. But there's nothing to do in St. Paul, so I used to come over here. So, where are you from?"

"Richfield. Where are you from, Doris?"

"Worthington," Doris replied pridefully.

"Worthington? Where the hell is that?" Molly asked.

"It's in the Southwest corner of the State. About an hour

from Sioux Falls."

"Like nowheresville, it sounds like," Molly replied.

"Oh, it isn't that bad. Hanging out at Lake Okabena was fab."

Molly looked at Doris as if she had two heads.

"Girl, if the best thing about where you're from in Minnesota is that it had a lake, you're in some serious need of entertainment. You can't throw a rock in this State without hitting a lake."

"I know, but," Doris attempted to protest but was cut off.

"No buts, Doris. I've now taken it as my personal responsibility to show you two what a good time really is. Let's go to Bridgeman's."

So Doris and Karen followed Molly to the southeast corner of 4th Street and 14th Avenue and entered Bridgeman's – an ice cream shop. And while the ice cream sundaes they ordered were phenomenal, it was the buzz and the energy of the patrons, nearly all college-age, that made the place electric. But for Karen, what really drew her attention was the young man who had served them – his nametag announcing his name as Tad.

"What's with you, Karen?" Molly asked as Karen was gazing off in the distance.

"Earth to Karen," Molly announced when Karen didn't respond.

"Oh, I'm sorry, I was just," she began, only to be interrupted by Molly.

"You were just drooling over that hunk who served you. What kind of name is Tad anyways?

"I don't care. I'll return this sundae and take a bite of him instead," Karen replied salaciously.

"Oh, listen to you. Suburban girl's all hot and bothered and wants to make the soda jerk her old man." Molly taunted.

Karen blushed.

"I wouldn't kick him out of bed for eating crackers," Doris remarked before taking a bite of her sundae.

"Jeez, you guys don't get out much, do you? I have to pee," Molly said, getting up from the table.

"I'll go with you," Doris chimed, tearing herself away from her half-eaten dessert.

"Try not to drool all over the table while we're gone, Karen," Molly smiled.

Karen, who had hardly touched her ice cream, tried to make a dent in it to keep from staring at Tad. Only to have someone ask her a question.

"Is there something wrong with your sundae?"

She looked up to see Tad standing at her table.

"No, no, it's fine," Karen replied, flustered.

"Because if you don't like it, I'll be happy to make you something else," he added.

"No, really, I was just talking with my girlfriends and didn't have a chance to eat it. It's great, I'm sure."

"Okay. I'm Tad, by the way," he said.

"I know," Karen blushed.

"Did I introduce myself before? I do that sometimes."

"No, it's the ah, uh," she pointed to his nametag.

"Oh, right. I forget I'm wearing this thing. What's your name?"

"Karen," she replied shyly.

"Pleased to meet you, Karen. Do you go to the U like 99% of everyone in here?"

"I do. Well, actually, I just moved here. So it will be my first year."

"That's great. What are you studying?"

"I'm studying to become a teacher. Do you go to the U?"

"Yep, I'm in my third year. I'm studying the performing arts."

"Oh, like acting in theatres? My grandpa was an actor. I used to go and see him when he came to town," Karen brightened at the memory.

"Cool. I've been to a lot of plays at the Guthrie. Death of a Salesman, Hamlet, A Christmas Carol."

"You saw A Christmas Carol? Like two years ago?" Karen asked excitedly.

"Yeah, why? Did you see it too?"

"Yes, and my grandpa played Ebenezer Scrooge!"

"Your grandpa is Cyril Frost? I saw him. He was great!" Tad exclaimed, stunned at the coincidence.

"Oh my God! You remembered his name? And we might have been there at the same time," Karen replied, equally shocked.

"Wow, small world. What's your grandpa doing now?"

Karen's moment of joy screeched to a halt, and Tad could tell by the sudden change in her expression that his question had caused her pain.

"I'm sorry," he said before she could even answer. "I didn't mean to upset you."

"That's okay, how would you know? He died last year."

"I'm really sorry to hear that, Karen. Hey, I better get back to the counter before I lose my job. But would you consider going to see a play with me next week? I have tickets to see Shakespeare's As You Like It."

"I'd love to," she replied, her sadness suddenly displaced

again by joy.

And just as her grandmother and mother had experienced before her, Karen experienced that rare magical connection that sometimes happens between two people. When the sun, moon, and stars all miraculously and mysteriously seem to align.

When Molly and Doris got back to the table, there was no mistaking that Karen had experienced a transformational moment.

"What's gotten into you?" Molly asked.

Karen's smile could have lit up the deepest, darkest night. And before she could say anything, Molly knew.

"Oh, never mind, I know exactly what's gotten into you."

# CHAPTER 73

The pressure of bearing the name Enoch Slaughter, even when you're the fourth iteration, is intense. So while Enoch IV was content to sow his wild oats, his father had other ideas and expectations.

"When are you finally going to settle down and give your mother and me a grandson?"

"Jeez, Dad, I'm only 19 years old. Can't I have a little fun?"

"It looks to me like you've had quite a bit of fun. You know, you have other responsibilities."

"I know, I know," he replied exasperated. "Get married. Have a son. Name him Enoch. Carry on the family name. I've heard it a million times."

"Well, then, what are you waiting for? Get to it," his father encouraged.

"What's the rush? How old were you when you got married?"

"That's not the point."

"It is the point. Weren't you like 23 when you married Mom?"

"Those were different times. This is a new age. Everything is being done sooner, faster. So stop sticking it in anything that moves. It's time to find a good girl and get serious. How about that McMaster girl?"

"Dawn McMaster? That redheaded checkout girl at McMaster's Grocery store?"

"Yeah, she's gorgeous. She seems smart and friendly. And let's just say she has better melons than their store's produce section," he said with a smirk.

"Jeez, Dad, don't be disgusting. She's like, what? Sixteen?"

"I speak the truth. And besides, your mother was 17 when I married her. So better get crackin' before someone else picks those melons, son."

Despite his father's creepy fascination with Dawn McMaster's womanly orbs, Enoch IV took his advice. Visiting the store on three consecutive days.

"Well, hi again," Dawn said enthusiastically when she saw him. "You've been here more this week than in the previous month."

"Yeah, I keep forgetting stuff," Enoch IV said bashfully.

The real reason being he was trying to get up the nerve to ask her out. Something about her made him uncharacteristically timid. He'd see her flaming red hair, bright green eyes, and incandescent smile set in her face of pure porcelain skin and choke on his words. It was as if she was some untouchable goddess he didn't deserve.

"You should make yourself a shopping list. Not that I mind seeing you," she said, her eyes smoldering with desire.

"You like seeing me?" he asked. Then immediately wondered why he had said that out loud.

"Well, technically, I said I don't mind seeing you. But I'd go as far as like," she laughed and smiled.

"Would you go as far as to go out with me some time?"

"Is that why you're in here for the third day in a row? You wanted to ask me out?"

"Well, ah, yeah," he said, blushing.

"So you don't really need these groceries, do you?"

"No, but I want to go out with you," he smiled.

"Are you sure you don't have to come back a fourth time?" she grinned, knowing she was now just stringing him along.

"I'm positive," he replied, anxious for her answer.

"Well, I guess they do say that the third time's the charm. So I'd be happy to go out with you."

And to his father's credit, Enoch IV found that Dawn was everything he had said, gorgeous, intelligent, friendly, well-endowed, and unclaimed.

While Dawn's parents William and Trisha McMaster, supported their relationship, it wasn't without one big reservation – the double-edged sword of associating with the Slaughters. On the one hand, they had power, privilege, and wealth. Which was all well and good if you remained on their good side. But woe to the individual or family that disappointed the Slaughters. So as long as the relationship between their daughter and Enoch IV was satisfactory, they were safe. Knowing that if the relationship went south, it could spell doom for their store and their time calling Slaughter home.

One other person in Slaughter had a big reservation about Enoch IV and Dawn's relationship. And she was not about to sit still and watch it blossom.

# CHAPTER 74

Karen didn't wind up spending much time in her 10 by 13-foot dorm room after all. Her relationship with Thaddeus "Tad" Searmont quickly flourished. And following their date to see the Shakespeare play, she became almost a permanent fixture at the off-campus house that Tad and two of his friends had rented. The only times Karen would spend in her dorm room were on those evenings before she had an early morning class – which was rare.

When they weren't in class, they hit the town. Going to plays, movies, concerts, or clubs to go dancing. Other times they'd go swimming or have picnics at one of the many lakes in and around the Twin Cities. They saw the Beach Boys at the Minneapolis Auditorium. And even saw The Beatles at Metropolitan Stadium. But most of the time, they were just content to hang out at Tad's house. Karen would help him learn his lines by reading from the scripts he was given, and they'd throw occasional parties for their friends and classmates.

As good as Tad and Karen's relationship was, she was hesitant to tell her mother about it. Fearful that doing so may jinx the relationship. Or, more likely, that she'd insist on meeting him. Elsa was the classic worrying mother who needed frequent reassurance that her daughter was safe and doing well. And Karen just wasn't ready to subject Tad or their relationship to that kind of pressure.

The fact that Karen was rarely at the dorm when her mother called didn't help. There was one phone in the hallway, shared by all the students. Karen had been careful to tell her dorm mates not to tell her mother about her boyfriend, but one of her neighbors slipped up on one occasion. The following morning, when Karen arrived at the dorm to get ready for classes, her mother was standing outside her door.

"Mom, what are you doing here?"

"Waiting for you. Where have you been? At your boyfriend's place?"

"Ah, yeah. How did you know?" she said, caught off guard and unable to come up with an alternate alibi.

"One of your friends told me when I called last night. Why haven't I heard about this boyfriend," she said, spitting out the word boyfriend as if it was a dirty word.

"I was going to tell you," Karen began.

"When Karen?" her mother exploded. "What? Am I not important enough to know about your life? Is he some kind of drugged-out hippy?"

"No, Mom. He's not some drugged-out hippy. His name is Tad, and he treats me like I'm royalty. He's studying to be an actor, like Grandpa," she blurted out angrily as tears came to her eyes.

"Oh, honey, I'm sorry. I was just so worried," her mother backpedaled, seeing she had upset her and misread the situation. "Forgive me," she said as she wrapped her arms around her daughter.

"Why don't you trust me?" Karen snuffled. "Why would you think I'd fall in love with some low-life?"

"You're in love with him?" her mother said in shock.

"Yes, Mom. I've been seeing him for almost 6 months. He's a Junior and rents a nice house with two of his friends. That's where I was. Now, can I get ready for class? I promise I'll bring him over to meet you soon, okay?"

Her mother relented and gave her another hug and apology before leaving. The cat was now out of the bag, and it somehow tarnished the shine on her relationship with Tad. Something about having to subject Tad to her mother's judgment didn't sit well with her. Now every conversation she'd have with her mother would undoubtedly include a question and an assessment of the health of her relationship with Tad. Followed closely by her judgment, whether Karen wanted it or not. Relationships were difficult enough without all the outside voices offering their unsolicited opinions. Karen loved her mother and knew that she meant well. But this was her life and her relationship, and she wanted complete control of the wheel.

If only life and relationships were that easy. But unbeknownst to Karen, her mother wasn't even in the car, let alone have her hands on the steering wheel. No, her life was being piloted by a much more invasive and controlling entity. And that individual was about to make an indelible mark on Karen's life and destiny.

# CHAPTER 75

Enoch IV's relationship with Dawn radically changed his behavior. And in most people's eyes, including his parents, this was a welcome change for the better. Instead of the wild and crazy young buck speeding through town seeking new adventures or another revolving-door romantic conquest, he settled down. Yielding to Dawn's decidedly more domestic interests and pursuits.

She liked to read, sew, do jigsaw puzzles, play board games, and watch TV. But just because she was a homebody didn't mean she wasn't in tune with the times. Her favorite book was The Feminine Mystique, and she had strong opinions on equal rights for women.

As she still lived at home with her parents, Enoch IV often found himself at her house under the watchful eye of her parents. On occasion, Dawn would come to Enoch IV's parent's home for dinner. And on rare occasions, Dawn's parents would have an outside meeting and leave them alone in the house. Allowing them the opportunity to make out.

The first few times they were alone, Dawn set strict rules of hugging and lip kissing only. Enoch would invariably try to push those boundaries, but she deftly and firmly fended him off. It was an exercise in restraint that Enoch IV wasn't used to, and it tested him mightily.

Just as he was near the end of his rope and beginning to

think that perhaps Dawn was frigid, she loosened the rules. No, a more accurate description would be that she threw the rulebook out the window. Before he knew what was happening, she was all over him, like some wild woman. Suffice to say, Dawn was the furthest thing from frigid and even encouraged Enoch to do a few things he hadn't ever thought about or tried before. All he could think was that if this is what a liberated 1960s woman was all about, he was liberation's biggest fan.

The following day, Enoch IV approached his father, flush with excitement.

"Dad, I want to ask Dawn to marry me, but I don't know where we will live."

"Well, that's great news, son! I told you she was a keeper."

"Yeah, but I don't want to be married and living at her parent's house."

"Have you saved any money to buy a house?" his father asked.

"A little," he replied, which was a lie as he had hoped to use what little savings he had to buy a motorcycle.

"And have you bought her an engagement ring yet?"

"No," he said sheepishly, suddenly realizing he hadn't tallied up the cost of his grand plans.

But as was so often the case, his father baled him out.

"Well, I'll be happy to help you out. But you'll have to put up all your savings."

"Yes, sir," he said dejectedly.

"Marriage and buying a house are big responsibilities, son. It's time you learn the value of a dollar and pitch in. Your mother and I can't pay your way forever."

"I know," he replied. Then, thinking about all the money he had foolishly burned through modifying his Mustang, fixing up his truck, and on girls before he met Dawn.

"Have you decided where and when you'll propose?"

His face brightened. Happy to be able to talk about something other than his sorry financial status.

"Yeah, I was going to take her to Lover's Leap at Canisteo and propose there."

"How appropriate. You're not going to actually leap, are you?" his father asked.

"No. It's just a pretty spot, and I thought she might like it."

Canisteo was a large and deep pit lake formed from the inactive Canisteo iron ore mine pit northeast of Slaughter. Lover's Leap was what locals had named an outcropping from which brave or foolish souls would jump and plunge 60-feet into the water. Enoch IV had done the leap several times. And as long as the water levels were high, this didn't pose too great a risk. However, a few kids over the years had lost their lives or been paralyzed from leaps when the water was shallow, or they failed to jump out far enough from the edge.

"Have you asked her father for her hand in marriage?" his father asked.

"What? People don't really do that anymore, do they?"

"Well, when Anna's older and some guy wants to marry her, he damn well better ask me," Enoch III blustered, referencing his 13-year-old daughter.

"I guess I could," he replied, his tone betraying a lack of commitment.

"No guessing about it. Just do it. He'll appreciate and respect you for it."

"Okay."

And in the ensuing days, Enoch IV bought a ring and met with Dawn's father. As his father had predicted, William McMaster reacted favorably when Enoch IV stammered through his request for permission to marry his daughter.

"Well, that's mighty mature of you, young man. And not easy to do. I know, I had to do it myself to marry Dawn's mother. Dawn's never been more content, and I hope the two of you have a long and happy life together. You have my permission."

"Thank you, sir. I promise to do my best to keep her happy."

When the day finally came for Enoch IV to pop the question, he was filled with so much nervous energy he couldn't sit still.

"What's with you? You're acting like you have ants in your pants," Dawn said as they were sitting at the dining room table doing a 1,000 piece jigsaw puzzle of the Golden Gate bridge.

"I think I just need to get out, take a walk, and get some fresh air. Let's take a break. I know a perfect spot to take a little hike."

"But we haven't even finished assembling the border," she protested.

"We'll do it when we come back," he countered.

"Oh, all right," she said reluctantly. "But I don't want to be gone long."

She told her parents, and Dawn headed for the door. Mr. McMaster gave Enoch IV a wink and silently mouthed, "Good luck."

Twenty minutes later, they were hiking up the path to Lover's Leap. Dawn had never been to Canisteo. But it seemed like the marriage proposal gods were all working in Enochs' favor as the sun began to descend, creating a brilliant palette of colors on the horizon.

"Oh, Enoch, it's so beautiful here," she gushed as they crested the top of the path. "How did you know about this?"

"I used to come here in the summer and jump into the lake."

“From here? That’s crazy. You could have killed yourself.”

“Yes, I know. It was crazy. But you want to know something that isn’t crazy?” he asked.

“What?” she asked in anticipation.

Enoch bent down on one knee, reached into his pocket, and as he started to pull the engagement ring out, he began.

“Dawn McMaster, you are God’s most beautiful creation, and I want to spend the rest of my life loving you. Will you marry me?” he asked, holding the ring out for her to see.

She was so shocked that she raised her hand to her mouth, took a step back, and caught her heel on a rock. It caused her to pitch backward. Then, when she took another step back to try and regain her balance, she failed. And before she could utter a word in response to Enoch’s question, she fell backward, over the edge of Lover’s Leap. All Enoch heard was a scream followed by the sickening sound of her body bouncing off the cliffside rocks and a final splash.

Enoch didn’t want to look, but he had to in the hope she survived somehow. He vomited before he even got to the ledge. And when he looked over and saw her broken body floating facedown in the water, he got sick again. He seriously contemplated joining her in her watery grave.

The brilliant colors of the sky had suddenly grown dark and ominous. Mirroring Enoch’s emotions as he wrestled with the will to live and the guilt of causing Dawn’s death. He let the ring fall from his fingers and watched it descend until it was gone, just like the woman he loved.

If only he had known who the real culprit was, but he didn’t. She was tucked away in her little white house, her Bible cracked open to the verse from Deuteronomy that had caused Dawn’s “accident.” The same verse she had used 60 years earlier to punish the ward staff who had abused her at Fairdale Falls State Hospital.

"To me belongeth vengeance and recompense. Their foot shall slide in due time: for the day of their calamity is at hand, and the things that shall come upon them make haste."

# CHAPTER 76

Karen and Tad's relationship continued to flourish. Even after Karen made good on her promise to bring him over to meet her parents. Elsa and Klaus liked him, and to Karen's surprise, her mother didn't call her incessantly for a report on the health of their relationship.

The real shock came at the end of the school year when Karen told her parents she was moving in with Tad. She anticipated World War III, but they didn't even bat an eyelash. And instead, bought them a new living room set as a housewarming gift. Having heard from Karen about the ragtag, mismatched furniture that Tad and his roommates had lived with for years.

Karen had done well in the first year of the University's two-year teaching program and was interning as a teacher's aide for a summer school program at a local elementary school. Tad's acting career got a boost when he was invited to participate in a Summer Theatre series in town before his senior year. Thus, the arcs of their education, employment, and relationship seemed to be moving forward in a complementary and progressive fashion.

"Where do you see us a year from now?" Tad asked one evening as he was holding Karen in his arms after they had made love.

"Together," she said with a smile.

"Well, good. But I was hoping for a little more detail."

"I guess it depends on where we can get jobs. Do you want to stay in the Twin Cities, or would it be better for us to move somewhere else?"

"I'm perfectly happy with staying here. We both grew up here, and our families live here. When we get married and have babies, it will be nice to have family around. What do you think?"

"I'm good with that."

Karen and Tad had frequently discussed their future together, and both had been on the same page, seemingly from the moment they had met. Karen didn't even get upset when her mother would risk asking her about when they were going to stop "living in sin," as she put it.

"We're going to wait until after we graduate to get married, Mom. It's just a piece of paper. It's not like it's going to change anything between us. We're already committed to each other for life."

"And grandbabies?"

"Jeez, Mom. I'm sure those will come in time too. We have careers to consider first. We don't want to bring our children into the world without being able to afford to care for them."

"Children? You plan to have more than one?" her mother asked excitedly.

"Yes, mother. We've talked about having 2 or 3. We'll see. Now relax. It will be a few years before you can spoil them rotten."

Like her grandmother and grandfather's relationship, Tad and Karen's union gave you that rare sense of permanence, stability, and enduring passion. That no matter how the winds blew, they would always be together and be able to adapt.

Such was the case during their final year at the University. Karen and Tad's schedules were much more demanding, and their time together was significantly limited. In addition to his full course load, Tad auditioned and landed a part in a play at the Guthrie Theatre. Meanwhile, Karen's schedule was divided between interning as a teacher's aide in the mornings and classes in the afternoon and early evening. As a result, being together awake at the house without somewhere to be was a rare occasion. Nevertheless, they made the best of it, knowing that this was temporary and that the reward of a lifetime together awaited them after graduation.

The free time they did have together was frequently spent making plans for their wedding and deciding where they wanted to live. Their parents had no shortage of opinions on both matters. And Elsa and Klaus naturally tried to convince them they should find a home in Richfield. However, they didn't like the cookie-cutter suburbs in which their parents lived. Hoping instead to find a home in town, preferably close to one of the many lakes.

And as luck may have it, Karen learned of a perfect opportunity through a teacher at the school where she was interning. The two-bedroom bungalow was on France Avenue in the Linden Hills neighborhood, just a few minute's walk to either Lake Calhoun or Lake Harriet. She rushed home excited to tell Tad, only to find him in bed with another woman.

She was beyond shocked. She ran out of the bedroom. And out of the house, despite Tad's pleas for her to stop so he could explain. There was no explanation he could give that would have her change course. She was devastated, and rightfully so. They had spent nearly two years together, making plans for the future. Now they were shattered.

Karen jumped in her car and, through tear-filled eyes, made her way to Richfield. Elsa and Klaus were as stunned as she was and welcomed her to stay with them. She was in no condition to do otherwise. She confined herself in her childhood bedroom for two days, unable to eat or sleep. Tad had tried repeatedly to call and talk with her, but Elsa had intercepted the calls and finally told him to stop calling.

Her life was thrown into disarray, and Karen had all she could do just to finish the last two weeks of her schooling. She didn't even attend her graduation ceremony, not at all in the mood to celebrate anything. Tad's infidelity defied explanation. All Karen could think was that he must have been unfaithful all along. And somehow, she must have had her head in the clouds not to recognize it.

But this time, Hagatha had employed a new verse to end Karen and Tad's idyllic romance. As Karen ruminated about her uncertain future, her great-grandmother celebrated. She had sent an adultress to dose Tad with a drug and tempt him into the compromising position in which Karen found him. Thus, adding a verse from Proverbs to her armamentarium.

"For the lips of an immoral woman drip honey, and her mouth is smoother than oil. But in the end, she is bitter as wormwood, sharp as a two-edged sword. Her feet go down to death, her steps lay hold of hell."

# CHAPTER 77

Kathleen Flanagan was the last remaining descendant of Enoch Slaughter's youngest brother Abraham. She had been Slaughter Elementary School's 7th-grade teacher since before World War II. Though she had never married, it was not by choice. Kathleen would have been happy to welcome a suitor at any point in her adult life. But, perhaps unfairly, she was judged by one unfortunate defect – a raised hairy mole on her chin. Other than that, she was intelligent, kind, God-fearing, and not unattractive. That is if you could somehow pull your eyes away from the bushy blemish on her face that cried out like a beacon demanding your attention.

To Principal Fred Markson, Kathleen Flanagan's more significant defect was that, as a teacher, she was hopelessly stuck in a bygone era when the times demanded a more flexible educator. As a matter of fact, Principal Markson had specifically been hired to bring Slaughter Elementary's faculty into the new age. His predecessor, Swede Larson, who was now the School Board's Chairman, had retired ten years earlier. Recognizing that the school needed an infusion of new blood and new thinking to satisfy the children and the parents of the Baby Boom generation.

However, the out with the old, in with the new credo, was a challenge to implement, even with the Board Chair's support. Slaughter Minnesota was like many small towns in

America. The more things changed in big-city-USA, the more small-towns tried to preserve what was familiar and tried and true. If it ain't broke, don't fix it was the motto. In other words, Slaughter townfolk valued consistency and how things were always done more than change and what was shiny, new, and innovative. The last thing Slaughter residents and Mayor Enoch Slaughter, Jr. wanted was to be over-run by hippies, drug addicts, and rock-and-roll!

Principal Markson had met repeatedly with Ms. Flanagan to encourage her to loosen up a bit in following the woefully archaic curriculum. However, she refused to budge.

"Damn rule-follower," he exclaimed to himself after she had exited his office following another failed intervention. "She'll probably want to teach until she dies. God, I hope not. But if so, let's hope she goes sooner rather than later," he said in frustration.

And he was right. Ms. Flanagan did want to teach until she died. What he didn't anticipate was that shortly after expressing his exasperated hope for her early demise, she was diagnosed with a cancerous and inoperable brain tumor. After that, it was hard for Principal Markson not to feel tremendous guilt every time he saw Ms. Flanagan. And he saw her often as she had made the courageous decision to continue teaching despite the pain and her terminal condition.

She even encouraged Principal Markson to recruit a teacher so that she could mentor her replacement. However, he couldn't get himself to post the position. Even though it would have been prudent to do so. Recruiting qualified teachers to come to Slaughter, Minnesota, wasn't easy. But every time he thought about advertising for the job, his conscience got the better of him. It was just another reminder that he had hoped for her passing. So instead, he over-compensated and declared the last month of the school year as Ms. Flanagan Appreciation month, hosting a series of events in her honor. She responded to the recognition with customary class and humility. Then died in her sleep on the last week of the school year. Finally, freeing Principal Markson to advertise the teaching vacancy.

Fortunately, since it was the end of the school year, he had the entire summer of 1968 to find her replacement. He needn't have worried. Hagatha Ketchel's plan was going according to Hoyle.

# CHAPTER 78

Every morning Elsa tried to motivate Karen to get out of bed and apply for a teaching job for the next school year. And every morning, Karen would say, "Maybe tomorrow."

"You know, you've been saying maybe tomorrow for two weeks now," her mother chided. "Before you know it, tomorrow is going to be the first week in September, and all the teaching jobs will be filled."

When Karen didn't respond, Elsa began rattling off teaching opportunities from the help wanted page of the newspaper. Like she had done every other morning.

"Mom, just stop," Karen shouted, finally irritated enough to show emotion other than despondency. "I don't think I want to get a job here in the Twin Cities."

"Why do you say that? That's been your plan all along, hasn't it?"

"That was Tad and my plan all along. But now the thought of living and working in the same town as him makes me sick to my stomach."

"Well, it's a big town, Karen. The chances of seeing Tad are slim. Plus, there are plenty more fish in the sea. Young men who will treat you right and not cheat on you."

"Ugh, Mom. I don't even want to think about going out

with men right now. I think I'm going to try to find a teaching job somewhere else?"

"What? Where?"

"I don't know. Maybe I'll go to Duluth and be close to Grandma," she said, off the cuff as she really hadn't thought about it.

"Well, I'd rather have you here, but being close to Grandma would be fine, too."

And with that, Karen started to come out of her grief. The more she thought about getting a job in or around Duluth, the more she could see the light at the end of the tunnel. But instead of taking her mother's advice and calling her Grandma Hilda, she elected to conduct her job search independently. Reasoning that she didn't want to get her grandmother's hopes up if she didn't find a job or elected not to take one if offered.

Each day, she'd go to the Public Library and peruse the help wanted ads in the Duluth Herald. Finally, after a week of fruitless efforts, an ad caught her eye.

"Exceptional 7th-grade teaching opportunity in a small, affluent community. Enjoy the freedom and flexibility to use your teaching skills to the fullest. Live in a town small enough to know your neighbors but big enough to offer many big-city conveniences. Nestled in a pine forest within easy driving distance to Duluth, the Boundary Waters, the headwaters of the Mississippi, and some of the best recreation and vacation spots in the State."

She made a copy of the ad, and when she got home, typed up a letter of interest and sent it with her resume to the Post Office Box address in Duluth.

"Why do you think they didn't give the name of the school or the town?" Karen asked her mother.

"I don't know, honey. But it sounds really nice. Maybe they just didn't want people flocking there. I bet if you ask your

Grandma, she'd know what town they're referencing."

"I don't want to do that. They might not even want a new teacher just out of school, and then Grandma will have gotten her hopes up for nothing."

What they didn't know was that Slaughter Elementary had hired a marketing firm to help them advertise the position. The agency recommended a blind ad. Reasoning that Slaughter was a respected name in the community but not widely known across the state. In short, not mentioning Slaughter guaranteed that people wouldn't be immediately put off by a name that in common usage connotes something horrifying versus appealing. Of course, the ad did embellish or take certain liberties with its claims, as marketing agencies are inclined to do. Like what was considered "easy driving distance." And, of course, it also didn't mention that the pine forest the town was supposedly nestled in was being aggressively harvested. But you did what you had to do when you lived in Slaughter.

Two weeks passed, during which Karen continued to pour over the help wanted ads in the Duluth Herald – to no avail. She also hadn't received a response to the letter of interest she had sent to the mystery 7$^{th}$-grade opportunity. She went home dejected, thinking she might have to bite the bullet and try to find a job in the Twin Cities.

"Karen? Is that you?" her mother called from upstairs when she came through the door.

"Yeah, Mom. It's me."

"A Principal Markson called while you were out. He wanted to speak with you. I left his number by the phone."

"Thanks, Mom. I'll call him back!" Karen replied enthusiastically, feeling a glimmer of hope.

She was so excited, she had to redial the rotary phone twice after making errors in dialing. Finally, making the connection, she wished she had gone to the bathroom before calling. She was about to hang up to go relieve herself when a female voice answered.

"Slaughter Elementary School, this is Klara Baumstamm. How may I help you?"

"Ah, yes, Ms. Baumstamm. I'm Karen Garber. I understand that Principal Markson called earlier wanting to speak with me. Is he in?"

"That's Mrs. Baumstamm, and unfortunately, Principal Markson is out of the office at the moment. However, he did leave me instructions to invite you to come to Slaughter and interview for the vacant 7$^{th}$-grade teaching opportunity."

"Oh, that's great news. Thank you. I'd be delighted. But where exactly are you located?"

"Slaughter is 12 miles northeast of Grand Rapids."

"Oh, I thought it was closer to Duluth," Karen responded.

"Does that mean you're no longer interested in the position? Because if you're not, I have several other candidates I'm trying to schedule."

"No, no, I'm still very interested. I was just under the impression it was closer to Duluth."

"Okay, then. Would you be able to be here a week from tomorrow?"

"Yes, that will be just fine."

"Very good. I will send you a letter to confirm along with the schedule of interviews. The letter will also include lodging information. The school will be picking up all of your food and lodging expenses, so no need to worry about that. You will be responsible for your own transportation here, however. Does that pose any problems?"

"No, Mrs. Baumstamm. That is very generous. Thank you."

"We will see you a week from tomorrow then. Good afternoon, Ms. Garber."

"Good afternoon, Mrs. Baumstamm," she replied and was about to add another thank you, but Mrs. Baumstamm had already hung up.

Karen's cries of joy brought her mother rushing down the stairs to find out what all the excitement was about.

"They're going to interview me for that 7$^{th}$-grade teaching position!" she said excitedly.

"That's great, honey! I was hoping that was what the call was about. What's the name of the town?"

"Slaughter," Karen replied. "Have you ever heard of it?"

"No. And who would name a town Slaughter? It sounds like something out of some slasher movie."

"God, Mom. Don't say that. I don't want to have nightmares before I even get there!"

Causing Elsa to kick herself for her poor choice of words. And hoping they wouldn't trigger her daughter to have night terrors like those she and her grandmother experienced.

"How far is it from Grandma's?" she asked, shifting discussion away from the town's awful name.

"I don't know. It's 12 miles from Grand Rapids."

"That's not close to Duluth at all. I thought the ad said it was within easy driving distance?"

"It did."

"Well, I don't call what must be at least 70 some odd miles easy driving distance."

"Really? It's that far from Duluth?"

"Yes."

"Well, it's just an interview. I might not even get the job. The lady I spoke to said they have a few other candidates. And even if I do get an offer, I don't have to accept it if I don't like it there."

The revelation of Slaughter's distance from Duluth, however, did little to dampen Karen's enthusiasm. She was just happy to have an opportunity that wasn't in the Twin Cities, where there were constant reminders of Tad everywhere she went.

# CHAPTER 79

Enoch IV sank into a deep depression. So much so that his father had to ask the Mayor, Enoch, Jr., to pull some strings to get his son extended time off from his job. Requesting a leave of absence for a mental illness was a stigma the Slaughter family couldn't abide by. Admitting that the Founder's great-grandson had an emotional condition would scar Enoch IV's reputation and the family's name forever.

Instead, the Mayor requested that the mining company allow Enoch IV a 3-month leave to work on a Special Project. In return, he'd compensate the company handsomely, recognizing their need to temporarily find a replacement. The company was more than happy to grant Enoch IV the time off and accept the Mayor's generous remuneration.

Meanwhile, Enoch IV, who was determined to kill himself, had been moved to a secure room at the Slaughter Mansion, where a team of doctors and nurses provided round-the-clock care and supervision. They, of course, had been commissioned by the Mayor, were well compensated, and required to sign non-disclosure agreements.

Enoch IV felt responsible for Dawn's death and now also felt like a coward that he hadn't leaped to his death in response when he had the chance. The treatment du jour was a medication called Tofranil. Electroconvulsive therapy (ECT) had fallen out of favor in the 1960s. However, some doctors still employed it in patients who didn't respond to Tofranil.

After Enoch IV had been on medication for two weeks with no appreciable progress, the doctor's added ECT treatments 3 times a week for 4 weeks. Unfortunately, one of the side-effects of ECT is memory loss, which in Enoch IV's case, may have ironically been what started him on the road to recovery. By the 12th and last ECT treatment, Enoch IV no longer remembered Dawn McMaster or that he had watched her fall to her death.

While you couldn't say that Enoch IV had returned to normal, he at least didn't have a desire to kill himself anymore. He went back to his job at the Taconite Plant in Hibbing. He didn't, however, return to being a Casanova with the ladies. He didn't avoid them, but he also didn't pursue anything deeper than very surface-level acquaintances. He still wanted a motorcycle, but he had lost his daredevil spirit. He had a vague sense that something was missing in his life but couldn't put his finger on what it was. His full recovery would take a couple of years, culminating when he would meet a sexy school teacher at a dance club in Grand Rapids on his 21st birthday.

# CHAPTER 80

By the time Karen rolled into Grand Rapids the evening before her interview, she was too tired from her 4-hour drive from Richfield to consider taking a spin through Slaughter. Not that she ultimately slept very well, once at the hotel. She was too nervous and excited. Each time she'd start nodding off, her mind would think of another question she might be asked. And instead of giving in to her exhaustion, she rehearsed in her head how she would answer the question. Eventually, she did get some sleep, but it was far from optimal.

It took a shower and a couple of cups of strong coffee to get her feeling at least somewhat prepared for the gauntlet of interviews scheduled to begin at 8:00 a.m. She was anxious to tour the "affluent community" that was "nestled in the pine forest" before her interview. So she hopped in her Ford Falcon and got to Slaughter an hour before she needed to be at the school.

While Slaughter didn't appear as affluent or nestled in the woods as she had imagined, it definitely was small-town America. And for Karen, it fit the one important criterion she had – it felt worlds away from Tad, the Twin Cities, and the painful memories they carried.

Touring Slaughter didn't take all the time she had allotted. She drove down Main Street and through a couple of neighborhoods. She saw an impressive mansion on a hill which she imagined was what prompted the affluent descriptor. Next, she drove by the High School and Elementary School, which she found impressive, if not oversized, for the community. Her tour complete, she decided to kill some time by taking a stroll through the park she saw when entering the town.

While standing by the statue at the park's entrance, reading about the town's Founder, she was interrupted by wolf whistles. Turning to see the source, she saw a car full of teenage boys. Two boys were hanging out the windows. One yelled, "You're a fox," while the other followed with, "Will you have my baby?"

She couldn't help but find their comments amusing. They were the typical teenage testosterone-fueled shenanigans she was sometimes subjected to in the Twin Cities. And it was a harbinger of things to come. What she wasn't aware of was that her fashion choice for the day would continue to turn heads. Some would be titillated, but more would see it as a transgression and be offended. While a mini-skirt and sandals may have been the typical uniform of the day for women in the Twin Cities, it was distinctly not in Slaughter, Minnesota. A fact Karen would eventually realize when it was too late to do anything about it.

They say that when interviewing for a job, you always want to be sure that you make an impression that people will remember. If that was the case, Karen Garber would have been offered the 7th-grade teaching position when she walked into the conference room. When Mrs. Baumstamm led her into the room, everyone breathed a collective and very audible inhalation. Most combined this respiratory reaction with looks of disdain. A few male teachers, including Principal Markson, gazed with delight, bordering almost on desire.

At this exact moment, Karen realized that fashion that played well in downtown Minneapolis didn't necessarily play well in Slaughter, Minnesota. If she could have, she would have hit the rewind button to take her back to when she was naked in front of her hotel closet, selecting what to wear that morning. Instead, all she could think was, "I should have worn my knee-length shift dress."

It was a good thing that Board Chairman Swede Larson wasn't there. He probably would have declared the interview over right then and there, as he was the most militant of Slaughter's fashion police. It was due to his insistence that Slaughter Elementary students were still required to wear school uniforms. And teachers were expected to look professional and dress conservatively.

Nevertheless, Principal Markson introduced her enthusiastically to all the teachers she would meet with throughout the day. Most of the teachers around the table took one look at Karen and knew she was toast. Regardless of Principal Markson's enthusiasm, they knew she'd never get the Board Chairman's approval. As a result, most relaxed, put away all their challenging questions and prepared to watch with delight as the floozy's hope for the job went down in flames.

Karen's one-on-one interviews with the teachers were a tale of two types of reactions related to the interviewer's gender. Women educators gave her a cold reception, seemed indifferent to what she shared, and usually ended their meetings early. Male teachers, with one exception, gave her a warm reception, hung on her every word, and often exceeded their allotted meeting time. The only exception was Bruce Buffington, Slaughter Elementary's 5$^{th}$-grade teacher. He seemed offended she occupied the same space with him and was either critical of what she shared about her training and experience or uninterested.

As the teachers completed their meetings with Karen, they shared their observations with Principal Markson. And by mid-afternoon, just before she met with him, the teachers had overwhelmingly voted thumbs down by a tally of 5 to 2. Principal Markson debated whether to cancel her meeting with Board Chairman Larson scheduled directly after his time with her. He knew that it would be an uphill battle to get Swede's approval based on her appearance alone. It wouldn't reflect well on him to waste the Board Chair's time on a candidate the teachers had so thoroughly rejected.

But before he could make a decision, Ms. Baumstamm knocked on his door and escorted Karen into his office. He could have requested a private moment with Ms. Baumstamm to instruct her to cancel Swede's meeting, but he was distracted by the goddess before him. And as she approached, smiled, and extended her hand in greeting, he found everything about her mesmerizing and exciting. This obviously had nothing to do with whether she was qualified for the job or not. However, he was hired to cobble together a teaching staff that would breathe new life into the curriculum.

"So nice to meet you, Principal Markson," she said, shaking his hand as her sweet floral perfume worked its magic on his olfactory system. Causing his limbic system to fully engage his pleasure centers.

"Oh, the pleasure is all mine, Ms. Garber," he replied.

"Please call me Karen," she said, her skirt riding up her legs tantalizingly as she took a seat on the other side of the Principal's desk.

"All right, Karen. And please call me Fred," he replied, his eyes glued to the peek-a-boo act her skirt was doing as she slowly crossed her legs, putting a temporary end to the show.

"How did you feel your meetings went today?" he asked, his eyes making their way back to meet hers.

"Well, some of them went really well," she replied and paused.

"And others?" he prompted.

"Others didn't feel like they went as well. I think I

may have made a mistake wearing this outfit. They seemed offended."

"Well, we do have a relatively conservative dress code here compared to the Twin Cities. But how would you have known that? I think you look just fine. Besides, I'm hiring for a person's ability to teach a more up-to-date curriculum, not what they choose to wear."

"I appreciate that, Principal Mark, I mean, Fred," she said, blushing as she uncrossed and recrossed her legs.

"So convince me you're the right person for the job. How would you modernize Slaughter Elementary's curriculum so that our students are better prepared for today's world?"

"Well, if given latitude to augment the required curriculum, I'd make sure that in every subject, there would be some attention to how that teaching translates into how things are today. And where things seem to be going in the future."

"That sounds good. Can you give me an example of what you mean?"

"Sure," she said, bouncing excitedly up in her chair, causing her breasts to bounce with her. "For example, most science curriculums don't include the last 10 years of space flight. No Sputnik, no creation of NASA, no Alan Shepherd, no John Glenn. I mean, in a few months, the Apollo program will launch a rocket to the moon! How can we say we're teaching our children when their education is stuck in the 1950s?"

"Excellent example, Karen. Now, let's talk about the meeting you'll be having with our Board Chairman, Swede Larson."

"Okay," she said, surprised he didn't want to ask her more questions.

"Swede is old-fashioned when it comes to things like clothes and manners. But he's all in favor of augmenting our old, tired, and outdated curriculum. So he is not going to react well to what you're wearing."

"Should I go back to the hotel and change? I have a more conservative shift dress," she offered.

"No, there probably isn't time for that. And being late for your interview with him would be even worse. How about making up some story about why you couldn't wear your more professional outfit?"

"You mean, like lie and tell him the waiter at breakfast accidentally spilled my food all over it?"

"Well, normally, I wouldn't condone lying, but in this case, we don't want him to disqualify you for something that has no bearing on your ability to teach. As it is, I'm sure I will still have to convince him that you're the right person for the job."

Karen couldn't believe they were having this conversation. It was as if he had already decided to hire her. And now they were conspiring together to convince the Board Chairman.

"I can do that if that is what you want me to do," she said.

"Yes, I want you to do that. Let's role play. I'll be the Board Chair. Pretend you've just walked in the door. What do you say?"

Karen couldn't help but feel like she was now auditioning for a part in a play. She fought off her thoughts of those times she played a role in assisting Tad to learn his lines. She got up from the chair, strutted to the door, and turned around to approach Principal Markson. He stood up, barely able to keep his mind on the task at hand.

"Good afternoon, Mr. Board Chairman. I apologize for my inappropriate outfit. My business dress got soiled this morning when the waiter tripped and dumped my breakfast on it. I didn't have the foresight to pack another outfit. So I had to wear this. I hope you will forgive me."

It wasn't so much her words as it was her acting skills that reassured Principal Markson that this scheme could actually work. Although Swede Larson was pushing 80 years old, he couldn't imagine any red-blooded American male resisting this sexy damsel in distress act.

Before she knew it, she was shuttled off to another office where Swede Larson sat awaiting her arrival. She entered and reprised her damsel in distress act, this time for real. And an hour later, Swede Larson emerged and disappeared into Principal Markson's office. While Karen sat waiting on pins and needles under the critical glare of Mrs. Baumstamm, who was clearly not a fan.

Karen didn't have to wait long before Principal Markson and Swede Larson exited the office.

"Congratulations, Ms. Garber. We'd like to offer you the job as Slaughter Elementary's next 7$^{th}$-grade teacher," Principal Markson announced.

Karen sprang up from the chair and bounced up and down with a cry of delight. Meanwhile, in the background, Mrs. Baumstamm nearly fainted and fell out of her chair. Karen couldn't restrain herself from giving Swede and Principal Markson hugs, which they didn't seem to mind. After Swede took his leave, Principal Markson invited Karen back into his office to discuss the details of her compensation, benefits, and starting date. She gave him another hug before leaving and bounded out of his office happier than she had been in months.

The drive back to Richfield didn't seem nearly as long, and her excitement had only grown in anticipation of telling her parents. Elsa's response was more muted than Klaus's upon hearing the news.

"Aren't you happy for me, mother? You'd love Slaughter. It's such a nice little town."

"Of course, I'm happy for you, dear. It's just so far away," she replied.

Which was true, but not the real reason she had reservations. You see, Elsa and Grandma Hilda both had been visited by nightmares the previous evening. Visions of Hagatha cackling evilly in the face of cataclysmic death and destruction while repeating the same phrase over and over.

"Slaughter the Slaughters. Slaughter the Slaughters. Slaughter the Slaughters."

# EPILOGUE

Where is the line between sanity and lunacy? And who's to say if and when that boundary will be breached? Some endure repeated insults to their human psyche over a lifetime and only seem to draw strength from it and grow in their compassion for others. Some go along swimmingly in smooth seas, only to lose their bearings when the slightest turbulence is encountered and never regain their way even when the storm subsides.

What happened to Otto and Ursala Ketchel's sweet, innocent little girl? Did things change the moment Enoch walked into her life? Did his greed and grandiosity slowly grind away at her goodness? Or was it a chemical imbalance due to her pregnancy or the postpartum period that prompted her psychosis? Or maybe it was the rejection? As if she deliberately disregarded his demands by having a daughter, thereby dashing his dreams and destiny.

And why did the word of God get so twisted in Hagatha's mind? Words she was raised on and drew comfort and inspiration from as a child. Holy and heavenly words meant to help and heal, not hellacious harangues intended to hinder and harm.

Was her path chosen or compelled? Why take her hatred out on children? Why form an alliance and corrupt her great-granddaughter? What did she hope to gain? How could a woman who grew so bitter be blessed with such a long life? Or be granted such destructive powers? Too many questions and not enough answers.

Just one irrefutable truth – Hagatha Ida Ketchel's reign of terror was not over. In fact, it was just beginning.

* * *

Thank you for reading Hagatha Ketchel Unhinged, the second book in the Slaughter Minnesota Horror series. The third book in the series, Hagatha's Century of Terror, is scheduled for publication on January 15, 2022.

Enter address below in your internet browser to view or order other books by this author.
https://readerlinks.com/mybooks/3464

# BOOKS IN THIS SERIES

*The Slaughter Minnesota Horror Series*
A series about what happens when you dare cross Hagatha Ida Ketchel. For those readers who grew up near that one scary house that they didn't dare pass or that strange neighbor they always tried to avoid.

## Old Lady Ketchel's Revenge

No one truly escapes their childhood unscathed. Especially if you grew up in Slaughter, Minnesota, in the 1960s and crossed Old Lady Ketchel's path.

## Hagatha Ketchel Unhinged

Twenty-four years in an asylum is enough time to really lose your mind. And arouse one to unleash the dark and vengeful thoughts residing therein.

## Hagatha's Century Of Terror

What does a crazy old lady in Slaughter, Minnesota, need on her 100th birthday? Sweet revenge, of course.

# BOOKS BY THIS AUTHOR

## Table For Four: A Medical Thriller Series Book 1

A blockbuster Alzheimer's cure. A murder and unexplained deaths. Two aggrieved parties meet by chance. Will they expose the truth, or die trying?

## Dying To Recall: A Medical Thriller Series Book 2

A suicide, a break-in, an ominous warning. Is it a coincidence? Or have Jackie and Curt unleashed the wrath of vengeful pharmaceutical executives?

## Memory's Hope: A Medical Thriller Series Book 3

The case against AlzCura intensifies until the FDA's shocking response to the data. Will the guilty parties walk, or will they be brought to justice?

## Aja Minor: Gifted Or Cursed: A Psychic Crime Thriller Series Book 1

Aja has disturbing powers. She feels cursed, but the FBI thinks otherwise. Will she stop a serial rapist and killer or become his next victim?

## Aja Minor: Fountain Of Youth: A Psychic Crime Thriller Series Book 2

Aja Minor goes undercover. The target, an international child trafficking ring. When her cover is blown, the mission and her life are in jeopardy.

## Aja Minor: Predatorville: A Psychic Crime Thriller Series Book 3

Solving a surge in assaults and missing children is Aja Minor's next test. But when the hunter becomes the hunted, will she get out of Predatorville alive?

## Old Lady Ketchel's Revenge: The Slaughter Minnesota Horror Series Book 1

No one truly escapes their childhood unscathed. Especially if you grew up in Slaughter, Minnesota, in the 1960s and crossed Old Lady Ketchel's path.

## Hagatha Ketchel Unhinged: The Slaughter Minnesota Horror Series Book 2

Twenty-four years in an asylum is enough time to really lose your mind. And arouse one to unleash the dark and vengeful thoughts residing therein.

## Hagatha's Century Of Terror: The Slaughter Minnesota Horror Series Book 3

What does a crazy old lady in Slaughter, Minnesota, need on her 100th birthday? Sweet revenge, of course.

## Loving You From My Grave: A Wholesome Inspirational Romance

He ran from his past. She's held captive by hers. Could love set them free, bridge their differences in age and race, and survive death?

## Little Bird On My Balcony: Selected Poems

A collection of poems that speak to the love, loss, longing, and levity of navigating young adulthood.

## Adilynn's Lullaby: Poems Of Love & Loss

A collection of poems about love and loss that provide hope and inspiration during some of life's most difficult times.

# ABOUT CHRIS BLIERSBACH

Chris Bliersbach is originally from St. Paul, Minnesota, and now lives in Henderson, Nevada.

Follow him on Amazon, Facebook, or join his mailing list at cmbliersbach@gmail.com.

Made in United States
Orlando, FL
21 July 2024

49370655R00173